THE
ELFIN
BARRIER

THE
ELFIN
BARRIER

PATRICIA GAGNON BENNETT

authorHOUSE®

AuthorHouse™ LLC
1663 Liberty Drive
Bloomington, IN 47403
www.authorhouse.com
Phone: 1-800-839-8640

Published by AuthorHouse   05/15/2014

ISBN: 978-1-4969-1334-0 (sc)
ISBN: 978-1-4969-1333-3 (e)

Library of Congress Control Number: 2014909104

CHAPTER ONE

Brandy Wells awoke to an incredible headache.

Rubbing her temples, with the tips of her fingers, she wondered where she was. Slowly, she looked around, trying to focus her blurred vision in the surrounding darkness. The first thing she noticed was her crumpled, red truck, quickly followed by the miracle that she was still inside the cab securely belted into place, and finally that she was amazingly alive. Just what had happened to her and her truck? A shadow stepped close to the open space that was once the window beside her, and was now a pile of broken glass. A face leaned in and a hand pushed the mass of tangled brown hair away from her large, equally brown eyes. It was her best friend; her only friend, Steve Rixx.

Suddenly she remembered in a rush of jumbled thoughts.

She had been driving home from work, a job she hated, but had to have as it paid what little bills she incurred. Heck, her boss didn't even know her name. He was constantly calling her "Betty". Traveling down the secluded dirt path that served as her road, she noticed a car barely pulled to the side. It was Steve's beat up old Chrysler. Upon stopping, she noticed nothing but black silence. Glancing at her cell phone she knew there wouldn't be any service, and the flashing symbol verified that fact.

The road only led to one place, hers, so she continued slowly on, looking for her friend in the darkness.

Recently, solitude was all that she ever wanted, and with her home, she got just that. When she was a teen her parents had bought a very large parcel of land in these secluded woods to make their new home. At first she had been appalled. How could she, one who had been raised in a big, thriving, alive city, ever be expected to live out in the boonies? In time though, not only had she lovingly grown to accept her fated, but she had meshed easily with the peaceful and quiet surroundings that the woods had to offer. She and her parents had indeed found their sense of paradise.

Her security had not lasted for as long as she had hoped. In a flash her world crumbled. An auto accident a few years earlier had robbed her of her parents. For weeks she kept to herself, not wanting to leave the haven that had been built around her. As she rambled for hours in the surrounding woods, she would often wish herself gone as well. It wasn't that she was lonely, for the silence soothed her. She hurt. She hurt to the core of her being. In time though, the serenity of the birds, the animals, the wind, and the rain healed her broken spirit and she once again found the happiness that she had known in her home. That was then, and this was now.

As she had anticipated, she spotted Steve a little further down the road. She easily recognized his short, blonde hair and his strong, tall form dressed in blue jeans, red checkered, flannel shirt, and white hi-top tennis shoes. Turning, he squinted his blue eyes at her headlights and began to wave frantically as if she couldn't see him or know that it was him.

"What on earth are you doing out here at this time of night?" she asked as her friend clambered into the passenger side door.

"Well, in case you forgot, Miss Hermit, today just happens to be your birthday, and I just happened to remember that you have a particular fondness for chocolate." Smiling, he produced a box wrapped in gold foil from beneath his shirt and handed it to her.

"Steve, you are something else," Brandy said, laughing at him. His smile was infectious, especially after a rotten night of work. "You don't know how much I appreciate this, or how much I really needed it today."

"I didn't think anyone should be alone on their birthday, especially when they are turning the ripe old age of . . ."

"Thanks for reminding me how old I am," she said, cutting him off. Grinning again, when he made a face she added, "By the way, what happened to your car back there?"

"I keep forgetting what a recluse you are and didn't have quite enough gas in the tank."

"Oh, and what were going to do once you got out to my place?" she asked, cutting her eyes at him.

"Well, I sure didn't think you would throw me out after bringing you candy. Chocolate candy at that," Steve said with great exaggeration, giving the best pitiful look he could muster.

"Well, maybe not," she said, laughing again and shaking her head at her friend. Focusing her attention back to the dark road, she noticed a flash in the shadows before them.

"Hey, what was that?" she asked.

"Where?" Steve leaned forward, squinting in front of them.

"Up there." Brandy released her right hand from the steering wheel and pointed forward.

"Wow! It's a bear. A really big bear!"

"That's no bear," she said flatly. Frowning, Brandy tried to make out the shape that they were getting closer and closer to.

"You're right. You know, it looks kind of like somebody riding a horse that has horns on its head." But when the creature turned into the beam of the headlights and began to charge at them, he grabbed Brandy by the arm. "Damn it! It is a person riding a horse with horns on its head."

At the exact same moment, Brandy also realized what was rushing toward them. It's eyes seemed to glow red in the brillance of her truck's headlights. Just before the apparition reached them, she pulled hard on the steering wheel, swerving the truck to the right of the road. The tires hit the soft sand on the side of the path and lost all friction. Losing control, the vehicle spun wildly towards the trees, finally coming to a hard and sudden stop. Then there was blackness.

"Well, that explains the headache," she mumbled miserably pulling herself back to the present. Steve yanked heavily until her door opened and helped her from the crushed auto.

"Wow, that was some ride," he said, glancing nervously about them in the dark. "You don't suppose our weird looking buddy is still out here, do you?"

"So that was real?"

"Yup. Unless, that is, you and I have the same hallucinations." Looking over his shoulder, he sighed in relief. "No sign of Bigfoot, but that doesn't mean he couldn't still be out there. I really don't want to wait for him to come back. So are you ready to move?"

"Yeah. Is there any hope at all for my truck?" Brandy asked, looking at the crumpled mass of steel.

"None. I would say it's totaled beyond repair."

Brandy took a deep breath and shook her head. "Well, I guess I shouldn't complain too much. We are both still alive and not too terribly damaged."

"And we are alone." Steve grinned boyishly, trying to sound romantic and lightening the seriousness of what just occurred.

"And you're crazy." Brandy laughed back, knowing that his joke was nothing more than that, a joke. There would never be anything romantic between. There love was that of a brother and sister. "Don't forget about our friend out there," she added, pointing into the darkness.

"Don't remind me. C'mon, let's make tracks."

They started off through the woods in what they hoped was the correct path to her house. She knew that taking the road would be at least a five mile walk, so they reasoned that going through the woods would be shorter. They also knew that the creature could just as easily be on the road as well as in the trees, since that is where they had seem him, so they mutually agreed upon the shorter route. The moon was clear and bright as they walked along. The soft leaves that piled beneath their feet cushioned their steps and hushed their progress. The air was cool and Brandy breathed in the crisp freshness of it, marveling at the few twinkling stars that she could make out between the branches overhead.

"How much farther do you think we have to go?" Steve asked quietly, some time later, not wanting to speak above a whisper. The clearness of the night had suddenly disappeared and they had walked into a heavy, thick fog that had settled close to the ground.

"I'm not really sure. To be honest, I'm not very good at measuring distances. It sure seems like we've gone an awfully long way already."

Steve stopped abruptly, listening into the dark night. Suddenly he turned his head and peered far into the trees. "What was that?"

"What was what?" Brandy asked, unexpectedly feeling a bit nervous for she had heard nothing.

"I can't say for sure, but I know I heard something up there," Steve said, pointing his finger in front of him.

"Well, since you heard it first, you go first," Brandy said, gripping his arm tightly and nudging him along in front of her.

"Thanks a bunch," he whispered to her over his shoulder.

As they crept along through the shadowy moonlit trees, Brandy had to agree that she too now heard something up ahead in the distance. And whatever it was, it was getting closer with each step that they took. Suddenly Steve stopped.

Walking closely behind, clutching his sleeve, Brandy nearly knocked both of them to the ground when he halted.

"Sorry," she mumbled apologetically at her inattentive clumsiness. "What is it?"

"Look up there between the bushes. There is a light of some kind. Like a campfire. I didn't know people camped all the way out here. I mean there is no way to get a car or anything like that in here. Is there?"

"No, there's not," Brandy said, nodding her head in agreement. She felt irritated at this development. What was someone else doing in her woods? Her sanctuary?

They silently parted the bushes and peered keenly through the gap. Brandy gaped in amazement at what she saw. There was a group of horned horses off to the left side of the fire, just like the one they had seen in the road. As she stared at them she realized that they were larger than ordinary horses and had twisted horns coming out of the tops of their heads beside their ears. Their manes and tails were scraggly and thin, and tangled with small branches and leaves. In front of them was a circle of tall hideous creatures. Their skin was a dull, scaly gray, and their eyes glowed a bright reptilian yellow. Their forms were mostly human, yet in a grotesque, lumpy sort of way.

"Are those goblins?" she whispered mostly to herself. Even more amazing than the goblins was what she saw in the center of their ring. "It's an elf," she breathed out softly.

"A what?" Steve asked, glancing at her as though she had lost her mind.

"I know, I know," whispered Brandy, grinning excitedly. "I can't believe it either, but look at him. It has to be an elf. He looks just like all the books say: tall, graceful, yet muscular, pointed ears and all. And so handsome, too," she added with a closer look at the elf. His hair was long and as dark as midnight sky. He stood a bit over six foot and his lean body was well muscled beneath his brown leather clothing. His skin was lightly tanned in contrast to his hair, and his light green eyes danced fiercely in the light of the fire that burned on the ground.

"You sure know how to make a guy feel good," Steve mumbled with a sarcastic smile.

"I didn't mean . . ." Brandy began, but was cut off by a cry from the outskirts of the circle. She shifted her gaze across the circle of goblins to the outlying trees. Suddenly a lone goblin emerged, dragging another unwilling form along with him. It was a female elf.

"The prize catch didn't elude us for long," snarled an armor clad goblin as he shoved the slim girl elf into the ring of his cohorts.

"It's a girl," Steve whispered softly. He felt anger building in him at the mistreatment of the fair headed elf girl. "Those dogs, how dare they throw a girl around like that," he ground out. Suddenly he was ready to fight. Not knowing why, but he instantly felt obligated to rush to this girl's aid.

"Steve, wait!" Brandy hissed as her friend stood and began moving into the clearing.

It was too late. Steve had already taken up a fallen branch as big around in thickness as his arm, and was headed for the circle of gruesome goblins. There was complete silence when he was spotted. The horse creatures stopped their snuffing and pawing at the ground to examine the new scent with interest. The goblins glared at him with savage amusement, and the elves regarded him with absolute amazement.

"Great," Brandy mumbled miserably to herself. "You sure know the time to play hero, Steven Rixx." She looked around and picked a large limb for herself, following him out into the clearing. Her presence was met with the same reaction as Steve's, only more evidently so.

"Good going, Sir Gallant. What in the hell are we supposed to do now? Ask for their autographs and then act like we are going to be on our merry way? I don't think so," she snapped irritably at her friend. "You could have given me some kind of warning, you know."

"Sorry, Brandy. I don't know what came over me, but when I saw how they treated the girl, I just couldn't help myself," Steve said apologetically. He glanced again at the elf girl in the center of the ring, who smiled appreciatively obviously understanding his words.

Brandy opened her mouth to scold Steve again like one would a child for his actions, when one of the goblins pointed a long, scaly, clawed finger at them. "I thought you took care of those pitiful humans," he yelled at another of the creatures. "Kill them at once, or it will be your head on the end of my sword and not these puny elves!"

"Is he speaking English?" Steve asked in amazement.

"Sure sounds like it to me. How can that be?"

"I really don't know. Maybe we are in your dream after all."

Brandy looked at Steve as two of the goblins rushed at them. "It's been fun," she snorted sarcastically at her friend. "I don't know how, or why, we can understand these guys, but I'm not going down without a fight."

"I agree and I know you can fight like an alley cat when cornered, so let's show them," Steve said. He smiled reassuringly to her, lifting his branch club high above his head.

Brandy took a deep breath and steadied her feet as the first goblin approached her, She wrinkled her nose in disgust at the stench of filth that he gave off. "You need a bath," she shot at him when he reached her. The goblin swung his sword at her with a monstrous shriek. Brandy deftly fell to her knees just as the blade whistled over her head. When she did so, she brought her club around in a vicious two-handed swing, making contact with the creature square in the center of his mid section. The creature fell to the ground with a thud, moaning, and trying ineffectively to gain his footing once again.

"Don't even think about it," Brandy said menacingly. "I've still got my club here, and I'm not afraid to use it." Thank heavens he believes me, Brandy thought desperately to herself when the goblin eyed her warily and stayed where he was on the ground, he too seeming to understand every word that she uttered.

Glancing over at Steve, she saw that he too had disarmed his opponent and had him pinned to the ground with threats of more punishment yet to come. "You were right," she said with a grin. "Not as bad as it looked."

"Well, there are still the others, but they don't act as though they can make up their minds on what they are going to do," Steve replied, nodding his head at the remaining four goblins.

Following his gaze, Brandy saw that the goblins talked softly amongst themselves in words that could not be understood. They looked to their fallen comrades and without saying anything else, they turned and headed back into the woods, their horse beasts following obediently behind.

"Get back into the trees with your smelly friends," Steve ordered the fallen creatures, taking Brandy's hand, drawing her away from the goblin that lay on the ground in front of her.

Slowly the two goblins got to their feet and eyed the humans warily.

"Go on. Get out of here before we change our minds," Steve shouted harshly at them, swinging his club in their direction.

"Your actions will prove to be a fatal mistake, human," hissed one of the goblins as they retreated back into the shadows of the woods. The pronunciation of their words were slow and made Brandy's skin crawl.

"I guess that means we won for now?" asked Brandy, turning to Steve, but he had already left her side and was striding over to the elfin girl who still stood silently by the small fire.

Steve approached the girl confidently, but for once in his life he fumbled badly for words when reaching her. He had never seen a girl more beautiful before. Long shimmering ivory hair that fell nearly to her knees, luminous light sky blue eyes, and a slim graceful body. His tongue felt twenty times too large for his mouth as he desperately tried to speak to her, completely unaware of both Brandy and the elfin girl's companion staring at him.

"Are you alright, miss?" he stammered awkwardly.

"Who are you and how did you gain entrance into our Elfin Woods?" demanded the girl's companion, angrily and stressing the word 'our'.

"Who are we? Well, who the hell are you, Mr. High and Mighty?" Brandy shot back hotly, indignant of his attitude and completely forgetting how attractive he was.

The elf girl laughed at her companion and smiled brightly at the humans. "Please pay him no mind, he is irritable all of the time. I am Princess Carina of the Elfin Woods and this is Forrest. Who are you?"

Steve smiled at Carina. "I am Steve Rixx and this is my good friend Brandy Wells. She is not usually grouchy, but she sure can have a temper at times." Steve grinned at Brandy with a wink, and then turned his full attention back to the Princess.

"What did he mean about gaining entrance into your Elfin woods?" Brandy asked Carina. She was still shaky from the auto accident, then she had almost been killed by some goblin creature, and now she had some handsome wise-mouthed elf guy telling her that she was invading their woods. She had always thought of them as her woods.

"Every once in a very great while the barrier between your world and ours thins in spots. When this happens, it is possible for humans to enter into our realm," Carina explained.

"What kind of barrier?"

"It's a barrier comprised of magical spells that separates our two realms."

"Can we get back across?" Brandy asked.

"I don't know. You see the barrier only thins for a very short while. And it only happens on extremely rare occasions. Then it . . . , well . . . , in essence heals itself," Carina said.

"We came here to make sure that nothing was able to slip through, but it seems we were a little late," Forrest said darkly.

"Seems to me you were in the process of getting your butt whipped by some ugly reptilian creature," Brandy shot back with a glare.

"Wait. Listen," Steve said, putting his hand over his friend's mouth. "Do you hear something in the bushes?" he asked walking toward the edge of the trees with his club gripped tightly in his hand.

"What is it?" Brandy whispered to him.

"I don't know," Steve began, then stopped suddenly when the group of goblins rushed out of the bushes at them brandishing weapons. "Damn, I think we're really in trouble now."

"You can say that again," Brandy stated, glancing behind herself. "It seems as though our elf buddies didn't want to stick around for the encore of this fight."

"What?"

She turned to tell Steve that the pair that they had aided were no longer present, but never got the words from her mouth. A sharp flash of pain raced across her head. Her knees buckled and the last thing she saw was Steve being dragged away by the goblins. Then nothing but absolute darkness.

"We must help them, Forrest," Carina said from their hiding place in the thick bushes, as she watched the human Steve being dragged away by the reptilian monsters, and the female knocked senseless to the ground.

"Why? They are only two stupid humans. They should have minded their own business," the dark haired elf replied.

"And if they had, it would have been us being dragged away by those horrible creatures and not them. They were only trying to help. Besides they seem friendly."

"Do not be fooled. You know as well as I that humans can not be trusted," Forrest said harshly.

"Do I? And why is that?"

"Because they are humans."

"That makes no sense, and I do no care," Carina snapped back. She turned to the woods behind her and gave a shrill cry into the night. Within moments a sleek brown hawk landed lightly on a branch nearby. She walked over to the bird and spoke quietly to it. The bird cocked his head in understanding at the princess' words. With one small squawk from its bright yellow beak, the bird lifted his wings and took to the night sky.

"I am going to help the girl with or without you," Carina stated angrily, facing Forrest as if in challenge.

"Very well, Princess," he gloomily replied, cautiously following her into the clearing to where Brandy lay unconscious on the soft dry grass.

"We must take her back to our village. She may be seriously hurt," said Carina as she knelt beside the fallen human girl.

Forrest silently nodded his agreement as he easily lifted Brandy into his powerful arms. Her silky chestnut hair softly tickled at his chin as he quickly glanced into her round, creamy and very pale face. 'She is attractive for a human,' he grumbled grudgingly to himself in silence. In noiseless quickness the two elves made their way back to their horses which were tethered in the trees. Nervously, the equines snorted their greetings to the two elves who rode them, and sniffed with caution and excitement at the newcomer that Forrest carried.

"Humans in the Elfin woods," Forrest muttered, shaking his head, as he mounted his horse with ease, despite carrying the girl. "This is not good."

Chapter Two

"My head," Brandy mumbled sleepily. She rubbed her head, keeping her eyes closed, not wanting to brave the sunlight yet. "Will it ever quit hurting, or am I doomed to have a headache forever?"

She struggled to a sitting position and struggled even harder to open her eyes. Painfully she adjusted her sight to the dimly lit room. It was sparsely furnished with a pair gracefully carved wooden chairs and a matching table. The floor was covered with woven rugs, that were the colors of leaves in the fall. The walls were bare and made of a rich colored wood, which filled the room with an inviting, warm scent.

"Hello," Carina said cheerfully from a corner of the room, her voice open and friendly. She came and sat next to Brandy in a small hickory chair that was beside the bed.

"Oh no. I thought it was all a bad dream." Brandy groaned, flopping back down on the bed of brightly colored cushions and blankets. Her eyes snapped back open when the realization of where she was truly registered. She sat back up like a bullet being shot into the sky, ignoring the persistent and protesting pain that raged uncontrollably in her head.

"Where's Steve?" she asked, her fingers going to the place on her skull that hurt the most only to discover a large bump.

"Do not worry, I am having him followed. We will be able to find him," the princess said confidently. She smiled and patted the human girl's hand reassuringly.

"How are you having him followed?" Brandy asked dubiously. "And how will you know where he is being taken?"

"I have a hawk trailing him. Their eyes are very keen and he will do a very good job. He will then communicate to others of his kind and they in turn will tell me of your mates general location," Carina explained.

Brandy gave a short laugh that came out like more of a snort. "Steve is not my mate, he's my best friend. I love him dearly as a brother, but definitely not as a husband. That would most certainly be an unruly match."

"How charming," Forrest sneered with a sarcastic voice, from the doorway where he stood listening.

"What is your problem? I mean, you have shown no gratitude for being helped last night or anything. And besides, what have I ever done to offend you?" Brandy snapped in a rush at the handsome elf, instantly regretting her actions and words. Even though he infuriated her easily with two syllables, she was drawn to his eyes. They were like nothing she had ever seen before. His black pupils were surrounded by a golden canary yellow, and that in turn was rimmed by a brilliant jade green. They were somewhat dark and forbidding eyes, but she sensed that they held a spark of liveliness and excitement somewhere deep in their depths, no matter how hard he seemed to try and hide it. An excitement, she found surprisingly to herself, that she would love to experience.

Forrest was taken aback by the human girl's tone. Her deep brown eyes danced with the fire of rage. Slowly a smile played across his lips. The human girl definitely had a spirit, and fear did not dwell within her as he thought it did in most humans. Yes, she was curious indeed.

Brandy tore her gaze from the penetrating look and grin that she received from Forrest. "How is it that you have a bird following Steve?" she asked, looking once again to the friendly face of Carina, not at all realizing that she had already asked that question.

"I can talk with birds and understand what they are saying back to me."

"I have read that elves have many magical powers, so is it common among your people to talk with animals, and other things?" Brandy asked, shooting a quick glance back at Forrest, who had remained in the room listening to their conversation. She half-way expected some kind of sarcastic comment to her question, but he remained silent, as if studying her.

"Some of us have the ability to talk with animals, others are healers and still others tend to the trees and plants. For the most part, those in our village do not possess magical powers."

"I always thought all elves had special powers," Brandy commented quietly. It was kind of nice knowing that many of them were just ordinary people like herself.

"At one time all elves did posses, as you phrase it, magical powers. I believe that since our time span on this land is much longer than for yourself," Carina began, "that our extended lives have made us a little lazy, and our confidence in what we can do has paid the penalty."

"Could be." Brandy nodded in thoughtful agreement. "The mind is the most powerful tool that we hold. If it is not used to its full potential, the body as a whole suffers."

"Precisely," said Carina with a smile at Brandy's insightfulness to what she herself thought all along.

"Interesting," Forrest murmured almost to himself. He glanced keenly at the human girl again. She spoke intelligently. Another quality that he felt sure humans could not have.

"By the way," Brandy began, "how am I able to understand your speech and you can understand me?"

"A very long time ago, there was no such barrier between our lands. Elves and humans interacted all of the time. Their cultures coexisted very peaceably together. As the humans strived more for power and control of all around them, our elder magic users erected that barrier to, well, separate our worlds. It is written in the stories of old that we should try to always keep the knowledge of the human world among us. For there have been times in the past when elves have traveled into your world to collect knowledge or to seek out one of our own who have chosen to stay among you. So from our youth, we are taught the language of humans that reside on the other side of the barrier from our own clans.

"Oh." Brandy sat silently for a moment, trying to absorb all that had happened over such a short span of time. Elves. Elves that she could understand and that looked so very much like herself. But then there were the others. There were the hideous creatures that she could also understand and that had taken her friend. Were their reasons for knowing her language the same as the elves, or for something far more sinister?

"I really appreciate your hospitality," she began, struggling to sit up on the side of the bed, "but I must find Steve. Maybe your bird friends could point me in the right direction, and I will be on my way."

"Do not worry. We have a group preparing to leave to go in search for him," Carina said, placing a comforting hand on Brandy's shoulder.

"Count me in," said Brandy, standing up quickly, then just as quickly sitting back down holding her head in her hands. The pain made her vision swim and prickled the roots of her hair. "Do you have any aspirin?" she groaned.

"Aspirin?" Carina asked quizzically, looking to Forrest to see if he had understood what was requested of them, receiving only a puzzled look and a small shrug in return.

"Something for a headache," Brandy explained, tapping her forehead lightly with her finger.

"Of course," Carina smiled in understanding. Reaching to the tray that she had carried into the room, she handed Brandy a mug of hot liquid.

Brandy gratefully accepted the cup and tentatively sniffed it. It smelled of mint. She easily drained the flavorful contents and was pleased to find that not only did it ease the pain in her head, but also seemed to return the strength to her tired and battered body. "That was good," she complimented.

"I am glad. Here is some food, eat it while I go and get you some clothing to travel in," Carina said. She rose from her chair with a smile and departed the room, Forrest following closely behind.

"She can not accompany the search group," Brandy heard Forrest's protests echo off of the walls as he and Carina made their way down the hall. Just like a guy, she thought to herself. With a grin she turned her attention to the plate of food that sat on the small carved wood table beside her bed. The tantalizing aroma of the meal teased her stomach to a loud grumble.

She looked carefully at the plate, trying to recognize any of what it held. With a shrug she decided to go with her hungry stomach and began shoveling the food into her mouth, much to her complete satisfaction. The taste she could not identify, but it was very good.

A short time late Carina returned with her arms full of clothing. Forrest still followed her, complaining the whole while.

"How was your meal?" the princess asked with a smile.

"I don't know what it was, but it was excellent."

"I'm glad you enjoyed it. It was a mixture of fish, herbs and vegetables. Now, I have clothing for you. These will prove practical in blending in with the surroundings as well as being light and comfortable," Carina said holding out a set of clothing for Brandy's inspection. She noticed that they were similar to what the princess wore. A long soft brown leather shirt and form fitting pants with black stitching. There were no buttons or zippers, instead the clothing was held together with leather ties.

"Dress quickly," Carina said. "The others are waiting to depart."

Brandy began to pull her bright purple sweatshirt off, when she realized that Forrest made no move to leave the room. "Do you mind?" she asked indignantly, a light shade of red creeping up warmly on her cheeks.

"Mind what?" Forrest asked blankly, not understanding what she meant.

"Leaving while I change clothing."

Forrest laughed heartily at her request. "We of the woods have no need for such modesty. Besides, I am sure you have nothing that I haven't seen before."

"Fine," Brandy retorted hot-temperedly. Her embarrassment gave way to anger. She pulled her sweatshirt agitatedly over her head and flung it to the floor. After kicking off her canvas tennis shoes, she unzipped her blue jeans and carelessly tossed them aside. All that remained was a pair of white cotton bikini underpants.

Forrest's eyes opened a bit wider. He looked closely at the girl before him. Her creamy skin glistened softly in the pale candle light of the room, as did the delicate highlights of her long thick hair, that cascaded like a waterfall down her back. Her limbs were well toned and slightly muscular. Her breasts and hips were fully rounded and ripened to the full maturity of womanhood.

He was uncomfortably aware that his heart seemed to beat faster within his chest, and that his blood roared uncontrollably in his veins. She was not at all like what he had seen before in other elfin women. She was strongly built, yet delicate. The two differences complimenting each other. When he realized that he was staring, it was too late, she had noticed.

"Just like everyone else," Brandy smirked, her anger ebbing, as she noticed his open gaze of admiration of her figure.

Forrest mumbled something unintelligible before he hurried from the room, his face darkening as he all but fled.

"That does not happen everyday." Carina laughed, as she finished helping Brandy tie the last strap of her shirt into place.

"What?"

"Getting the take on Forrest. He thinks he is so superior sometimes." Carina grinned mischievously. "It is nice to see him humbled."

"I think he could be a lot of fun if he would just loosen up."

"You are probably right, but that has never been his way. Well, we had better hurry and get going," Carina said leading the way down the corridor.

"Are you coming also to search for Steve as well?" Brandy asked, following Carina and glancing at the brightly woven tapestries that hung from the walls. They depicted elves who favored Carina in some way or another. They must be her family or past relatives, she thought.

"Yes."

"I'm glad. You're very kind," Brandy admitted to her new friend.

"Thank you. I am very fond of you also, but I must confess that I am very interested in your friend Steve," Carina grinned impishly. "I was somewhat gladdened to hear that he was not your mate."

"Well, he is interesting." Brandy laughed. Steve had that effect on almost every girl he met. She couldn't believe that it worked on elves also. Well, why not, she reasoned silently to herself, we are not that much different. In fact we are very much alike.

"The creatures that took Steve," Brandy began hesitantly, "are they goblins or what?"

"I do not know the word goblins, but we call them gobioids. They are very horrible creatures with cruel temperaments."

"I see," she murmured, following close behind Carina. Brandy hoped that her dear friend was alright as the princess led her through a large open room that echoed with every step that they took, and then outside into a sun brightened courtyard.

All around the courtyard there were flag poles, from which brightly colored pieces of cloth waved happily in the breeze. Scattered throughout the yard were other elves of all ages. From young children to those who had seen many decades of life. The cottages, shops and building were wonderfully hand carved masterpieces. She had only seen such marvels in drawings. She wondered if the artists had ever crossed the barrier as she had. In the center of the village, was the tallest structure, from which she and Carina had emerged. She assumed that was the princess and her family's home. As she stepped further into open yard, she came in full view of all those before her. As all eyes focused in her direction, and a hush settled over the people.

She hesitated as her earlier confidence quickly left her. She felt like an animal on display at some zoo exhibit. Much to her surprise, Forrest materialized at her side. Wordlessly taking her arm, he escorted her to the center of the yard where a large platform stood imperiously. Seated on the dais was the one whom Brandy assumed to the ruler of these elves, and Carina's father, for the princess looked much like this man, except that his hair was darker. As if to prove Brandy's thoughts to be true, Carina left her side and bounded up the steps of the platform, hugging the man warmly.

Forrest led Brandy to the steps, then stopped and bowed reverently. "My lord Corona, this is the human girl that we came across in the wood."

"Brandy Wells, your highness," Brandy said with a smile before Forrest could continue. She walked up the stairs and extended her hand in greeting.

A murmur arose from the surrounding elves at her action. Forrest started to protest the human's behavior when Corona held up a hand for his peoples silence. "Our human friend is new to our land. Show her some patience," he said as he took her outstretched hand and bade her to sit in the chair next to his own.

"I would like to hear about your land and its many ways, but I can tell from my daughter's look that it will have to be another time." Corona smiled affectionately at his child.

"Perhaps when you find your friend you will honor me with tales of your land."

"With great pleasure," Brandy promised.

"My lord," began Forrest, "I must ask reconsideration in allowing the human girl or your daughter to accompany us on this journey of search."

"Father, I am well trained in the arts of defense and can well hold my own safety against a foe." Carina turned to her father with a beseeching tone. "Besides, I am the only one who can talk to the birds so that we may know of the other human and the gobioid's location."

"And I can take care of myself," Brandy added quickly, jumping from her seat, and sending a dark look at Forrest. "Steve is my best friend and I'll not desert him," she pleaded to the elf lord seated before her.

"How can you take care of yourself? You do not even know how to defend yourself. You will be easy prey for the gobioids," Forrest argued back. "Have you ever used a sword? Or what about a bow?" he continued with a taunting hint in his voice. He grabbed a crossbow from a guard who stood nearby and waved it at Brandy.

Brandy gave the elf a blank look. Without betraying any emotion, she took the crossbow from his hand. She then accepted the arrow that the guard eagerly held up to her with a small encouraging smile. Notching the arrow on the tee, Brandy rested the stock against her shoulder.

"See that flag pole over there?" she indicated to the pole that was the farthest away from them across the courtyard. "I'll try for it." She winked at Forrest, carefully took aim, and pulled the trigger. The arrow gracefully cut through the distance between the dais and the pole, striking home with a resounding thud.

Forrest eyes widened as words of admiration filtered through the crowd like wildfire. Carina squeezed her arm gleefully. "Well done," she whispered happily.

Carona's eyes smiled warmly at Brandy and he gave a small nod of approval. "I do believe you can take care of yourself. Keep that bow, for it suits you well. May all of the arrows that you loose be as well guided as was your first."

"We must leave," Carina began again and before any more objections could be placed in their way. "We are losing valuable traveling time." She pointed to the heavens. The sun was already beginning to reach the center of its journey across the clear blue sky. She was very glad when her father pulled her close for a hug and led them down the steps to the grass.

Brandy stared about as Carina and her father said their good byes. She marveled at how warm the sun felt on her face. How beautiful the woods were that surrounded them. How fragrant the air smelled and how her life had become so odd in the span of one night. Her thoughts settled on Forrest. Why does he dislike me so, she wondered. I find him so fascinating and attractive, yet he is so resentful of me. I would like to get to know him, but will he let me?

Her thoughts were abruptly interrupted by Forrest himself. "Are you going to stand here daydreaming, or are you ready to leave?" he snapped.

In a sudden childish and spontaneous response, Brandy stuck her tongue out at him. He stared at her with shocked amazement. She said nothing, but hurried past him to follow Carina to where a group of elves and horses waited at the gates of their village.

Forrest intently watched her pass and shook his head in puzzlement. Humans are most curious and unusual, he thought to himself as he too walked slowly towards the rest of the group.

When Brandy reached the small group, Carina took her by the hand and introduced her to the others that were waiting. "Brandy this is Draco, Volan, and Puppis."

The other elves smiled courteously and eyed the human with open interest, and although the only physical difference between themselves and this newcomer was the shape their ears, they were candidly curious of her of mannerisms and actions.

Brandy too looked at the three elves with honest curiosity. Puppis was a very slight and petite elf girl. Her hair was the color of flame, and she offered Brandy a warm and friendly smile. Volan had boyish good looks with bright eyes that peeked out beneath a mass of tangled yellow hair. He bowed to Brandy with a flourish and came to her side to help her onto her horse.

"Thank you," Brandy murmured appreciatively as she settled into the cloth saddle that covered the horse's back. Her eyes studied the last of the elves, Draco. He was short and stocky with large powerfully looking hands in which he held a massive two sided axe. He was older than the rest of the group. Probably to keep us in line, she thought. Works for me, she smile as she watched him easily hoist the huge weapon over his shoulder and swing lightly up onto his horse.

"You can ride, I trust?" Forrest asked a little too loudly as they readied to depart.

"Honestly, not as well as I wish I could," Brandy admitted quietly. "I will keep up."

"You had better." With that Forrest led his horse under the tall gate and into the shady woods, the others followed closely behind.

Puppis turned in her saddle and smiled to Brandy. "Do not worry about him, he is not very nice to anyone."

"Thanks." Brandy smiled back. She didn't know whether she should feel any better or not, but tried her best to shrug off Forrest's remark.

As the village disappeared from sight behind them and the branches of the trees closed up all around them, Brandy sighed. "Hang on Steve, we're coming," she whispered into the wind blowing gently above her.

Chapter Three

"I wonder where our elf buddies are?" Brandy asked.

Steve followed her glance behind them. They were no where to be seen. When he turned his head back to the noise, the six goblins once again stood before him. He couldn't believe that they were able to move so fast, but they did. In seconds, two of them seized him with scaly hands while a third hit Brandy on the back of the head with the flat of his sword. Steve watched her sink to the ground like a limp rag doll.

"Brandy!" he yelled frantically, when he saw that she didn't move after the blow. He began fighting against his captures with renewed strength and curses, but it was hopeless. The goblins swarmed over him like ants at a picnic. They held his arms and legs, dragging him through the underbrush. The branches grabbed cruelly at him, tearing his clothes as well as the exposed skin of his hands and face.

After a short hurried trip, the goblins carelessly threw Steve to the ground. He took a deep breath and jumped to his feet, ready to flee. Just as quickly as he regained his footing, one of the creatures swung a massive arm at him, sending him back to his knees. Shaking his head, he struggled to clear his vision.

"Damn, you guys mean business," he muttered.

The creatures gave a chuckling wheeze. "Gobioids, we are gobioids," the largest of the group informed him.

"I'm so impressed," Steve muttered. He shook his head in wonder as he studied them more closely for the first time.

They were even more horrible than he had originally imagined. Their skin was dull and scaly, and their eyes gleamed wickedly in the pale moonlight. Worst of all was their stench. They smelled of death. He actually found himself wishing more and more for any avenue of escape.

"The human you requested," said the largest of the gobioids to someone that Steve could not see. He appeared to Steve, to be the one with authority over the others, for he and only he spoke to the hidden one.

"Bind the human to a travel beast. Try not to damage him too greatly," said the hidden voice harshly.

Steve did not like what the hidden one implied when he told the gobioids to try and not damage him too much. As they reached their rough, cold clawed hands toward him again, he decided not to put up a struggle. Surprisingly neither did the gobioids. They deftly tied his wrists and ankles together with a long leather strap. One of the largest gobioids easily hoisted Steve over it's muscled shoulder and carried him to the nearest horned beast.

"Boy, I thought you guys were aromatic," Steve muttered to the gobioid, wrinkling his nose in disgust, as he was placed standing again. Then shaking his head at the beast he added, "but these four legged creatures take the cake."

Leveling his yellow eyes at the human, not understanding the meaning of his words, the gobioid finally spoke. "They are called Agouti."

"Agouti," Steve repeated very slowly, trying to say the word as the gobioid had done. So this was what he and Brandy had seen before the wreck of her truck. They did indeed look similar to horses, only a few hands larger. They had short horns that curved inward on the top front of their heads. Their eyes were dark and unblinking, and their coats were somewhat shaggy and course in texture. They snorted loudly and shuffled constantly, eager to be on their way.

"Yes, agouti," the gobioid said again, nodding his head. He reached out and easily lifted Steve up to the back of the beast, tossing him face down across the animal.

"I can ride, you know," Steve called out to his captors while they mounted their beasts and headed into the dark woods.

"No more talk," grumbled one of the gobioids, raising his massive hand in warning.

Steve firmly closed his mouth and looked away. Gee whiz, he sighed silently. Not at all friendly. He tried to joke to himself. Humor had always been a comfort to him in difficult times. This was definitely one of those times. He clung desperately to the back and underside of the agouti with his tethered limbs. Every jolting step that the animal took riddled pain throughout his mid section. He could feel the blood rushing to his head, and he fervently hoped that their trip would be a short one, but he knew that it probably wouldn't work out that way.

He was right. He soon lost track of time. When they stopped the sun was shining down through the tree limbs. He let himself slither down the side of the agouti and crumpled on the cool ground below him. He was exhausted, and it felt good not to be moving.

"Up!" commanded one of the gobioids.

Steve opened his eyes and stared warily at the creature before him. He had a retort on his tongue, but held it back. He didn't know if his body could withstand much more torture. He struggled into a sitting position, and could go no farther.

The gobioid said nothing, instead it shoved a heavy leather pouch, with a spout on it, into his bound hands. "Drink, and be quick about it," he barked.

Steve did not hesitate. He wasn't sure what the drink would be, but his mouth and throat was so dry that he did not care. He was surprised when he tasted the liquid and eagerly welcomed the water that filtered through his lips.

"That's enough," said the gobioid, abruptly pulling the flask from Steve's grasp, before he could get his fill. He then grabbed the human and flung him back over the agouti.

As they traveled on, Steve looked at the leaves that covered the floor of the woods and the low bushes that were in view of his eyes. They looked the same as the leaves and bushes that were near his home. Only he was used to looking at them from a normal point of view. Why had he been taken, Steve wondered. When he and Brandy had come upon them in the woods, the gobioids had been attacking the elves, but he had been the one who was now their prisoner. Why? Whatever the reason behind it was, he knew for sure that it wasn't going to be beneficial to him.

But wait. What about Brandy? He was thankful that she had been left behind. He wondered how was she? The blow she had take had been powerful. Was she even alive? Of course she is, he thought angrily. Don't even think such a stupid thing. Brandy was strong and feisty. He was positive that she was alive, and that she was looking for him. She would never let him down. She would find him, Steve knew that beyond anything else. Only for now he would have to hang on.

When they finally stopped again, it was dark. The sun had long since disappeared behind the trees, casting shadows all about. Steve felt a hand grab him roughly by the back of the shirt. He sailed from the agouti and landed heavily on the ground.

"Damn it," Steve yelled angrily at his captors, not caring about the consequences of his words. "Think you can do that any harder?"

"Probably so," one of the gobioids said with an amused laugh. He reached for the human male, oblivious to the sarcasm in which the words had been spoken.

"Enough Braakk," commanded a voice. The voice that Steve had first heard when he had been captured.

Turning his head, Steve expected to see another gobioid, instead his eyes came to rest on an elf. A tall, darkly tanned elf, with black hair and blazing coal black eyes. "You're an elf . . ." he stammered foolishly, trying to make sense of what was happening.

"Surely you did not expect another one of these dull witted creatures, did you?" he asked in a mocking tone, gesturing to the gobioids who stood numbly in his presence.

"Well, I didn't expect an elf," Steve countered.

"Why ever not?" the elf asked, raising a surprised eyebrow.

"Because those were elves back in the clearing that your goons were attacking. I kind of thought you were the good guys."

"Do you mean to tell me that humans do not attack and fight other humans," mocked the elf, grinning sarcastically. He motioned to a gobioid standing close to Steve. "Cut his bonds," he ordered.

Steve was stunned by the elf's word, but he was grateful to be having his binds removed. His wrists and ankles were swollen, bleeding and hurt terribly. Outwardly he would show no signs of his discomfort, but inwardly his joints screamed in agony.

"Who are you, and why did you attack the other elves?" Steve asked as he stood and tried to regain the circulation and use of his numb limbs.

"I am called Chameleon, and why I was there is really no concern of yours," the elf said imperiously, brushing off the human's question.

"Then why did you kidnap me? It's against the law where I come from."

Chameleon laughed loudly. "There is no law here except for my law. Look around," he said, motioning to the gobioids with a careless and sweeping wave. "They obey me and only me, and as for kidnapping you, I did no such thing. I have no intention of holding you for ransom. You are a very precious commodity to me for now and that is all you need to know. When your use is over, then so shall you be."

"Great. So you're going to kill me."

"Not exactly," said Chameleon, turning his back on the human. "There are other things worse than death."

Steve stared in horrified wonder at the elf. Chameleon was speaking to the surrounding gobioids in a language that he could not understand. This is really bad, Steve thought. I think I'm beginning the adventure of a lifetime and I end up being gobioid bait, and the prisoner of some smart ass elf. Boy, wouldn't my friends be jealous of me now, he thought disgustedly. And just what did 'not exactly' mean?

He looked around, trying to decide from which direction they had come, but it was no use. His ride on the agouti had done nothing more than to further confuse him as to where he was. He had no idea from where he had come or where he was going.

"The master says you need to eat."

Braakk's rough speech interrupted Steve's thoughts. The creature shoved a wooden bowl of food into his still tingling hands. Steve held it to his nose, bracing himself for some horrible smell, but it was not there. Instead what greeted him was an aroma that was delicious. His stomach grumbled greedily as he realized just how hungry he was.

"Thanks," Steve said with a nod. "You got a spoon or a fork?"

"Use your hands," he grunted, but not so harshly this time. Braakk pointed to a large tree stump that laid felled on the ground. "Sit there."

Steve sat obediently, resting his back against a thick limb that was still attached to the tree. Braakk squatted in front of him and tied his feet together again, but much looser than before.

"Thanks, much better than before," Steve said appreciatively, wiggling his feet.

Braakk quietly studied the human in front of him for a moment. "Just eat," he muttered as he turned and shuffled back to join the other gobioids who had gathered around a small glowing campfire.

Steve looked in his bowl. The food appeared to be some sort of green vegetable. He was glad, for he didn't want to know what kind of meat that these creatures would eat. Steve chewed slowly so as to make his meal last longer for he doubted that he would get seconds. While eating, he keenly watched the gobioids, who in turned kept an eye on him. Every so often one of them would look at him, make a comment in their guttural language, and they would all laugh. He figured that he must seem odd to them, and easy to poke fun at, but he really didn't care to hear what their comments were about. He was sure that they wouldn't be pleasant. Then he reasoned, if their positions were reversed, his comments probably wouldn't be that nice either.

Removing his gaze from the gobioids, Steve scanned the area for Chameleon. He was no where in sight, it was as if he had disappeared again. He thoughts were a jumble of confusion as to why he had been taken. One thing was for sure, he didn't really want to know after his talk with the dark elf.

A short while later Braakk left the group of gobioids and approached Steve. Wordlessly he took the bowl from Steve's hand, rebound his wrists, and turned to leave.

"Now what?? Steve asked curiously, before Braakk could walk away.

"You sleep," Braakk said matter of factly, pointing at the ground.

"No bed time story?" Steve joked like a small, mischievous child. Acting idiotic was his way of coping.

"No. Just sleep," Braakk said dryly.

Steve chuckled lightly as he settled down to the ground. He rested his weary shoulders and head against the fallen tree. His body felt tense and very tired after his long ride, and he hoped that sleep wouldn't elude him for long. Unfortunately that wasn't the case. For what seemed like hours, he laid in his place looking all about himself. As he once again found himself staring into the surrounding woods, he felt as though someone or something was out there watching him back. Then he caught a slight movement in the tree branches above him. He laid as quietly and still as possible. He shot a quick glance at the gobioids. They were oblivious to anything save their own loud conversation and crude noises. Glancing back up into the branches he saw a large hawk sitting there, looking intently at him.

"Scared by a bird," Steve reprimanded himself with a laugh. "What a wimp I'm becoming."

"Do not be frightened," the bird squeaked softly, hopping down from its perch to sit close to Steve's head on the log.

Steve's eyes bugged out in alarm. The bird had talked and had understood it. Not only that, but it had made an intelligent sentence. And, it said 'don't be frightened', but right now scared was sounding pretty good.

"Steve," the bird began urgently. "Please do no be afraid. It is me, the elf girl that you saved in the clearing yesterday. My name is Carina."

"Great," Steve mumbled miserably. "I meet the girl of my dreams and she turns out to be a bird. Why me?"

The bird giggled, ruffling it's brown feathers. "I am not a bird, I am just talking through it. Are you alright?"

"Just a bit bruised, but other than that fine."

"I am glad," Carina said. "Your friend Brandy is well. She is with us."

"But where are you?"

"We are close by, and we have more elves with us to help you. Please do not despair."

"Trust me, I'm not going anywhere," Steve chuckled holding his bound hands up. He looked at his captures, fearful that they would hear him, but they seemed to immersed in their own conversation.

"Do you know where they are taking you?" Carina asked, the bird hopping nervously from foot to foot every time it glanced at the gobioids.

"No. They haven't said. By the way, who is this other elf, Chameleon? He seems to be the leader of these creeps. Is the name familiar to you?"

The bird stopped its prancing and stared intently at human. "I must go now," Carina said in a soft voice. "I can only use the bird for a short while. Please trust in me. We will come for you." With the last word spoken the hawk flapped his large powerful wings and floated off to another tree.

Steve smiled contentedly and settled back comfortably against his tree. He closed his eyes and took a deep relaxing breath. Brandy was safe and well, he had talked to the princess, and most importantly, he was not alone.

CHAPTER FOUR

Brandy stared anxiously at Carina. The elf girl sat before her, cross legged, with her eyes closed. She wished she could hear what unspoken words were being said and unheard, but were floating around in the princess' mind. Instead, she was just sitting there watching, and not being able to do anything.

The group had ridden the rest of the day away in almost complete silence. Silence was usually Brandy's friend, but it today it wasn't. Today it had been her worst enemy. The lack of noise made her want to scream out at the stillness at the top of her lungs. The quiet made her brain conjure up all kinds of terrible visions of what may be happening to Steve. The concern she felt for her friend was slowly eating away at her insides. When the sun had begun to sink, they stopped to set up camp. Carina said that she would try to locate and make contact with Steve. Brandy had eagerly agreed, and yet now she wanted the princess to talk to her and tell her what was going on, instead of waiting.

After what seemed an eternity, Carina opened her sky colored eyes and blinked them heavily several times. Rubbing the sides of her head with gentle strokes of her fingertips, Carina squinted into the fire light. "That always gives me a pain in my head," she complained softly.

As the others gathered around Carina, Brandy could contain herself no longer. "Where is he? Is he okay? Those scaly snakes had better not have laid a clawed hand on him . . . ,"

"Calm down." Carina cut into the human girl's flow of words with a smile. "Your friend is fine. And even better news; he is very close by, maybe a days ride ahead. That is much better than I had expected, for the agouti are faster than our horses. The gobioids seem to be in no hurry."

"We can take six gobioids with no trouble," Volan said with a confident smile at Brandy. "We should have your friend back in no time."

"There is something else," Carina added with a note of concern creeping into her voice, looking at the elves before her. "Chameleon has him."

"Heavens help us," Puppis whispered quietly, making a gesture in the air before her. Volan said nothing but shook his head, and Draco picked up his large axe and began sharpening it with renewed vigor.

"What? What's wrong? Who is this Chameleon?" Brandy asked, searching each of their faces for an answer.

"He is an evil one," Puppis said gently, taking Brandy's hands in her own trembling ones. "Your friend may be in grave danger."

"Then let's get going. We can leave right now and probably catch them by tomorrow." Brandy jumped to her feet, but the others remained where they were. She stared at them in confusion. "Well, what are you waiting for? A written invitation?" she demanded.

"You do not understand," began Carina slowly. "Chameleon is evil. He has turned his back on all of the ways of the elfin folk. He has traded the goodness in his soul for the knowledge of darkness that all should have sense to fear. He has joined the forces of the Dark Queen Lacerta. She allows him to command all below him."

"You mean he's an elf, like you are?" Brandy asked.

"No." Carina shook her head firmly. "He is nothing like we are. He has changed into something sinister and frightening. His being is corrupted by evil and power, no matter what the cost to others."

"We should have guessed it was him when we first encountered the gobioids," Forrest said darkly, breaking the silence of his brooding. He held no liking for humans, but in the grasp of Chameleon, even he felt for the human male.

"Well, if you won't help him, then I will go on alone. I don't care who or what this Chameleon is, I won't run from him. He has Steve and I refuse to give up hope. This Chameleon will just have to kill me," Brandy said angrily. She turned and went toward her horse. She would help Steve no matter what the consequences or the price. He was the only family that she had. She felt her face burning hotly as tears of frustration threatened to escape her eyes. She had no idea where to begin looking for Steve, but she would be damned if she was going to sit around and do nothing to help him.

"Do not cry child," said a hoarse, gruff voice.

It was Draco who came to her side. He put his strong arms about her weary shoulders and pulled her close to his burly chest in a comforting hug. Gently he stroked the back of her hair the way her father used to, making Brandy feel like a small insecure child again. As her tears fell freely, dampening Draco's shirt, he continued softly.

"The horses must rest, and so must we. We worry for your friend for we know his capture. Please have faith in this; your friend is still alive which means that he has a value to Chameleon. We will reach him and none here will give up trying," Draco promised, giving Brandy a reassuring nod.

Brandy slowly looked to the others who each in turn nodded their agreement at Draco's words. Finally her eyes rested on Forrest. Instead of looking away, he met her gaze fully. For the briefest of moments he gave her a small encouraging smile.

"Perhaps we should rest now," said Draco, wiping Brandy's face with a soft cloth, then returning to the fire where a pot of stew bubbled invitingly.

"Good idea," Volan agreed, good naturedly patting his stomach with a large smile.

"I think we girls shall eat a little later," Carina said with a quick glance at Puppis who seemed to instantly understand and approve of her unspoken plan.

"Where are we going?" Brandy asked as Carina and Puppis each took one of her arms and began leading her from the camp.

"Close to here is a warm spring fed lake. Its waters will soothe your muscles and make you feel much better." Puppis smiled kindheartedly.

"That is an even better idea than food," said a grinning Volan from his place by the fire. "Maybe I should come and guard your clothes. You would not want to misplace them."

"We can take care of ourselves, Volan, and so can our clothes. You stay put," Carina warned with a laugh and a wag of her finger.

Puppis expertly navigated through the dark shadows of the trees. The moon overhead offered little light as they traveled forward. The leaves lightly caressed Brandy's face with soft gentleness and a slight breeze whispered melodiously through the branches.

In a span of mere minutes they emerged through the trees to the very banks of a lake. Brandy stared in wonder at its peaceful appearance. Its surface could have been dark glass for not a ripple disturbed its silent slumber. The moon's reflection shone gracefully off of the lake, spraying the water with the brilliance of a million diamonds. The vision before her was already soothing her frazzled nerves.

"Come on," Carina said eagerly, removing her clothing and tossing them in a pile by her feet. "The water is much better if you get in it."

Brandy quickly undressed and followed Carina and Puppis to the still waters. Hesitantly she placed her foot into its calm darkness. Carina was right, Brandy thought, the water was at perfect bath temperature. She dove into the calming warmness, gracefully cutting through its depths like a fish. As she surfaced she laughed gleefully, the stresses of moments ago melting from her shoulders. "This is incredible. How does it stay so warm?"

"The elders say that the water comes from the deepest part of the ground. I do not really care how it stays warm, only that it does," Puppis replied, then laughed, splashing loudly in the tepid comfort that surrounded them.

Brandy closed her eyes and savored the relaxing feel the enveloped her body. She rolled slowly in the calm spring fed pool, letting its gentle touch caress her body. Time and time again she dove deep into the depths of its dark waters, then rushed happily back to the surface just as her air supply diminished. All her problems that had haunted her earlier seemed much easier now. Maybe all would be well.

"If you stay out there much longer you will truly turn into a fish," Carina called to Brandy from the shore.

Brandy looked around in wonder. She had been so wrapped up in her delight of the swim that she had not realized that she was far out into the lake, and that the others had already returned to shore. "I'll be out in a flash." Brandy smiled across the water with a waving her arm in reply.

With strong strokes she quickly propelled herself toward the shore, swiftly eating up the distance to land. Oblivious to all around her, Brandy was startled when she felt something brush against her leg. Instantly she stopped swimming and treaded water. Peering around at the dark liquid that surrounded her, she saw nothing and laughed to herself. Goof ball, she chided silently, it was probably a fish. Again she turned toward land and began swimming. After a few strokes something touched her legs again. This time it wasn't a light brush, it was more like a thump.

Her heart began beating wildly, fear gripping tightly at her insides. All she could think of was all of the horrible shark movies she had ever seen. It always started with a brush against the skin, then a thump, and then it was all over. Glancing around for a dorsal fin, she shivered inwardly. There was something down there, she thought. Anxiously her arms stroked deeply at the water, desperately trying to eat up the remaining distance between herself and safety. The security of land seemed like an eternity away from her. Her breaths came in ragged gasps as she struggled feverishly on. Suddenly something slick lashed around her left ankle and pulled her beneath the surface. Water rushed into her open mouth and up her nose. Frantically she kicked with her free foot at whatever groped her other limb. The slimy creature loosened it grip on her and Brandy swiftly pulled herself to the surface and fresh air above.

Breaking the plane of the water, Brandy coughed and sputtered trying to breathe air instead of water. She struggled on toward the shore hoping that her assailant had left.

"Help!" she screamed in a ragged voice. "Help me! Something's in the water."

Carina and Puppis turned at Brandy's distressed cry. At first they could not comprehend what was happening, but quickly understood when they looked past her. As Brandy swam frantically toward them, a ripple shot through the water like a well aimed arrow. A long sleek body tracked the human girl who floundered in comparison to its own gracefulness.

"Heavens help her," Puppis cried. "It is a guivre."

"Hurry, back to camp and get the others," Carina ordered, pushing Puppis off in the direction of their bivouac. She turned her full attention back to Brandy. "Swim faster Brandy, faster," she yelled as loudly as she could. She could see the guivre raising its head from the waters behind Brandy. It had honed in on its prey and now it wanted to finish the chase.

Brandy heard Carina's words of encouragement and doubled her efforts to speed up. God, please help me, she prayed silently. Only fifty more feet. You can make it, Brandy, she reassured herself. Her arms screamed in protest at the torturous pace that they were going, but they would not fail her now. She would not let her body fail her.

With only short distance to go to safety Brandy chanced a quick look behind her. What she saw stopped her dead in her tracks. Fear paralyzed her limbs with numbness. If it weren't for the fact that her feet could now touch the bottom of the lake, she would have surely sunk and drowned before the creature could even have taken her. A huge head with large glassy eyes stared down at her from a neck that rose at least six or seven feet above the water. Its orb shaped yellow eyes, with a midnight black pupil slit, regarded her with menacing coolness. The moonlight reflected a rainbow of colors off of the creatures scaled body. It had two short white horns on top of its head, and many rows of sharp teeth filled its wide mouth.

The creature leaned closely to Brandy and deeply sniffed at her, rustling her wet hair that floated all about her in the water like strands of loose silk. Lifting its massive head, the monster hissed loudly into the night. The noise of the beast shook Brandy back to her senses. She must get away. Slowly and as inconspicuously as possible, she began backing up toward the shore. If she could get into some shallower water, maybe she could sprint the rest of the way to land. She knew that the odds were not in her favor, but she would rather try than be a passive hors d'oeuvre to this creature. Brandy counted ten steps backward, the water had receded to her elbows. The creature continued to hiss into the night sky. If only she could get a little farther back then she would be able to run. Suddenly she felt something grab at her back. A scream of fear tore from her lips as she whirled around to face her newest attacker. Her mouth fell open as she realized that she looked into the gem colored eyes of Forrest. Involuntarily she flung her arms around his neck and hugged him close, trying to ease the trembling that had invaded her tired limbs.

"You are safe now, child," Draco's voice said to her from beside Forrest.

Brandy smiled happily at the sound of his voice. "What about that, that thing?" she stammered, glancing at the huge snake like beast that towered over them.

"Do not you fret a bit about him. He and I are about to have a chat and find out why his is still out and about at this time of year," Draco reassured her as he patted her shoulder.

"I don't understand," Brandy began as Forrest easily lifted her in his arms and carried her from the water. "This thing is a friend to the elves?"

"Well, not exactly," Forrest explained, trying not to notice how securely and trustingly the naked human girl snuggled in his arms. "We have an understanding with them on when we can and can not use the lakes and rivers that they occupy."

"Thank the heavens you are safe . . ." Carina began, but was cut off as Forrest walked past her without stopping, taking Brandy's clothes from her hands.

He halted by a large bush and gently returned Brandy to her feet. "For your . . . Privacy," Forrest stammered, quickly shoving Brandy's clothes to her, and turning his back while she hastily dressed.

"I can't thank you enough," Brandy murmured, tying the last of her shirt lacings in place. "I thought I was a midnight snack for that thing. You guys definitely seem to grow things a lot bigger in your side of the mist."

Forrest said nothing, only nodded his head silently and walked back toward the others who stood with Draco by the lake side. Brandy hastily pulled on her soft leather short boots and hurried to catch up. She didn't want to miss any of this conversation.

"Are you alright, child?" Draco asked with fatherly concern.

"Yes, I'm fine now, but what was that thing?"

"That was a guivre," Volan answered quickly. "Ill tempered creatures when you invade their water."

"You were lucky," Puppis added, "he was a small one."

"A small one," Brandy gasped in wonder. "It must have been nearly twenty foot long. I would hate to have seen its father."

"They are twice that long when fully grown," Volan said with a nod.

Brandy looked at Draco. "You said that you and the guivre were going to have a chat, can all of you talk to those creatures?"

"No," Draco said with a small smile.

"Draco is the only elf in our woods with the ability to talk Dragon speech," Carina said proudly of the elder elf.

"That makes sense," Brandy said, tapping herself on the forehead. "I should have guessed. Draco is the name for the constellation of the Dragon.

Draco laughed out in amusement of the human girls declaration. "You are very correct indeed. I did not think that humans looked to the stars much anymore."

"There are some of us who do nothing but look to the stars and dream," she said quietly.

"Dreaming is a good thing," Carina said and smiled at Brandy.

"Sometimes, sometimes not." Brandy smiled wistfully back.

"What did you learn from the guivre?" Forrest asked. This human girl disturbed him when she spoke. Her voice had the most unusual effect on him, and he did not like it. Humans were supposed to be the enemy; that's what he always thought. More and more he was not hating this human, but finding himself intrigued with her. That was something that disturbed him greatly indeed.

"Yes, the guivre. What did it have to say?" Brandy echoed Forrest's question. Even though the creature had come inches from making her a late night snack, she was greatly interested in it.

"First of all, he apologizes for trying to eat you. He has never seen a human before, and your scent confused him greatly. That is why he was making so much noise."

"Well, I guess I can forgive him," Brandy said a little uncertainly. "I've never seen his kind before either, but I wouldn't have eaten him."

"Has he seen Brandy's friend or any of the gobioids?" asked Volan hopefully, stifling a snicker at her comment.

"No. I asked him about that also, but he has not seen anyone until the females invaded his waters."

"What is the guivre still doing in this lake?" Carina queried. "He should be in his den by now."

Draco cleared his throat and took a deep breath. "Well, I am afraid that the news is not very good at all. It seems, according to the dragon, that Lyra has not sent word of Spring. In fact none of the dragons that the guivre has come in contact with has heard anything from Lyra as of yet."

"You realize Spring is only four days away," Puppis said worriedly.

Volan nodded in concern at his friend's words. "What will happen if Lyra does not do her work and Spring does not arrive?"

"Wait! Who is Lyra and what does that have to do with why that guivre tried to eat me?" Brandy interrupted in confusion, looking to each of the elves whose faces held serious anxiety.

"Lyra is the Keeper of Spring. It is her duty to bring the woods and all of the elfin lands out of their slumber of winter," Carina began.

"Usually the dragons are the first to know of Lyra beginning her work, for she contacts them before any of the other creatures so that they can prepare for their long sleep," continued Puppis.

"So can you contact this Lyra and find out what is going on?" Brandy asked Carina.

"No. It is not that easy. Lyra is not an elf; she is much more. She has many, many magical powers. She is almost as old as time. She cannot just be found, only she can seek one out," Carina answered as well as she could. It was hard for her to explain that in which she grew up knowing about. That which all elves knew about.

There was a long silence as the elves grappled with words in which to describe Lyra to Brandy. Finally Forrest broke the wall of unspoken words which surrounded them. "I believe you humans would call her Mother Nature."

Brandy said nothing, but silently mouthed the words that Forrest had spoken. When she was little she had believed in Mother Nature, but now it was nothing more to her than a childish nursery rhyme. She knew that the seasons were controlled by the weather and the atmosphere, not some magical person. What about here? Very little of what she had encountered in this place had been like how it was at home. Maybe the seasons here were controlled by this Lyra. All of the elves who stood before her believed so.

"I always thought Mother Nature was a fairy tale," Brandy stammered awkwardly. As soon as the words left her, she wished she hadn't spoken them. The looks of the others were of disbelief at what she had said.

"Figures," Forrest said sarcastically. "Humans think that elves are fairy tales as well."

"That's not fair," Brandy retorted. "I can't help what has been taught to me. You think all humans are bad and not to be trusted, but that's not true either."

"Enough, children," Draco broke in with his fatherly tone. "Let us return to camp and sort out some kind of plan. There is much that must be discussed."

"Yes," Carina agreed instantly. She knew that Brandy was trying to absorb all that she was seeing, hearing, and learning, and that it must not be easy for her. "The fact remains that Lyra appears to be missing or lost. We must make a plan."

What of Steve, Brandy thought despondently as she followed slowly behind the others. She plucked leaves from the tree branches in frustration. She felt their anxiety and alarm at the news from the guivre, and she wanted to help, but that meant turning her back on Steve, and that she couldn't do. She knew that if she had to, she would continue on looking for Steve by herself.

CHAPTER FIVE

Brandy wandered slowly through the dark damp corridors. She couldn't remember how she had gotten to where ever it was that she was, only that she was there. Occasionally a torch would appear in the long hallway and give the surrounding gloom some light for a moment, then it would vanish and the darkness would once again reclaim her. She gingerly reached her hand out and touched the wall with her fingertips. It felt cold and slimy, like a giant earthworm, but it was a wall none the less. A faint murmur in the distance before her caught her attention. She strained her hearing to try and make out some of the soft syllables that floated in the air before proceeding further down the dark path, but could not. Taking a deep breath, she headed boldly for the sound, keeping her hand on the wall beside her for guidance and reassurance that something in this place was real and solid.

A glimmer of light appeared ahead of her, growing slowly in size with each step that she took. The murmuring had ceased and now silence reigned dominant in its place. Brandy halted in an open doorway. She had reached the source of the light. It came from a fire pit in the center of a massive room. There were no windows in the room, even though the ceiling must have been three stories tall. There was nothing on the left side of the room save for a stairway that winded from the floor to another corridor nearly at the top of the room. The damp block walls were empty and free of any decorations and no rugs or capeting covered the floor so that they could have kept the coldness of the outside from creeping in.

Brandy felt an involuntary shiver snake its way down her spine as she turned her gaze to the right side of the room. A long smooth ebony table made of marble stood imperiously on top of a thick, lush fur that had been dyed crimson. At least she hoped it had been dyed and not originally that color. What stood behind the table caught her attention and held it fast. It was a crystal. It hung suspended in air, neither touching the floor with its base nor held to the ceiling by ropes or chains. It just seemed to float there, unmoving, as if being held steadfastly by unseen hands.

Brandy's heart pounded loudly in her ears as she approached the huge glistening crystal. Her eyes were transfixed on the floating rock. She stopped before the marble table and placed her hands on its smooth, glassy surface. The coldness of it surprised her and sent goose bumps rushing up and down her arms. Shivering despite the warmth that the fire pit gave off, Brandy hugged her arms close to her. Her hands felt as though they had been burned with ice. She stared deeply into the thick depths of the crystal and blinked tightly several times at what she saw.

A body? No, a lady! Brandy inhaled quietly. She quickly rounded the table and stood before the crystal. Hesitantly she placed her hand lightly on its shining surface. The instant her skin made contact, the lady's eyes opened wide. At first she jumped back, but then stepped forward again. Her gaze was drawn to the lady's face. Her skin was flawlessly smooth, her features were perfectly proportioned, her silver white hair streamed to her bare feet, and her eyes were the color of thunder clouds before a wild storm. The lady was simply dressed in a soft green, yellow and blue gown that hung loosely from her shoulders to her ankles.

"Brandy Wells, daughter of my human children. I am pleased you have come," the lady said softly. Her voice was like the music of the trees in Brandy's ears. The trees from her home.

"Have we met before?" Brandy asked in a small timid voice. Though the lady's lips had not moved her words had been clearly heard within Brandy's mind.

"Not in the elfin realm, my child. We have spoken many times in the human woods."

"I don't understand. The only people in the woods back home were my parents before they died. Then I was alone," Brandy said, shaking her head. The tears of longing for her parents were building in her eyes. Who was this lady? Why was she saying such things, and bringing back memories that she had tried so hard to forget?

"You came to me many times in the dark coolness of the trees and spoke of your heart's feelings. I always listened to you and was happy when you too accepted those feelings." The lady smiled warmly at Brandy, fixing her gaze intently through the crystal.

"I guess I never really felt as though I were truly alone," Brandy whispered in new understanding at the lady's words. She had continuously felt as though there was someone else in the trees with her after the loss of her parents. Someone who was listening with compassionate silence.

"Who are you?"

"Here, I am called Lyra."

"Lyra? You're Lyra?" Brandy asked in disbelief, nearly shouting the words. "How can this be? You are supposed to be the Keeper of Spring, or so the elves tell me. What are you doing in a crystal? Has someone imprisoned you here? Are you hurt?"

"She is my ornament for the moment," a cold voice declared from behind.

Brandy whirled at the sound. Descending the stairs was an elf. He was tall, slender, yet forceful in his walk. Energy seemed to glow from the depths of his black robes. His hair and eyes were darker than coal, almost a blue black color. The only light that emanated from him was the pearliness of his teeth as he grinned cruelly and triumphantly at her.

"Excuse me?" Brandy asked in amazement. "Do you know who this is?" She pointed to Lyra suspended behind her.

Chuckling contemptuously, the dark elf seemed to draw amusement from her comment. "Of course I do, little human girl. Those puny elves you associate with think she is some sort of all powerful spirit. Bah, they don't know what real power is."

"I am sure that they are much more powerful than you are!" Brandy spurted the words out hotly and indignantly.

"Do you even know who I am?" queried the elf, not at all bothered by her retort.

"From what I can see, you're nothing more than another smart ass elf who doesn't know what he's doing," Brandy shot back angrily.

The darkly dressed elf threw back his head in laughter. "My, my. Not very pretty words coming from such a lovely mouth. I am Chameleon," the elf announced regally.

Brandy snapped her mouth tightly closed against the words that hung there, threatening to escape. This was the dreaded elf Chameleon. The one who was so evil and feared. He did not seem much different from the others, except that she could sense something in the air that was not quite right. This elf definitely had powers, for how else could he had captured Lyra and keep her here. Yet more importantly to her, he had Steve, so she would have to be careful.

Chameleon grinned at the silent dismay that filtered across Brandy's face. "So, I take it you have heard of me?"

"Oh, yes, but I wouldn't be so sure that it was flattering," she replied hotly, walking over to face the elf. His presence was intimidating and she had to quell the urge to flee, but none the less Brandy held her ground before him. "Where is my friend, the other human, Steve Rixx? And what have you done with him?"

"You do have a sharp little tongue on you," Chameleon said with a smile. "You could prove to be some temporary fun around this drab place. I am afraid that is going to have to wait. I have other things planned for you at the moment."

Ignoring his words, Brandy continued. "I said, in case you are a little deaf, where is my friend . . ."

"I heard you the first time." Chameleon thundered. He cut her off with a dark look that bespoke of much worse. His glance warned her not to push too far.

"You need not concern yourself with him. At this moment, he is fine, and if you wish for him to remain so, then carry a message back to your pitiful elf companions. I want Carina brought here to me immediately."

"Where is here?" Brandy asked, with arms outspread, looking around her dank surroundings.

"This is my home. Do not worry, they will know the way," Chameleon said with a grin that made her cringe.

"Brandy do not listen to him." Lyra's voice urgently broke into the conversation. "He means her nothing but harm."

"Silence!" Chameleon roared, flinging his arm in the crystal's direction. A flash of lightning flew from his fingertips and struck the stone's smooth surface. Lyra flinched as the bolt hit, stilling her words and closing her eyes once more in some sort of forced sleep.

"What did you do to her?" Brandy asked in a horrified whisper. Could he truly be more powerful than the Keeper of Spring, she thought.

"She is what you would call stunned. She tends to annoy me at times, and I do not like to be annoyed," Chameleon said with a warning look that spoke volumes.

"So it seems," Brandy uttered quietly.

"Now, as I was saying. I want you to bring Carina here or you will never see your dear human friend again. By the way, if you thought that the guivre gave you a scare, then your friend can expect much worse."

"What do you mean by that?"

"Just ignore my words and you will find out." Chameleon smirked in a way that dared her to test the seriousness of his words. "Now it is time for you to leave."

"You still haven't told me where Steve is," began Brandy, but that was all she managed to get out. For a second a dark shadow caught her eye at the top of the stairs. It look like a woman dressed in black and silver clothing, but she couldn't be sure. In a blink she was gone.

When she looked back to the dark elf, he mumbled a few words she could not understand and waved his hands in the air. Brandy felt some unseen claws grab her from behind. She knew they must be claws for their nails piercing her skin was all to real. The hands pulled her effortlessly from the room and down the dark corridor, the complete reversal from the way she had come. Then complete darkness surrounded her again. She fought the urge to scream in absolute terror. She would not give into her fear. The knowledge that for now Chameleon did not want her dead gave her strength. For that she was thankful.

CHAPTER SIX

The sound of voices filtered through the haze of sleep and opened Brandy's eyes to the early morning sun peeking through the tree branches overhead. She sat up and stretched her arms over her head, rubbing her eyes, and yawning loudly. "So I'm still alive," she mumbled to herself. "Amazing."

She stood and stretched again. She wondered if what had happened during the night was real or only a dream. How could it have been real? She was still here with the others, and yet on the other hand it had seemed so real, too real.

"Maybe I'm just losing it," she grumbled, running her fingers through her long tangled hair.

Yawning and stretching once more, Brandy winced at a sudden pain that rippled across her side. Gingerly she lifted her arm and shirt and stared at what she saw. Six small puncture marks, like pin pricks, lined her rib cage. Quickly checking her left side she saw similar marks. "How?" she mused out softly. The end of her dream came floating back. Unseen claws had gripped her and pulled her back from Chameleon's castle. So it really hadn't been a dream at all, but a frightening reality. This were getting stranger and stranger in this realm. First there were elves and gobioids, then dragons, and now dreams that actually hurt you. What next?

Slowly she wandered to where the others sat around their dwindling camp fire. Should she tell them what had happened or should she keep it to herself? Before she could decide, Volan made a space for her between himself and Puppis, pulling her down into a sitting position.

"Good morning," she said, trying her best to sound cheerful with a weak smile.

"Dawn of the day to you," said Volan with a grin. "Not used to sleeping on the ground?"

Brandy laughed at his question. "No, not really. I miss my soft bed and warm blankets."

"So do I," agreed Puppis, smiling ruefully. "I truly enjoy hunting and scouting trips, but I always look forward to the time when we return home and the comforts that it holds."

"Well, I hope it was not too bad," Carina said handing Brandy a mug of hot, mint smelling brew. "Hopefully we will not be out here too long."

"Yes, I'm anxious to find Steve."

All the elves were quiet for a moment. Brandy looked at each of them in the face, studying them intently, and still they said nothing.

"We are still going after Steve aren't we?" she asked, anger creeping into her voice. Were they going to abandon the search now that they were so close? Especially after they had all promised to continue on.

"Puppis and I are going with you," Volan said wrapping a brotherly arm about her shoulders, smiling reassuringly.

"What about the rest of you?" Brandy asked abruptly, not attempting to hide the rude edge of her words.

"We will be going back to our clan. We must find out what has happened to Lyra. Much is at stake with her disappearance," Carina said gently. She knew the other elves could sense that she felt badly about leaving the human in the clutches of the gobioids, but she as well as they, knew that Lyra missing was very wrong. They had to inform her father of this so that the other clans could be notified.

"We must contact the other elves to see if any knows of Lyra's whereabouts. All of the clans depend on her greatly."

"Well, you don't have to go back to your village for that," Brandy said shaking her head. She hadn't wanted to speak of her nightmare, but evidentially fate had other plans for her. "I know exactly where Lyra is." All eyes widened in disbelief and focused intently on her.

"How can you know this?" Forrest asked.

"I know this is going to sound crazy, but I had the weirdest dream last night . . ." Brandy began.

"A dream? The dream of a human could surely hold no meaning for us," Forrest snorted scornfully, dismissing her words with a wave of his hand as if she were no more than a bothersome fly.

"Well, it wasn't really a dream. I must have actually been there," Brandy said, trying to ignore Forrest's remark. She was desperately trying to quell the urge to smack him across the head with the palm of her hand.

"You were here all night, and those of us who stood watch can attest to that. In fact you talked quite a bit in your sleep," said Forrest sarcastically with raised eyebrows.

"Keep quiet for once and let her tell the story," Carina hissed at the dark haired elf who sat near her.

Brandy said nothing. She shouldn't have opened her mouth in the first place. She didn't need help and she didn't need Forrest. She could find Steve on her own, and she would find him. She didn't care about Chameleon either. She knew he was dangerous, but her presence seemed to have sparked an interest in him. Maybe she could use that to her advantage when dealing with him.

"Go ahead, Brandy," Puppis urged. "Tell us of your dream. Here in the elfin woods, dreams tell us much about what is going to happen in the future, or what the past is trying to teach us."

"I don't know," said Brandy. She chanced a peek at Forrest, but he would not meet her glance.

"Do tell us," coaxed Volan, patting her on the back. "I could be very important to us all."

"Okay," Brandy hesitantly agreed with a deep breath. "At first it was kind of scary because I didn't know how I got there. I was in a long damp corridor. It was very dark. I heard voices ahead of me so I decided to see who was there and where there was. I ended up in a huge chamber. It must have been under ground, because the air was damp and cold, and there were no windows. There was a large fire pit in the center of the room, and a long black marble table that sat on a red velvet rug. Then there was a huge crystal that hung in the air by itself. It was like a massive egg. It glimmered in the firelight and was really something to look at. And there was Lyra."

"Where?" asked Puppis and Volan in unison.

"Inside the crystal."

"How could that be?" gasped Puppis in horror.

"I don't know." Brandy shrugged, shaking her head slowly, reliving the scene in her mind again.

"Are you sure it was she?" Carina asked eagerly, hoping that the human may have been mistaken.

"Yes, she was lovely beyond words, with this most unusual silver hair. She then spoke to me and told me who she was. I really don't think she was lying about that."

"Who could have done such a thing?" Volan wondered.

"Chameleon," she said flatly. She watched as the evil elf's name registered on those who sat about her. Their faces were mixed with emotions ranging from shock and fear, to the disbelief that still covered Forrest's handsome features.

The elves were silent for many moments. Finally Carina broke the stillness that enveloped them all. "This is even more reason for us to return to the clan. We can not dare to face Chameleon in his own surroundings."

"We have to go there," Brandy insisted, grabbing Carina's hands in her own and holding them tightly. "He said that if you do not come he will harm Steve, maybe worse. I really didn't like the way he said that last part, either."

"Why does he want the princess?" Volan asked defensively.

"I don't know," Brandy replied sadly, shaking her head and releasing the princess's hands. "Forgive me Carina. I can't ask you to go to Chameleon's den. I know he means you harm, Lyra said so. Steve wouldn't want you to risk yourself for him, he would rather face what is coming. You should go back to your clan and get help from your father. Just point me in the right direction and I will try to help Steve myself until you can return with reinforcements."

"I can not let you continue on by yourself. You and your friend willingly risked your own lives to save Forrest and myself in the first place. It is time that I returned the favor," Carina said sincerely.

"This is nonsense," Forrest interrupted loudly. "We owe them nothing. How do we even know if her dream was real? What proof do we have besides the words of a mere human?"

"Well, if you're so sure that I was asleep here all night, then how did this happen," Brandy yelled back at Forrest with flushed cheeks and blazing eyes. She lifted her shirt for all to see the marks that lined her pale skin. "When you carried me from the lake last night, I think you can agree that these were not on me. You surely got a close enough look."

Forrest said nothing, but narrowed his eyes angrily at the human girl who sat across the small fire from him. Her words stung him deeply. He was even more disgruntled with himself that she had noticed how he had stared at her figure.

"I believe you," Carina said, with a nod of her head. "I will accompany you to Chameleon's castle."

"I forbid this." Forrest stood up angrily, flinging his cup to the ground. "You are princess of the elfin clan of the woods. You can not put yourself into such needless danger. As protector of the royal house, I forbid this."

"You forbid? You forget your place. I do not care what you forbid," Carina snapped back coldly, authority ringing loudly in her usually gentle voice. "Chameleon wants me for some reason, that only he seems to know. If we had taken a stand with the humans from the beginning, this may not have ever happened."

Forrest opened his mouth to argue his point back, when Draco raised his burly strong hand to silence the two quarreling elves. He had remained silent while all had spoken and now remembered something that had been nagging at the back of his memory since his conversation with the guivre the night before. "Enough of this bickering, children. There is an old tale that must be told. Maybe it will clear some of the mystery that surrounds what is happening here."

Grudgingly Forrest flopped himself back down to the ground. He said nothing for Draco was an elder of the clan who had lived many tens of years longer than the rest of the present company and had seen and learned many things. Even he knew that respect of the elder was of most importance to all elves.

Draco took a deep drink from his mug, set it in the leaves at his feet, and cleared his throat. "There is a tale of many, many centuries ago. Far, far before the oldest elder in any of the clans. It is a tale that begins with the beginning. Our great lands were once only filled with the way of the Spring. Lyra was the only all powerful force that inhabited our lands. Things were peaceful and calm. The white sleep of winter did not exist. The land was forever green and alive. And it remained that way for a very long time, but there were some who grew restless with the simpleness of it all. They went searching for something else."

"It sounds perfect," Brandy said. "What else could anyone want?"

"Change. And change was the elfin world's enemy. Because from change there is discontent, and discontent will breed evil. It was not long before the evil force grew stronger and stronger. Spreading our ever farther. Reaching with it's greedy hands. This change is what the elders of the time saw in the human world, so it was thought that by putting the barrier into place they could quell such things in our own lands."

"Why did not Lyra fore see this change and put an end to it before it grew?" Carina asked in bewilderment. She was curious for she had never heard the story of how evil came to be a part of their lives and lands. It seemed a story that the elves had seem to have forgotten.

"I do not know. I suppose it is that she had never been faced with evil before. Her innocence and spirit of trust and friendship did not allow for such things as evil in the beginning. Alas, the elves had taken a taste of change and were not ready to let it go."

"What happened? When she did realize that something was wrong?" asked Puppis, eagerly waiting to hear the rest of the tale.

"In all of the clans, not just ours, elves left and traveled far to the south. It is said they followed to where they felt they heard another voice. A voice that offered then greater powers and opportunities."

"What was the other voice?" asked Carina.

"It was later found out to be Lacerta."

"The Dark Queen?" gasped Puppis, her eyes widening in alarm. She covered her mouth with her hands, as if the spoken name would make the queen appear.

Draco nodded.

"Who's that?" asked Brandy, looking at each of the elves in turn.

"She was once as Lyra is. Some think she was even Lyra's sister, but I am not sure. The ancient tale speculates that Lacerta tired of being in Lyra's shadow and sought out to increase her own power and followers."

"Like Chameleon," Volan said quietly.

"Yes, like Chameleon," agreed Draco somberly. "For through the ages, some have still heard the call of the Dark Queen. In time, creatures that were strange and unusual to the elfin clans began appearing. Dragons, guivres, gobioids, and other beasts like the agouti. At first no one was too concerned with these occurrences because they felt sure that Lyra would protect us as she had always done so."

"It was too late by then, wasn't it?" Brandy asked. She knew what Draco's answer would be before he even said it. Humans had been doing the same thing for thousands of years. Thinking themselves safe, then finding out that they should have acted sooner.

Draco nodded silently. His eyes rested on the tiny flames that struggled to keep alive in the ring of rocks in front of him. After a few moments of silence he slowly continued. "When the gobioids attacked, none was prepared. Many elves lost their lives. The numbers of the creatures was great and they held no care for whom they killed; the old, children, those who were unable to protect themselves. Their only goal was to eliminate all elves who stood in their way. The elves were not warriors, so the annihilation seemed all but certain."

"What did they do?" Carina asked, tears glistening in her sky colored eyes at the thought of so many of her kin being needlessly butchered.

"They did what all elves do when cornered. They fought back. Only they fought better than the gobioids even though only a few had any fighting skills at all. Some who had joined Lacerta came back to us when they realized what her means were. Unfortunately they were few. Finally, all of the clans united and formed one massive fighting unit. Within weeks they had the gobioids pushed back to the gloomy, cold south from which they had crawled forth. The elves learned a very painful lesson that day. Once evil has been let loose it can never be completely turned back and eliminated, so that is why there is winter. Lyra keeps winter with us every turn of the seasons as a reminder of what happened to the elfin clans in those early days, and a way to share with the new beings that had inhabited our lands, for many of these beings were not evil in nature, only different to what elves were used to."

"What happened to Lacerta?" Puppis asked quietly.

"It was told that she extended too much of herself in the power that she used to control the gobioids, and that when they failed in their attack on the elves some of that power took its toll on her. She disappeared after that, and occasionally one of her followers, such as Chameleon, becomes very powerful in their own right and causes trouble for the one or two of the clans."

Brandy said nothing. She looked to Forrest, his eyes meeting hers. Did he believe the story that Draco had just told? She could not tell, for no emotions betrayed what his thoughts may have held.

"What has this tale to do with what the human girl tells us of?" Forrest asked, breaking the silence that had ensued. He nodded his head in her direction, his question confirming that he still did not trust what Brandy had said.

"It has everything to do with what Brandy has told us. As the gobioids and their evil forces were brought down it was then foretold that one day, one who would be a very powerful servant of the Dark Queen, would imprison Lyra and take his revenge against all elves."

"How? How can this be?" Volan asked. He knew he would not like what the answer to his question was going to be.

"It is said that a female princess of truest elfin blood will be sacrificed on the eve of Spring and that elfin blood will be the force that binds Lyra for an eternity," Draco replied, looking directly at Carina. "And you are the princess of truest elfin blood. For your ancestor was the one who united and led all of the clans into battle against the gobioids. You are the only elf maiden to be born of that line."

"That's why he wants you," Brandy said quietly. She was ashamed that she had thought they were going to desert her. She did not want them to accompany her now. The risk was too great for Carina.

"Then we must ride for Chameleon's castle, for Spring is only three days away," Carina said firmly, standing abruptly as if there were no further room for discussion. "We do not have time to return to my father. Lyra must be freed before Spring or the damage could be irreversible."

"I disagree, princess. You must return to our clan and tell your father what is happening," Forrest argued. "He must be informed, and the farther we keep you from Chameleon, the better."

Carina started to protest, but Brandy cut her off as she rose to her feet. "I must agree with Forrest, Carina. The clan will be safer for you," she said. Then pulling the princess close for words that she could only hear, Brandy continued. "I am glad to have you as a friend and I tend to like to protect my friends. Besides, Steve was taken with you from the first moment that he saw you, and he would get a little angry at me if something happened to you without being able to have the chance to show off for you first." Brandy smile affectionately at Carina and was pleased when she returned that smile.

"You are right," Carina conceded. "I just feel responsible for what has happened to Steve. And I too was taken with him from the beginning," she added softly, grinning impishly.

The two giggled as they turned to face the others. "I will be returning to the clan to talk with father," Carina stated. "Volan, you will accompany me. When we tell Lord Corona of the news, we will follow you to Chameleon with ample reinforcements."

"I should return with you, princess," argued Forrest. "It is my duty to protect you."

Carina ignored his comments with a wave of her hand. "I already told you I can take care of myself. Furthermore, who will you banter with if Brandy is not around. I do not believe that I have seen you this happy in years," she returned. A delighted grin spread across her face at the look of astonishment on Forrest's face.

CHAPTER SEVEN

"Up!"

The gruff voice ordered as it filtered through the sleepy haze that covered Steve's mind. He didn't want to wake, he was more than exhausted. He was having an incredibly unusual dream about some weird creatures and a breathtaking princess. A sharp, yet not too unkindly, kick in the ribs pulled him from his dreams. Groggily the unwilling human opened his eyes and tried to focus them on the shape that loomed before him. He scrambled back when he realized that it was a green, grayish reptilian face of a gobioid staring closely into his own. The creature laughed croakedly with amusement at Steve's reaction.

"Damn, don't you guys ever brush your teeth," Steve complained, yawning and rubbing his eyes tiredly. He glanced about and saw that it was still dark. How much time had passed, he wondered. Surely he had not slept the whole day away, for he felt confident that his captures would not permit that. He felt as though he had only been out for a few hours.

"Surprised you did I not," Braakk said in a snorting laugh. His fanged mouth grinning widely in levity at the human. "It is soon time to leave. Eat this," he added shoving a bowl into Steve's hands.

"What's this," Steve asked looking hesitantly into the wooden bowl. It was a creamy white concoction that once again amazed him with its inviting aroma. His captures were going all out for their prisoner.

"Porridge," Braakk struggled over the word. "I believe you humans eat such things, or so I was told." He hesitated a moment, glancing about to make sure none of the others saw his move, then pulled open one of the many leather pouches that surrounded his thick waist. Reaching in with a scaled claw, he removed a crude wooden spoon and stuck it quickly into the bowl.

"Why Braakk," Steve began, smiling brightly up at the gobioid. "I didn't know you cared so much."

The gobioid grinned at his compliment, then instantly returned sullen as he realized that his companions were giving him questioning glances. "Just eat!" he barked, but not very harshly. "We leave shortly."

Steve watched Braakk shuffle back over to the campfire that the gobioids shared. The others made remarks to him in their guttural tongue as he took his place among them. He guessed that they either teased or reprimanded him for his conversation with a human. Steve smiled as he slowly ate his porridge. He didn't like the gobioids for what they had done, and yet they were acting on the orders of Chameleon. He wasn't sure if that should make a difference at all. Perhaps there was help for Braakk and his bad manners, and for himself after all, but for now he was going to have to be very careful and watchful. He would learn as much about his foe as possible. Then, when the time was right, he would try to make his move against them and his captivity.

As he shoveled the last bit of porridge into his mouth, Braakk returned before Steve. "We leave now," he informed him.

"Tell me something, Braakk?"

"Perhaps," the gobioid replied, eying him warily. Chameleon had warned them not to be tricked by questions that the human may ask. He did not understand his master's distrust of this creature. To him they seemed relatively weak and defenseless. They were small, without much muscle, and they gave off a most peculiar odor. Plus they seemed to need a lot of food and had little endurance for riding.

"How long did we rest for?"

Braakk grinned at the question. They did not even ask such difficult things. "Half the night."

"That really isn't very much sleep for a growing boy, such as myself, that is," Steve said with a smile.

"That is all a gobioid warrior needs, so it is the same for you," Braakk said, pulling Steve to his feet by one arm, as if he weighed nothing at all. He then pulled a large blade from around his waistband and sliced the binds that loosely held his feet.

"If you say so," Steve mumbled, painfully stretching his stiff joints and muscles.

"Yes, I say so," Braakk replied. He shook his head at the human and led the way to the agouti who were tethered to a large tree trunk, greedily stripping the bark off the tree with their sharp teeth. They smacked loudly, foam dripping from their mouths, obviously pleased with the taste of their meal.

"Nice," Steve muttered, shaking his head in amazement at the eating habits of the beasts. He watched as Braakk untied the creatures and talked almost affectionately to them in soft tones of his rough speech. Braakk turned and faced Steve, expectantly holding a reign out in his direction. Steve looked blankly at him, not understanding what the gobioid had in store for him.

"You said earlier that you could ride," the gobioid indicated. "I am giving you the chance to prove your statement."

Steve grinned with anticipation at the thought. If he were able to control one of these beasts, then maybe, just maybe, he would be able to flee and try to find Brandy.

"But," Braakk continued as if picking his thoughts from the air, "you will still have your hands tied to limit your movement on the agouti. And I will lead your travel beast."

"Whatever you say, pal." Steve smiled agreeably. Perhaps Braakk was beginning to think of him as not too much of a threat. If he lets his guard down for one moment, Steve thought, I will surely take advantage of it. I have got to find a way back to Brandy and the others. They are close behind, so it shouldn't take too long, he assured himself with confidence.

"Where are we going to?" he asked tentatively, as if he were trying to make casual conversation instead of learning pertinent information.

"To the master's castle."

"The master?"

"Yes. He who allows us to live in his shadow. He who granted you the right to live."

"Do you mean that elf, Chameleon, that was around earlier?" asked Steve with raised eyebrows.

"Master is not an elf. He is all powerful and will take his revenge against the elves for the sake of our elders who he in turn serves."

"I see. Why doesn't your master travel with us now. He was here in the camp when we finished riding last night?" Steve was curious on how Chameleon seemed to appear and disappear whenever he wished.

"The master has control of all about us. He can become part of all that you see, and fly like part of the wind. For now he has left us and returned to the castle. His destiny is at hand and the predictions of the old one will soon be complete." Braakk stopped talking abruptly, glancing about himself. The look of one who had spoken far too freely to the inquisitive human played upon his features.

"Is that why I was taken?" Steve prodded Braakk to tell him more.

The gobioid eyed him warily. Maybe this human was only trying to trick him. "Enough questions," he barked shortly. "We ride now."

They traveled until the sun began poking its way through the dwindling branches that surrounded them. The terrain was becoming more and more sparse with every passing mile that the fleet footed agouti covered. Steve could see in the distance that there were no trees at all. Only flat, grassless, dry ground. Dark clouds loomed far ahead in the skies above, lightning flicking ominously in their depths. The air had taken on a chillier feel and the wind was beginning to intensify in velocity. Steve shivered in his saddle, but said nothing only pulling his flannel shirt closer to him. He would not appear weak before the gobioids at any cost.

The lead gobioid held up his hand, signaling that they were stopping for a moment. Steve remained seated and watched as the others dismounted. He knew what he must do. This may be the only chance that he would have to escape. There was a heaviness in the air that was growing more intense with each passing minute. A heaviness that felt foreboding to his immediate future. He would have to get away. He felt sure that once they left the woods he would never have a chance to flee, for then he would be too close to Chameleon's domain and too out in the open to blend into his surroundings and hide.

"We rest for a few moments now," Braakk informed Steve, back to his usual blunt and monotonous manner.

A light smile flitted to Steve's lips. Luckily he and Braakk had been at the back of the group, his path back would be made a little easier by not having to go over the others. Steve bent down in his saddle as if preparing to dismount, but instead he shot his bound hands out and grasped the long, heavy knife that was sheathed at Braakk's waist. Quickly straightening himself in the saddle again, he looked into the bewildered face of the gobioid.

"Sorry Braakk. I really hate to do this, but I can't let you guys take me to Chameleon," he said, somewhat apologetically, raising one foot and shoving Braakk heavily to the ground. Steve heard the air rush from the gobioid's body when he hit the ground. That would give him a bit more time to escape, he reasoned to himself. With a flick of the stolen knife he slashed the bonds that held his wrists. Then tucking the knife securely under his leg, against the saddle, he kicked the agouti into motion with his heels. Pulling hard around on the reins, Steve steered the beast back into the woods behind him, at full gallop. Thankfully, these beasts responded to commands exactly as a horse would.

The yells and confused shouts of the gobioids quickly faded at his back, but Steve was not about to chance anything. He kept the agouti, which seemed to travel much quicker than an ordinary horse, at a fast, breakneck pace for over an hour, until the seemingly tireless beast began at last to show signs of slowing. He hoped that he was traveling in a straight line, but he could not be sure, because everything looked the same. When he finally stopped, the agouti's sides labored heavily in its breathing, and thin coat of white sweat covered the coarse dark coat of the animal.

"Sorry, old guy," Steve said lightly, patting the agouti's neck, "but I'm sure that your friends will be most persistent in getting me back. We will walk for a while though so you can rest."

Steve dismounted and tucked the knife into his jeans, cutting a hole in them first so that the point would not pierce his own leg. He scooped up a large handful of leaves from the ground and wiped as much of the sweat off of the agouti as he could in a short period of time. The course coat of the animal seemed to make it more difficult to groom. He then took his knife and peeled a long strip of bark from the closest tree and handed it to the eager animal. While the beast munched, Steve led the way on foot, holding tightly to the animal's reins. He listened determinedly to any types of noises around him. He heard birds chirping, small animals chattering, and the wind singing in the trees, but he heard nothing to indicate that the other gobioids were close at hand.

The thought comforted him somewhat, but did not entirely ease his mind. They walked a short while longer, and then Steve once again mounted the agouti. He proceeded in the direction that he was going, for the trees had continued to thicken in presence. He reasoned that if he kept on at this route he would at least be heading away from Chameleon, and hopefully back towards Brandy and the other elves, and Carina.

The female elf fascinated him. Her beauty was, without question, intoxicating. Yet it was more than that. Her eyes seemed to have pierced the very center of his soul. He had dated many girls in the past, but none had made such an impression or lasting effect on him in many hours of conversation as had Carina in only a few minutes that they had been together. Her ivory hair reminded him of the whiteness of beach sand, and her eyes were like the color of the early morning sky. He blinked hard several times, but the vision of her face would not fade. So with a small satisfied grin he decided to enjoy her image.

The sun was high overhead when Steve halted the agouti near a trickle of a stream. He dismounted and let the animal drink its fill. He then knelt beside the little brook, filling his hands with the cool water, and splashing it over his head and face. He leaned back and let the chilliness of the liquid revive him and ease the tension in his head and neck. His knees protested loudly as he stood and regarded his surroundings. The barrenness of the plain and feeling of foreboding that he had seen only hours before had disappeared completely. He stood enveloped by many trees and thick underbrush. All seemed peaceful and quiet, but a small persistent nagging at the base of his neck produced shivers of uncertainty.

"Don't get careless, Steve," he said out loud in the silence that had suddenly filtered through the trees. "Stupid mistakes will get you in a lot of trouble. Not to mention that you will piss yourself off."

The agouti turned at the sound of Steve's voice and stared inquisitively at him. "Never heard a human talk to himself before?" Steve smiled squatting by the water again. "Well, get used to it. I do quite a bit of it." Shakings its head, the animal snorted and returned its attention to a piece of bark that it had been stripping from a tree nearby.

The agouti snorted again. "Noisy aren't you?" Steve asked. This time the creature ignored him. It stretched its horned head high into the air and breathed deeply, nostrils flaring. Its dark eyes flickered as its senses recognized the smell that floated on the air. The creature seemed to sense that something was close, and that something was recognizable to it.

The agouti opened its sharp toothed mouth and let out a shrill screech into the thick woods. Seconds later another screech broke the silent air in reply to the agouti's cry. The animal impatiently stamped its large hoofed feet and recklessly pulled his reins free from the branch that had bound it, bolting for the direction of the sound.

"Wait!" Steve yelled, jumping to his feet and rushing into the brush after the agouti. What had caused the creature to make such a horrifying sound? Why had it suddenly dashed off like that? He didn't know, but he did know that if he didn't get the animal back, it wouldn't take the gobioids long to catch up with him, for they were probably not too far behind.

A noise before him caused Steve to slow the progression of his head long rush forward. He cautiously approached a small clearing, which was bathed in sunlight, that had appeared between the trees and their branches. It was her, Carina. Steve stood motionless. Even though he could not see her face, he knew without a doubt by the color of her hair that it was her. She was talking loudly to someone, that he could not yet see from behind the many branches that blocked his full view, but he could not understand her words. Her tones did tell him that they were not happy or friendly words. He crept closer, foot by painstaking foot, until he reached the edge of the trees and had a clear view of the scene before him.

The agouti he had ridden was there, contentedly munching on something, probably more bark. Carina's back was still to him. Beside her stood another elf with long blonde hair, he held a sword in one hand and a knife in the other, but made no moves to use them. Then there were others. Dark hulking shapes that Steve had grown to know so well in the past day. Gobioids. Not any gobioids, but the ones who had held him prisoner. The ones who were taking him to Chameleon. How could they have caught up with him so quickly, he wondered.

He let out a deep sigh. He was not sure what to do, only knowing that he had to act. Before he could decide on his plan, the gobioids sprang to ferocious and instantaneous life in the clearing. Braakk and another burly gobioid grabbed Carina and twisted her arms behind her, quickly pulling the short sword from her hands that she attempted to use on them. The others rushed the male elf like a pack of angry wolves who had not fed in many a day. The elf slashed expertly at them, sending one of the gobioids to his knees in a puddle of greenish gore. Although he fought well, he was no match for the sheer force of the much larger creatures. As one managed to get close enough, he swung his massive club and sent the elf crumbling to the soft grass covered ground, completely unconscious.

"Volan!" Carina wailed in dismay, struggling to reach her fallen friend against the tight grip of the gobioids who held her fast.

"Shut that shrilly mouth of yours princess," threatened the gobioid who stood over the body of the fallen elf, "or your friend here will cease to breath."

"Kill him," urged another gobioid with an ugly gleam in his eye. "He took Shaek's life."

"No. The master will probably want him alive. And if not, then you can have him to do with what you please." The other gobioid grinned at the idea as drool dripped from his protruding fangs.

Steve watched angrily as the gobioids pawed at the princess with clawed hands, her yells of insults echoing through his brain. His silence had lasted long enough. It was time to act.

"Let her go Braakk," Steve ordered, making his way from his hiding spot and advancing on the gobioids with his knife in hand.

CHAPTER EIGHT

The five standing gobioids and the elf princess whirled at the sound of the voice. A human voice. A small grateful smile spread across Carina's flushed face as she recognized Steve's figure. The gobioids smiled also, but theirs were full of contempt. Two of the creatures advanced on Steve, clubs ready for action in their massive clawed hands.

"This is a surprise. We were chasing a stupid human and end up with that in which our master wanted most," sneered the largest gobioid, indicating the princess with a claw tipped finger. "You should have fled while you had the chance and were able to. Now you will become an easy meal," the gobioid assured Steve.

"Well, I think you're going to find this is one meal who won't lay down without putting up a pretty good fight," Steve taunted back. He knew that he held no real chance of surviving against the five gobioids in front of him, but maybe he could provide enough time for Brandy and the others to show up. Surely they couldn't be to far behind the princess and this other elf. Encouraged by this thought, he gripped his long knife tightly in his right hand and prepared for the two approaching creatures.

The gobioids yellow eyes gleamed wickedly at him as they came within reach. They stopped only a few feet in front of the human and laughed, slobber running down their scaly chins.

"Taber, you go first," said the largest creature in anticipation. "Don't gut him in too quickly, let us have some excitement, and well earned fun, first."

"As you wish, Rocc," said Taber with a drooling grin.

Steve took a few steps back. He narrowed his eyebrows in concentration. He had a few things in his favor. He was in good shape, much more nimbler than the gobioids, and he was much smarter than they gave him credit for. These were things that he was going to use toward his advantage. He knew that he would not survive against the sheer strength of the gobioid, so he was going to have to trick it, and maybe have a little fun of his own in the process to pay the creatures back for tying him up so tightly.

"Bet you can't catch me," he teased the gobioid who advanced on him. Tucking his knife back into his pants, he quickly scooped a small rock up from the ground and hurled it at the unsuspecting creature, hitting it square in the head. Then, like a rabbit, he whirled and ran back into the cover of the trees.

"Hurry up or you'll lose me," Steve yelled over his shoulder.

After a moment of confused hesitation the gobioid scratched his head, then followed, rushing recklessly into the dense brush. "I know you are in here, human. Why do you not make it easy on yourself and just give up. Making us angry will only make things worse for you."

"Didn't your buddy Chameleon tell you that we humans have something called tenacity and spunk. We don't like to give up, no matter what the odds are," Steve called to the gobioid. He had hidden himself in the trees and pulled a long thick branch back, holding it tightly in his arms. Only a few more steps and the gobioid would be right were he needed him. Come on, come on, he urged silently. He could feel the pressure of the limb pulling against him, but he refused to let go just yet. The gobioid was not quite close enough.

The creature stopped and listened intently to its surroundings, trying to locate the human, hearing nothing it took another step forward. Steve opened his arms, releasing the limb. Rushing forward with the force of a bullet, the wooden projectile caught the gobioid full front in the chest and face. The large unsuspecting creature was lifted from his feet and hurled backward. He landed on the ground with a resounding thud, eyes closed, and unmoving.

Steve cautiously crept forward, clutching his knife in hand, and kicked away the club that lay close to gobioid's hand. "You're not dead," he whispered to the still and silent creature, "but you ought to have one hell of a headache to remember me by." Returning to the edge of the trees he wondered what he was going to do with the others. They surely wouldn't be as easy to trick at the first one. When their comrade didn't return, they would be much more wary of him. As he looked past the single gobioid who was closest to him, to the ones who held Carina, he realized that his choice had already been made for him.

"Come out now human, or the elf dies," the raspy voice of the gobioid filtered to his ears. He held the princess around her middle with one strong hand and arm, and pressed a blade close to her pale throat with the other.

Steve heaved a heavy sigh when he emerged from the concealment of the trees. Rocc rushed to him, hastily removing the long knife and club, the club that his companion had once wielded, from Steve's unresisting hands. "Where is Taber?" he snorted with rage.

"Taking a nap," said Steve, indicating with his thumb over his shoulder to the trees. "He was careless."

"So were you," said Braakk harshly, approaching the pair with rough leather straps in his claws. "You make Braakk look foolish. This is not a good thing. Braakk tried to make your trip less painful, now you will pay plenty." The gobioid took the straps and cruelly twisted them around Steve's wrist before pulling them tight into knots.

Steve winced at the biting edge of the binds that cut roughly into his already sore skin producing a trickle of blood. He let himself be dragged, without much resistance, back to were the two gobioids, Carina, and the agouti stood, without saying a word. His heart sank when his eyes met the princesses, and he realized that he had no idea how he was going to get them out of this mess, or if he even could.

"Steve, I am so sorry . . ." Carina began, sadness filling her words, but was instantly cut of by the Gobioid holding her. He pressed the blade closer to her delicate throat, pricking it slightly.

Anger boiled to an explosive point within Steve at what he saw. It was one thing to beat on him, but to harm this innocent girl, that was too much for him to take. He pulled suddenly at Braakk's grip, releasing himself for a moment, but that was all he needed. He rushed straight at the gobioid who had injured the princess, knocking the creature to the ground, and landing heavily on top of him. Braakk quickly regained his wits and was on Steve in an instant, trying to pull the wriggling human from his shocked and struggling companion.

"Run!" Steve screamed at Carina, battling with his bound hands and free feet against the gobioids.

She hesitated, not knowing what to do. "I, . . . I cannot leave you."

"Damn it, run. There will be no other chance. I don't want you here, go get help." At her continued hesitation, he added in a callous tone, "you can do nothing here to help."

Carina whirled at his harsh words and fled into the trees with the fleetness of a graceful deer. Tears stung at her eyes just as the branches tore and stung at her clothing and exposed skin. Why had he been so harsh? She had only wanted to help him, the way he had helped her. Any elfin warrior would have been honored to have a maiden risk herself thus. Why was this human so different? Did not female humans risk their lives for those they cared for? And not knowing why, she held great caring in her heart for this human. So why did he treat he so?

She ran blindly on, not sure whether she was even headed in the right direction or not. Her breaths came as ragged gasps to her sore, dry throat. Her lungs screamed for her to stop, but she would not permit her legs to do so. She had to keep going. She had to find her father. He would know what to do. He could solve any problem that faced them. She did know that time was of the essence. And time was also her enemy. Somehow she would have to get help from her father and the clan and return to Chameleon's castle within three days. Could it be done, she wondered doubtfully. It would have to be; too much depended on it.

And what about Steve and Volan? Would the gobioid kill them both, or return with them to Chameleon? What of their fates now? Her questions haunted her as she ran through the shadowy trees. After what seemed an eternity, she slowed her steps to a walk, then stopped all together, leaning heavily against a tree for support. Her legs screamed in agony, and her mouth begged for some water. She stared intently around at her surroundings trying to get her bearings when she heard a faint rustle in the bushes near her. Startled, she froze, not able to will her exhausted body into running further.

"What are you doing out here alone, Princess Carina?"

Carina's skin prickled at the words that were spoken behind her, and the softness of the voice who spoke those words. It was Chameleon, she knew it without turning. A cold pale hand reached into her line of vision and gently, almost tenderly, touched her arm. The touch sent ripples of revulsion shuddering through her being. It was like being touched by death. With every ounce of will power that she possessed, Carina pulled her arm from his icy grasp and turned to face him.

"What do you want?" she managed to croak out at his composed and grinning stare.

"Why you, of course," Chameleon said, smiling smoothly, confidently. "I think you already know that."

"I will not go with you," she said evenly, ignoring his words.

"You really have no choice in the matter."

"I always have a choice," Carina said narrowly. She opened her mind quickly, before Chameleon could sense what she was doing, and urgently called to all of her winged friends that she could reach. "Help!" her mind screamed frantically. "I need your help, my dear friends." Their answer was instantaneous. A dozen feather creatures of different sizes and colors appeared suddenly from all directions around them. Squawking and screeching in loud unison, they answered the princesses cry of dismay.

They swooped at Chameleon's dark form, beaks flashing and taloned feet outstretched.

Their first assault took the wizard completely by surprise. He had not even realized what the princess was doing until she had done so. Pieces of his cloak were torn from him, and a few of the birds even managed to inflict minor wounds to his pale skin beneath. A single swoop was all they were allowed by the mage. As the birds readied themselves for another pass, Chameleon waved his long hands in the air, quietly breathing a few ancient words, and the birds disappeared save for a fluttering of a handful of bright feathers.

Carina cringed at his display. "What did you do with them?" she asked horrified at what she had just seen.

"They are gone." He laughed with a snap of his fingers. "Did you think that your weak abilities at elfin magic could be any match for me?"

She said nothing, but bit her lip to keep the tears that filled her eyes from falling. Her friends, that had always been there when she needed them, were gone. Needlessly sacrificed by this evil sorcerer to prove that he had power. Hate welled in her chest. She wanted to rip the wicked and smug grin right from his face and fling it back at him, but knew not how.

"Do you still feel as though you have a choice in whether or not you will accompany me back to my castle?" Chameleon asked coldly. Silence met his question, causing him to sneer at the indignant elf princess before him. "What I did to your birds I can easily do to the others. Your trusted friend Volan, and the human who seems rather taken with you. What a fool he has made of himself." The horror that he saw in the princesses eyes made him laugh loudly. "Yes, I have seen the way that he naively risks his life for you. A stupid, puny human who would not last a second in the darkest realms of evil against me. Is that what you want? Are you willing to give up their lives as well in your stubbornness? The end result will be the same. I will still have you, but what sacrifice are you will to pay in the end?"

The tears that were bottled up, fell over Carina's dark lashes and spilled down her pale cheeks. She could not condemn the others to who knew what. Despair gripped greedily at her insides, consuming her. "I will go with you, just as you knew I would," she whispered, barely spitting the words out hoarsely.

A smile of absolute pleasure spread across Chameleon's handsome features. He closed the distance between himself and the sullen, defeated princess in a few strides. Taking her cold, limp hand in his, he murmured a few old and powerful words. "Domsix cearac sivus xansth."

Carina's despondency was shaken into the realization that the trees that surrounded them had begun to shimmer. Their shape and form wavered before her very eyes until she could see nothing but the swirling masses of bright light streaked with the color of a rainbow. Within a blink of the eye, it was over. The light was gone, the trees were gone, the few pitiful feather that laid on the ground were gone. They now stood before the gobioid who had captured her, Volan, who had regained consciousness, and Steve, who stood battered, bleeding, and bound next to Braakk.

Volan and Steve marveled at the display that appeared before them. Steve knew nothing at all of magic and what it could accomplish. He was a realist. Everything around him had to have an explanation, and so far he had found none to explain the things that had been happening to him. Volan had only heard rumors of the power that Chameleon possessed. It seemed to him that all of those rumors were being surpassed.

"I see you finally have things under control here, Rocc," Chameleon said with a low menacing growl to the largest of the gobioid.

"Yes, master," he groveled, visibly shaken. "There will be no further trouble with these prisoners."

"Or from you."

"Yes, master. There will be no further trouble or inconveniences from me or my men. Er . . . your men."

Chameleon nodded his head and paced away from the princess and the others. Rubbing his hands together, he suddenly turned and faced the group once again. "Taber, relieve Rocc of his weapons," he commanded darkly. The gobioid did as he was told immediately, stripping away his comrades club and long knife in an instant, no hint of their friendship apparent in his actions.

"Come to me, Rocc."

The creature hesitated. Fear swept through him at the power that emanated from his master's eyes. He had expected a punishment for the princesses escape, but he feared this would be no ordinary punishment.

"You disobeyed me, Rocc," Chameleon began quietly, shaking his head slowly, then raising his voice he addressed the others. "It is not wise to disobey me. I think that a lesson is in order. I wish to remind all of you who is in charge, and who is the master." He raised a long slender finger and pointed it at Rocc.

At first the creature stared numbly at his master, not knowing what to expect. Then the fear that he felt spread across his features when he realized that this was to be no mere punishment. Unseen fingers circled his throat and began squeezing slowly and tightly. As the seconds ticked by the pressure increased. Rocc fell to his knees and begged Chameleon with his eyes to forgive him, for no sound could escape his lips. His tongue hung out of his mouth from between his sharp fangs as he fell to his back, his fingers tearing frantically at the unseen hands about his throat. His body begged for air, but none entered him. Slowly his twitching, fighting body eased until he laid still as stone on the ground.

Chameleon said nothing for many moments, but watched with a satisfied smile at the expressions that filled the faces before him. Advancing toward them, he looked directly at Taber. "I do not wish to be disobeyed again. Do you understand?"

"Absolutely, master," the gobioid said, nodding eagerly. "I will see to everything."

"Be sure that you do," Chameleon warned.

"You might as well take me out now, because I have no intention of bowing down and kissing your ass," Steve yelled angrily at the evil elf who strutted around before himself and the others.

Chameleon laughed at the human's outburst. "Your race surely lacks manners, but that is of no matter. I will be taking the princess back with me to my keep. The gobioid will escort you and this other prisoner. They will not be permitted to kill you, unless absolutely necessary that is. They will, however, punish you to the point that you will wish for death if you try to escape again."

Chameleon's tone was dark and ominous, but it was Steve's turn to laugh. "You talk like a big man with your dime store magic. I'll take my chances with your minions every chance I get, and don't doubt it for a second," he spat at the dark robed figure. "And by the way, if you ever want to drop the magic act, I'll gladly kick your ass like a real man, and put things back into perspective for you."

The anger that masked Chameleon's face at the human's words was quickly replaced by a mirthful grin. "I may just keep you alive a while longer, for when the prophecy is complete I believe I will let you amuse me and take you up on your challenge."

"Anytime," Steve promised.

The dark elf took Carina's arm and led her to the center of the small clearing. He turned and addressed the gobioid, "I will leave you to bring the prisoners to me. You will come across four others soon, take them prisoners as well. Two are only females so your chore should not be difficult. Make haste, the time of the prophecy is near." Then mumbling a few words under his breath, he and the princess shimmered, blending into the light of the sun that peered down, and then disappeared.

Chapter Nine

The group quickly broke camp, and after a brief farewell, went their separate ways. Carina and Volan headed back to the elfin clan of the wood, and Forrest led Puppis, Draco, and Brandy deeper south into the thick trees towards the edge wood and ever closer to Chameleon's shadowy domain.

Brandy followed last in line of the four riders. She wanted the solitude that being last offered her. Her thoughts pulled her millions of miles away from her companions. Where was Steve and what was happening to him? What kind of tangled web had she fallen into when she crossed that thin, sacred barrier that separated her world from that of the elves and gobioids? She obviously wasn't meant to be here, and at the same time it wasn't all that foreign to her. Draco and Puppis seemed to accept her presence on the trip and were very friendly to her, but Forrest ignored her openly. She didn't feel the hostility from him that she had encountered on their first meeting, but his chilly distance that he kept was more annoying to her than if he were to argue with her constantly, which she halfheartedly wished he would do.

They plodded on the whole day the same way. Wrapped in absolute silence. They did not stop for their midday meal, but opted to eat it while they traveled. About an hour before the sun would disappear for the night, Forrest halted his large black horse.

"We are very close to the edge of the woods, after that we will be in Chameleon's domain, and he will be able to sense our presence easily. We will stop here for the night to rest," he announced over his shoulder.

"Finally," Brandy mumbled to herself as she slid gratefully to the ground. Her back and fanny ached mercilessly. Her legs were cramped, and for many long moments she had to lean against her gray mare before the feeling would return to her tired lower limbs, permitting her the freedom to walk. And when she did walk, it was stiffly done for pin prickles raced wildly in her feet. Her horse nudged her gently in the back with her soft nose as if urging her to work the soreness out of her muscles.

"Thank you." Brandy smiled at the compassionate animal, stroking its silky mane. "I always knew horses where smarter than most people, and a lot nicer, too."

"It is part of their breeding," Puppis said, joining Brandy as they unsaddled their animals for the night.

"How can you do that?" Brandy asked, rubbing down her mare's coat with handfuls of grass and soft leaves until it shone in the waning sunlight.

"Many generations back, I am not sure how far, certain horses were noted to be very empathic towards their riders. They were bred only with other horses who displayed similar behavior. Soon all of our horses were the same way."

"Too bad people couldn't be like that."

"Maybe someday," Puppis agreed, nodding her head. Then with a grin she added, "but I doubt it."

"Probably so." Brandy smiled. She turned her attention back to her horse. "Well, old girl, you're all done." The horse nickered thankfully and wandered away to seek out some soft tendrils of grass to munch on.

"Should we go and collect some firewood or something?" asked Brandy pointing into the trees, and not wanting to feel useless, especially before the incriminating Forrest.

"No. Draco likes to keep his arm in practice, so he always does that. We can gather wild vegetables and fruits. Forrest will probably get a rabbit or some kind of fowl. Then we will have stew for our nights meal."

"Sounds good. I am hungry and stew will be a lot better than the dried stuff we have been eating since we left." Since we left, Brandy thought to herself as Puppis led the way into the quiet trees. That was only yesterday, and yet it feels as though it were almost a lifetime ago. It is like time stands still here in the woods, she shook her head slowly.

"Look." Puppis pointed, breaking into her thoughts. "You see those dark green leaves with the small white flowers in them? Those are a type of moer. They are very tasty and can be cook many different ways." They knelt beside the plants, Brandy keenly watching Puppis pull the leaves up, and shake the dirt from the roots of the plant.

"That's a potato," said Brandy, smiling with surprise in recognition of the plant. Things were again showing themselves to be more similar than not.

"Poe . . . ta . . . toe?"

"Sure. That's what we call them anyway. You can boil them, mash them, fry them, just about anything really."

Puppis laughed at the human girl's enthusiasm. "That is what we do to them too."

"Do you have carrots also? They are great in stew."

"What are car-rots?"

"It grows in the dirt like potatoes, or moer, and they're long, straight, and orange in color."

"Oh yes, we do." Puppis smiled, scanning the surrounding area with sharp eyes. "We call them krubi.

There they are. They usually grow in the same area as poe . . . ta . . . toes."

Brandy grinned at her new friend. "Very good," she complimented. "Now all we need is some onion."

"What is onion?" Puppis asked, raising an unsure eyebrow.

"You really can't miss them. They smell like, like, well I'm not sure what. All I can tell you is that they smell strong. Their tops, that grow out of the ground, are long and green, almost like heavy grass. Under the dirt is a white, multilayered bulb. That's an onion."

Puppis wrinkled her nose and laughed. "We just call that stink grass. Surely you do not eat it?" she asked in disbelief.

"It's good, really," Brandy protested with a laugh. "Let's just find some and I'll show you."

"I do not know if the others will like you putting it in our meal."

"We'll keep it a secret until after they eat it," Brandy urged the hesitant elf girl. "Then we'll tell. It's often better to not know than to be informed."

"Well, I do not know if I will like it." Puppis hesitated, not sure about what Brandy was telling her.

"Trust me. I eat it all the time at home, in fact most humans do. It won't hurt you, I promise," she assured the elf maid.

When they returned to camp, Forrest had a pot bubbling over the hot coals of their fire. Brandy had taken the liberty of cleaning and dicing the vegetables at the stream where they had washed them, and placed them back in the sack that they had carried. This way she would be able to put them in the pot without too much notice. When she finished, Puppis had returned with a sack full of sweet red berries.

"Smells good," Draco commented when they finally settled down to eat.

Brandy watched the others faces when they were all served. Puppis hesitated at first, but then timidly took a bite when Forrest and Draco ate the onions without damage.

"You are so right, they are good," Puppis said, with surprise and relief, to Brandy. "They taste nothing like they smell."

"What?" Forrest asked suspiciously peering into his bowl, moving the contents around with his spoon. What had this human put in their food?

"Onions," Brandy replied non-chalantly, with a little shrug.

"Onions?" Draco question without slowing down on his consumption of the stew.

"We call it stink grass," Puppis volunteered, then laughed at the disgusted face that Forrest made.

"You put stink grass in our food?" he asked angrily. "Are you trying to poison us?"

"Don't be an idiot," Brandy scolded him as if he were a toddler. "You don't eat the grass part, although some people do, you eat the bulb root beneath the ground, like moer and krubi."

"It is quite tasty," Draco complimented, helping himself to more of the stew out of the pot. "I had often seen animals of the wood eating the root and wondered of the taste."

"You are being silly!" Puppis laughed at Forrest again. "These are very good, and you should be open to try new things."

Forrest said nothing, but scowled at the elf girl who sat next to him. Grudgingly he ate the stew, not wanting to admit that he too found it very tasty.

After their meal, Brandy volunteered to take the utensils the short distance to the stream and wash them out. She also wanted the time alone to wash in peace. She was used to the solitary life that she had led for the past few years, and was not accustomed to having so many people around her, even if it was only a handful, at all times.

When the dishes were clean and laying on a cloth that she had carried to dry them, she pulled her boots off and stuck her feet in the cool relaxing waters. The chilliness of the stream caused goose bumps to erupt on her legs, but it felt good. She removed her shirt and splashed the cold liquid over her face, and arms, letting its refreshing feeling trickle down her neck and torso. She then took a heavy cake of soap, that Puppis had given her, and rubbed it into a rich lather, trying her best to clean the days grime off of her. After replacing her shirt, Brandy stayed by the waters edge kicking her legs and feet in the little stream. Suddenly a thought struck her. Were there guivres in little streams such as these? She peered into the water. It could not have been more than two foot deep, and she could see clearly to the sandy, pebble covered bottom even in the moonlight that had replaced the sun. Better not take any chances, she thought cautiously.

"You're going crazy!" She laughed out loud to herself, as she began to repack the bag that she had brought with her. When her task was finished, she pulled her soft boots back on and stood to return to camp. Her progress was instantly stopped by a limb cracking in the silent night that surrounded her. Her brain spun defensively. Who was there? She whirled around, peering wildly into the moon lit gloom, but saw nothing. Yet, the hairs on the back of her head prickled at the slight sound. She knew that it was not a friend who had broken that twig near her. It was definitely something else.

Stealthily as a cat, Brandy flung the bag over her shoulder and began picking her way through the trees back toward their camp. With every step she hesitated slightly to listen for anyone who may be near, or worse, behind her. Then, there it was again. Another branch cracked as the weight of a foot fell upon it. Brandy spun in her tracks only to find herself standing face to face with a huge ugly gobioid.

"So you are the little human girl that Chameleon spoke of," the creature said with a wheezing laugh, the stench of his breath nearly knocking Brandy to the ground.

"What's it to you toad face," Brandy yelled back loudly, hoping that someone from the camp would hear her. She did not have the crossbow that Corona had given her, it was with her things by the fire. She did have her knife that she had tucked into the tie at her waist. Would it be good enough to fight the gobioid off if she had too?

"You can yell all you like," the gobioid slobbered, smirking at her raised voice. "I made sure that I created a big enough disturbance on the other side of your camp so that the others would go investigate, before I left to come and fetch you."

"Come and fetch me?"

"Yes, my master requires your presence now."

"I didn't know you scum were such good little lap dogs. Do you lick his hand when he snaps his fingers too?" Brandy laughed in a taunting voice as she inched back away from the creature. She had to stall him long enough until she could run back to camp and hopefully have someone there.

"Say what you wish, human. My orders are clear, you are coming with me," the gobioid stated flatly, walking towards Brandy, and reaching for her with outstretched claws.

Brandy swung the bag off of her shoulders and heaved it at the advancing gobioid as hard as she could. It bounced harmlessly off his head, and brought an amused chuckle from his lips.

"That really did not hurt. Nor was it very nice," he said, with a laugh. He grabbed Brandy by the left arm with his massive hand, then turning to drag her forcibly behind him as if she were no more than a rag doll.

"Get your smelly paws off of me," she shouted angrily, trying without success to pull free from his grasp, and only causing him to laugh louder.

"You complain like a little bug," snickered the gobioid, dragging her farther and farther away from the camp with each long stride of his powerful legs.

"Well, this little bug can sting," Brandy retorted spitefully, anger beginning to boil within her. She pulled her knife from her waist tie and plunged it deep into the arm that held her. The creature howled in pain, releasing her instantly. She quickly snatched her weapon out of his arm and brought it down in an arcing swing on his other arm, opening a ragged gash, that spilled a greenish colored blood.

"You wretched demon. I will squash you like the little bug that you are," the gobioid shrieked in rage, madness stealing into his yellow eyes.

He rushed headlong towards Brandy, taking no precautions to protect himself, only thinking of hurting that which had caused him hurt. At the last second before he reached her, Brandy dropped instantly to her knees and stuck the blade deep into his midriff. The gobioid crashed to the ground, a loud bellow tearing from his fanged mouth. Brandy shuddered involuntarily from the sound. It was like she herself had been pierced in the heart the very same blade.

The creature moaned and writhed for a few short moments, and then stillness surrounded her.

Without being able to stop them, tears rushed to her eyes. She had never taken the life of any living animal before. Sure she had swatted flies, and stomped ants, but she had never taken a living, thinking life before. Even if this was some misshapen creature, it still had some feeble intelligence, but not anymore. Not because of her hand. Brandy wiped her face on her sleeve and turned her back on the crumpled mass. Slowly she recovered her bag and started heading toward the camp.

"Forget it. Let it go," she reprimanded herself loudly. "If you hadn't fought him off, you would be on your way to Chameleon by know, or worse. Then think of what kind of trouble you would be in." Brandy shook her head sadly, and look up to the sky at the stars that twinkled overhead. The brightness of them smiled happily at her, but did nothing to soothe her troubled, guilty conscience. She had taken a life. A life that was not hers to take.

"Behind you!"

The sound of Puppis's voice shattered the thoughts and feelings that raged through Brandy's being. She whirled around, just in time to see a massive clawed hand rushing toward her face. It was the gobioid that she had fought. That rat, she thought just as the fist made contact, he was faking. The blow lifted Brandy from her feet and sent her sprawling to the ground on her back. She laid there dazed, struggling to catch her breath, as she watched the other elves spring into action.

Draco swung his mighty axe, lopping off one of the creatures arms, before he too was sent crashing to the ground by the gobioid's other whirling limb. The gobioid went berserk with pain, but would not retreat. Instead it raged forward, intent on destroying any form that stood in its way to the human that lay on the ground. Puppis quickly filled the creature with half a dozen well placed arrows, but even this did not stop, or slow, the creatures advance. Finally, Forrest rushed at the gobioid, sword held firmly in both of his hands. He swung heavily at the gobioid, inflicting a horrible wound to its right leg. The creature staggered, but refused to fall. It flung its remaining fist ineffectively at the elf that stood before him.

"Master," the gobioid bellowed in pain. Even the creature knew that Chameleon would not come and save him. He was on his own to face that which was now imminent.

Forrest swung again, enlarging the hole in the creatures middle that Brandy had started with her knife. The gobioid went still as a statue. He turned his yellow eyes one last time on Brandy before those eyes saw nothing else, and fell to the ground. Unmoving and silent, forever.

CHAPTER TEN

"By the Mother of Spring, are you all right?" Puppis gasped, rushing to Brandy's side and gently helping her into a sitting position.

"I'm fine. I thought I had killed that thing. I have never caused death by my hands before. I didn't realize that . . ." Brandy began, struggling for words to describe what was going on and what she was feeling on the inside. She reached for her cheek, which throbbed in pain, only to find that she was bruised and thankfully not severely injured.

"Do not let it worry you, child," Draco said, gently patting her on the head., his simply gesture full of fatherly comfort. "It is over now, and he can not hurt you."

"Chameleon is still out there," Brandy said, looking around her and then to the others wide eyed.

"Did you see him?" Forrest asked, wiping the gobioid's gore from his long blade.

"No, but that thing said that Chameleon had sent for me," she stated, pointing to the crumpled mass of the fallen gobioid.

Draco let out a deep sigh as he hoisted his axe over his shoulder. "Then he knows we are coming. We must be prepared."

"Yes," agreed Forrest sullenly. He retrieved Brandy's knife from the gobioid, cleaned it, and placed it in the girl's shaking hands. After a brief glance at her dirty features, turned suddenly and headed back toward their camp.

"Come on, you will be fine," Puppis said in a soothing voice, helping Brandy to her feet.

"Sure, I will. Unless I keep getting hit in the head," Brandy grumbled, rubbing her aching temples. Slowly she walked, or almost stumbled back to the fire that was the center of their camp. She gratefully sank to her knees, and laid her head on her rolled up sleeping blanket.

"Are you well, child?" Draco asked, his voice full of true concern.

"Nothing that a bottle of aspirin and a weeks worth of sleep wouldn't cure?" she said, grinning through the dull throb in her head.

"Aspirin?" he questioned her with a frown.

"That is another of those human things that we have not figured out yet," Forrest said with a light smile.

A smile that Brandy couldn't believe. It had been a while since she had seen him smile.

"I will make her some wild mint tea, that seemed to help her the first time we found her." A short time later Forrest handed Brandy a cup of the promised minty brew, which she gratefully accepted and wasted no time in drinking it down.

"Thank you," she said sincerely to the elf, closing her eyes, the tiredness of the days events overtaking her.

"I think she has the right idea," said Draco wearily. "You children should get some rest. I will take first watch for the night. I do not think we should be too careful or let our guard down."

Puppis nodded her instantaneous agreement. "Wake me after your time is up, I will take second watch."

"Then I will finish up the night," said Forrest.

Brandy forced her weary eyes open and propped herself up on one arm. "Don't count me out. I will take the last watch."

"You do not have to," began Puppis, "you have really had quite a day."

"I'm part of this group aren't I?" When no answer of disagreement came, Brandy quickly continued. "Then I will take my turn at watch just like everyone else. I don't want any special treatments or favors."

"Fine," agreed Forrest. "I will wake you after my watch is over."

"Thanks," Brandy said, settling herself back down on her blanket. She did not even bother to unroll it, instead she curled up in a tight ball and fell almost instantly asleep.

"Welcome back."

Chameleon smiled eagerly at Brandy, who stood in the doorway of his great underground chamber.

She said nothing, but stared around in wonder. It was just like before. A fire roared in the pit, sending tendrils of warmth floating through the damp room. Lyra was still held, unmoving, in suspension, in the large flawless crystal. This time, though, she noticed something different. This time there was someone on the long flat marble table. A person. An elf. No, a female elf. It was Carina. Brandy recognized her long white hair. She was dressed in a plain white gown and slippers.

"What have you done?" Brandy sent an accusing glare at the dark robed elf.

"Nothing yet. The time is not right, but it is very close." He smiled with perfectly white teeth. "You will be here to see it. You will witness the change of partial power to total power for me and the one that I serve."

"Who do you serve?" Brandy asked, already knowing what the answer would be.

"My queen, Lacerta," he stated proudly. "I sense you know that already."

"Yes," Brandy admitted. "I saw her, when you brought me here before, in the shadows. Why does she hide?"

"She does not hide," Forrest said, smirking in amusement. "She observes. She is gaining strength steadily. You will meet her in time."

Brandy said nothing in return. She didn't like the way that Chameleon said things with such certainty. As if he had no doubt as to what the future held. She ran her eyes to the spot in which she had first seen the Dark Queen lurking, but found only emptiness. Her gaze then once again traveled to the still form of the princess laying on the table. She wondered if it were really Carina or another of the elf's tricks. She began to wander in what she hoped appeared an aimless manner.

"Let Carina go. She has done nothing to you," Brandy demanded loudly, in a voice that she hoped sounded confident.

"Yes, the princess is quite the innocent, but I am afraid that she figures prominently in my plans. For you see her ancestors had a lot to do with that. You do know the story, do you not?" Chameleon asked with a sarcastic smile.

"You're crazy you know. Absolutely nuts."

"You should not think that way, my dear. I have decided to let you become a part of all of this. I believe you shall make a worthy mate for me. Your life's fire is very strong, and that is good. Your strength will add to mine. Think of the powerful children we can raise."

"Drop dead," Brandy said flatly in a firm even tone. "I would never consent to being your mate. I would rather die first."

"I must let you in on a little secret. I have found that it is not very wise to say what you would do for a certainty until you have thought out all of the consequences that your answer and actions could have for yourself as well as others around you."

Brandy raised an eyebrow and laughed at the dark elf. "Are you threatening me? One of your toads already tried to do that tonight and I'm sure you know what that got him."

Chameleon grinned at the impetuous human girl before him. "He was nothing but a pawn. I was testing you, and you reacted just as I believed you would. You would rather fight than be easily taken. I like that very much. You resemble a wild animal, and like all wild animals, you will have a breaking point."

"Then why didn't you try and take me instead of sending your lackeys after me, or bugging my dreams for that matter?"

"Honestly, I would enjoy the challenge of it," conceded Chameleon with a slight nod of his coal colored head. "There is much here that takes my time. You will be joining me very soon, you can be assured of this."

"I don't doubt it, but it will not be in the way that you think. I will come here, and it will be to stop you."

"That may cost you your life, my little fire bug," Chameleon said softly, advancing on the girl.

"That's a chance I'm willing to take. What about you? Are you willing to risk your life on it?" she shot back defiantly.

Chameleon said nothing, but smiled triumphantly as he felt the human girl shiver in fright when his hand lightly brushed the bruise on her cheek. Her large brown eyes narrowed with apprehension when they met his cold. black gaze. Quickly she reached up and pushed his arm away from her with her hand.

"Don't touch me," she hissed.

"Do I frighten you?" He smiled lazily in challenge.

"No." Brandy lied badly. Her heart pounded wildly in her chest. This man frightened her more than any of her worst nightmares. She would rather die than admit that to him.

"I think I do," he said, laughing loudly. He reached out and twisted a chestnut curl around his finger. "I will see you soon, fire bug."

Brandy sat up abruptly and opened her eyes. She was back in the camp. Her breathing came in ragged gasps, and sweat trickled down her face and neck. Damn him, she thought furiously. She looked up and saw Forrest peering questioningly at her. He was already on watch, had that much of the night already slipped by, she wondered. Slowly she struggled to her feet and wrapped her blanket around as she shivered in the cool morning air. Picking up her crossbow, she walked quietly over to where Forrest sat on a log.

"May I join you," she inquired lightly.

Forrest answered with a small nod and pointed to the emptiness beside him. "You still have some time before your watch begins," he stated as Brandy settled herself on the hard lumpy log, placing the ready crossbow on her lap.

"Couldn't sleep. I dreamed of Chameleon again," Brandy sighed. "Or maybe I should say he interrupted my sleep again."

"Oh really?" Forrest asked, raising a skeptical eyebrow.

"I know you don't believe me, but I should tell you that he has Carina. She didn't make it back to your clan."

"How can that be?" he asked, without the usual skepticism in his voice.

"I have no idea, but he means to sacrifice her. Of that I am sure. Just as Draco told us in the story."

"What about Volan?"

"I don't know." Brandy shook her head slowly, searching her memory for all that she had tried to observe in Chameleon's chamber. "I didn't see him. Perhaps he is just being held else where in the castle."

"Probably so. I didn't feel his death," Forrest said quietly, almost to himself.

Brandy looked deeply at the sullen elf beside her. "What do you mean by that?"

Forrest gave her a wry smile. "You remember when you asked if all elves have magical powers? Well some of us do, but we keep them hidden from others."

"Why?"

"For some of us the powers are a curse, not a blessing or a helpful tool."

"So what does your magic do?" asked Brandy hesitantly after a moments silence when Forrest didn't elaborate further. She didn't know whether she wanted to know or not, but her curiosity was getting the best of her again.

"I sense death. It follows me like a dark, ominous cloud."

"You can tell when someone dies?" Brandy asked, shivering at her own question.

Forrest nodded his head. "That, and when someone will die soon."

"What a horrible burden to have to carry. I am very sorry," Brandy said softly. "Is there no one in the clan that you can talk to and tell of this?"

Forrest shook his head sadly. "No. And I would appreciate it if you would do likewise and say nothing of it."

"Of course, it is safe with me." For a few silent moments, Brandy stared intently into the fire. She wondered why, of all people, Forrest had chosen to share his long held secret with her. She whom he seemed to dislike and hold in inferior contempt. "Can I ask you something, if you don't mind?"

"Yes," the elf said, somewhat reluctantly.

"Why did you tell me your secret if you hate me so much?"

Forrest was taken aback. He had never found himself at such a loss of words as he did now at the human's blunt question. "I do not hate you," he stammered awkwardly.

"Then why do you treat me like you do? Cold and indifferent. You act as if you wouldn't care if I dropped off the face of the planet, but yet you have saved my life more than once."

"This is very difficult to say," Forrest began, running his hands nervously through his dark hair. "The first time I saw you, when you crossed the barrier to help us in the clearing, I sensed your death."

"What?" Brandy asked incredulously in a loud voice. Was he loony? "Are you saying that I am going to die soon?" she added in a low whisper.

"Probably so. I sensed that you would die while saving my life. So I did not want to get close to you in any way, hoping that the vision feeling would go away."

"And has it," Brandy asked hopefully.

"No it has not," Forrest said slowly, shaking his head sadly. "I am very sorry. I should not have said anything."

"Don't be. At least now I can kind of prepare myself, and try not to do something stupid, like save you," Brandy said, grinning at the elf. She returned her gaze to the fire.

So this is it, she thought. I guess I only get one shot at the adventure of a lifetime. Well, I might as well make the most of it. One things for sure, she vowed. I'm not going to be afraid of Chameleon or those creepy gobioids anymore.

And what about Steve? Would he live through whatever it was that they were facing. A silent tear trickled down her face at the thought of not clowning with her best friend anymore.

Taking a deep breath to quell her feelings, she felt a strange sense of calm settle over herself.

"What of Steve?" she asked Forrest, still staring into the fire. She could feel him looking at her with a questioning expression. "Will he die?" asked Brandy meeting his gaze.

"I do not think so."

"I'm glad," she said, sniffing away the last of her sorrow. "He's really a great guy. Lots of fun. I know you would like him if you gave him half a chance."

Forrest said nothing, but smile sorrowfully at the girl beside him. What had he done by telling her of his burden.

"Do me a favor, if I get dusted, that is?" Brandy grinned half heartedly, and continued at his nod. "Try not to pick on him too much. I think he likes your Princess Carina."

"I promise," he said, laughter lighting his eyes. How unusual this girl was.

"What of Carina and Lyra? Will they live through this mess?" Brandy asked, growing somber again.

"That I can not answer," Forrest said quietly. "Chameleon's magic is much more powerful than mine. He has blocked out all that concerns the princess and Lyra. I sense nothing at all in their regard."

"Then we shall have to wait and see what happens." Brandy smiled optimistically. "Well, I think we are going to be okay. You may actually be wrong," she added.

"Perhaps."

Forrest gazed thoughtfully at the human girl next to him. He put his arm around her shoulders and held her close. Her nearness felt good, relaxing, and comfortable. It was a feeling that he could grow very accustomed to, but how long would it be able to last, he wondered.

"Yes, Brandy. I think we will be," he whispered into her soft hair.

Chapter Eleven

Brandy watched the morning sun desperately try to break its way through the trees to the east. She and Forrest had stayed together by the fire and talked quietly for a while into the period of her watch. Finally she urged him to return to his sleeping blanket and get some rest before they would have to continue traveling when the sun rose.

She smiled in remembrance of their discussions. They had much in common, especially their need for solitude and quietness. She looked over at Forrest as he slept. A light peaceful smile touched the corners of his lips. She hoped that maybe she could be the reason for that smile. Her thoughts returned again to the ominous warning that he had given her. Would she really die while saving his life, she wondered sadly. It seemed to her that he was the one who had continuously come to her aid and not the other way around. Maybe he had gotten his wires crossed or something. Then she didn't want anything to happen to him, either. She decided that the best thing to do would be to try to forget about it and tend to the matters at hand.

She rose to her feet and walked a wide circle around the perimeter of their small camp. The others would be waking soon, and for that she was grateful. Every noise in the darkness had sounded like a monster attacking from the depths of the trees. She had quelled the urge a hundred times to rush to Forrest's side and shake him awake. She laughed to herself when she realized that her monsters of the dark had always turned out to be small night animals foraging hurriedly around for food before they themselves turned into a meal for something larger. Upon spotting her, many of the acted as if she were that something larger.

Just as Brandy was about to settle herself back down by the warm, friendly, small fire, a moving shadow in the depths of the trees caught her eye. She blinked hard several times and stared intently at the spot. She was sure that she had seen something, and yet she could see nothing now, only the faint glimmer of sunlight reaching its tiny specks of light into the dew covered branches. Was her imagination playing tricks on her, she wondered. Slowly she stood, holding her crossbow securely in front of her like a shield of safety, and advanced carefully into the trees.

"Maybe I should wake someone," she whispered to herself, gaining strength and encouragement from the sound of her own voice. "No you don't, because if there is nothing here you are going to really feel stupid, and make yourself look like a chicken."

She chuckled nervously when she glanced quickly around her and saw nothing but the shadows of the trees themselves and their gently moving leaves and branches.

"What a scaredy cat I am. I better get back to camp before anyone wakes up and finds me missing. They might think that I have finally lost my mind and took off raving like some lunatic." Brandy smiled, rubbing her eyes wearily. What I really need, she reasoned quietly, is a soda, a box of doughnuts, and a hot tub. That would fix things up perfectly.

Breaking through the last of the trees and back into the small clearing that made their camp, Brandy froze suddenly in her tracks. She stared numbly at what she saw. Gobioids. Three large, ugly, scaly creatures. Each of them brandishing large clubs and swords. They stalked to where each of the three elves slept soundly in their autumn colored blankets, depending on her to keep watch over them and to warn them of any impending danger. Damn, she couldn't even seem to do that right. As quietly as possible, she crept her way toward the unsuspecting gobioids. They did not seem to have noticed her presence yet. One thing was for sure, that wouldn't last for long. She sprang into the camp, like a panther pouncing on its unsuspecting prey.

"Hold it right there you reptiles," Brandy yelled as loudly as she could to the surprised creatures. Her sudden presence startled them for a moment, and that moment was long enough for the elves to be jolted from their slumber. They wasted no time rolling from their blankets and springing to their feet a little farther away from the gobioids than what they were only seconds previously. Only Draco had been able to arm himself as he rose to his feet and away from their attackers. Forrest and Puppis were not nearly as seasoned as he in the ways of being prepared for anything, so they stood facing their foe with nothing save their bare hands.

"Back away now, creatures," Draco warned with a low bear like rumble in his voice at those who stood before him. "Or you will have trouble using those claws of yours."

"We fear you not, old elf. You are the only one armed, and you will be easily overcome by myself or my comrades." The gobioid, who stood before Draco, laughed contemptuously at the elf's threat.

"He is not the only one who is armed. Now get back," Brandy challenged from where she stood. She held the crossbow tightly in her damp, uncertain hands. Butterflies danced wildly in her stomach, making it queasy. Images of the gobioid that had been killed the night before flashed in her mind. Nervous sweat prickled at her neck. Would she be able to fire her arrow at the jeering creature if need be? She hoped so, for she could not stand the thought that she would let her friends down. No, that was something that she couldn't do, she reminded herself.

"Unless of course that's what you want, an arrow sticking out of your thick ugly neck," Brandy threatened, instantly knowing now that she could do just that, because friendship overcame fear. The reassuring thought stilled her stomach and made her feel better, calmer, and more confident.

Another of the gobiods laughed. "Look, Taber, another human with too many words coming out of its mouth."

Suddenly stunned, as if slapped, Brandy balked at the creature's words. Another human. What did the gobioid mean by that? Could they be the ones who had taken Steve, or were there more humans here other than herself and Steve.

"Silence!" ordered Taber to the snickering gobioids who stood by him. He turned his attention back to the elves and human before him. "You can either surrender now or face the consequences of being maimed or worse."

Brandy looked to Draco. She would follow his lead no matter what he chose. She trusted his judgment, and told him so with a simple shrug of her shoulders when he glanced her way.

He smiled reassuringly at her shrug and faced the gobioids, squaring his shoulders and lifting his axe a little higher before him. "We will take our chances," Draco informed the creature that stood before him, receiving silent nods of agreement from Puppis and Forrest.

"As you wish," said Taber. He lifted his club and took a step forward, but that was a far as he went.

True to her word, Brandy lifted her crossbow and easily took aim. With a small whisk, and the span of a heartbeat, the long slim arrow cut a deadly arc across the distance of the camp. It embedded itself with a loud sickening thud into Taber's scaly, grayish neck. The creature instantly dropped its weapons and groped blindly for the protruding stick. Pain gripped greedily at his neck as he fell to his knees, trying to yell at the others for help, yet no sounds emerged from his tusked mouth. Only his eyes betrayed the fear he felt as his life's blood slipped from his wound.

"You die first, human!" yelled the gobioid who stood closest to his fallen comrade. He started closing the distance between himself and the meddlesome human, who fumbled for a new arrow, when a thunderous and commanding voice halted his progress.

"Stop, Coer!" the voice ordered. Coer did as he was told and remained as stone where his feet had landed. Brandy and the others strained their eyes to see who had spoken the words. Brandy gasped in horror as the speaker came into view. It was another gobioid. Only he was not alone as she would have thought. He was accompanied by two other unwilling prisoners. They were both bound by straps on their wrists and ankles, and were led by thick leather thongs wrapped tightly around their throats and dragged forcibly forward like unruly dogs.

"Steve!" exclaimed Brandy at the sight before her.

"Volan," Puppis mumbled sadly in dismay at her friend's predicament.

"Release your weapons instantly or your companions die," the gobioid stated simply. He held a long blade to Volan's throat. Draco lowered his axe to the ground, and Brandy dropped her crossbow without hesitation. Coer and the other gobioid who had originally faced them rushed in to kick their weapons away from them. In turn, they pushed

Brandy and Draco close to Puppis and Forrest, keeping them all under close watch.

"Braakk, what of Taber?" asked Coer, indicating the still, blood soaked form, of their former leader.

"Taber was a fool not to take his foe seriously. Leave him here for the carrion eaters to deal with. He deserves nothing more," the gobioid said, scorn lacing his words as he looked at his fallen cohort. "Chameleon would not have been as merciful as the human girl's arrow. It would do you two well to remember that," he added.

Brandy tried to rush to Steve's side, but was knocked to the ground by the claw of Coer. She remained where she was and glared hatefully at the creature who stood over her. Shooting her foot out like a striking snake, Brandy caught the gobioid just below the knee with her heel. His leg buckled under the impact of her blow. Cursing, or what she assumed was foul languare, his body went down with his injured leg. She pounced on the fallen gobioid and began plummeting it with punches from her small closed fists. Coer defensively hurled the light weight human off of himself like a bothersome insect, but not before she had opened a gash on his face.

As she spun about to continue what she began, loud crack in the air and a painful slap on her back broke Brandy from her mad assault on the gobioid. She took in a deep breath as the sting of whatever had hit her, sunk into her flesh. She halted in her struggle to punch Coer again long enough to look up at Braakk. He held a long multi stringed whip in his hand that contain a few strands of her hair.

"Perhaps you did not understand what I said," he began with a grumble. "You either cooperate or I will terminate your friend's life."

"Then you tell your pigs here to keep their crummy claws off of me," Brandy sputtered angrily, blinking back tears that threatened to escape her eyes from the pain that assaulted her.

"Do as you are told, and you will not be bothered by the others. Do you understand?"

"Maybe," Brandy conceded indignantly. Forrest walked to her and helped her to her feet, pulling her protectively by him.

"Do not provoke them so much," he urged with a whisper in her ear.

"I can't help it. They seem to bring out the best of my bad temper."

"Maybe if we are compliant they will let their guard down a little and we will be able to overpower them."

"I hope you are right," Brandy agreed softly, but deep in her heart she knew that the chances of that were going to be slim. They were not that far from Chameleon now, and he was certainly not going to let them escape his grasp.

"Bind them," Braakk ordered Coer and the other gobioid. With a menacing glare he added to Coer, "if you let your guard down one more time, I just might let the human finish you off if I do not do it myself first."

Coer said nothing, but quickly bound the elf girl's hands tightly. Then turned to the smirking human girl who readily held her hands out in front of her for him to bind.

"Enjoy this, slime. It's the last time you will find me so willing," she promised with a cat like grin.

When they were finished, the gobioid pushed them over to Braakk and the two other prisoners. "Should we put them on their horses?" asked Coer, indicating the animals that had cowered nervously around a tree since the gobioids and the much larger agouti had first appeared.

"No. Let them walk," Braakk said after a moments hesitation. He released his grip on Steve and Volan and tethered the four horses together on a long strap and tied them to an agouti. Then mounting his own beast he led the way from the camp. The humans and elves followed numbly behind as the two remaining gobioid mounted their travel beasts. The agouti who had lost their riders eagerly followed their own kind without question or hesitation.

"And remember," Braakk warned, turning in his saddle to look at his prisoners, "if you try to escape or fight, the one next to you will surely fall as a result of that action."

They traveled silently for many minutes. Brandy walked next to Steve and kept watching his face. It had a nasty bruise on one side and was cut on the other. His clothes were dirty and beginning to tear in many places. He walked with a limp, and his wrists were swollen and discolored. She was ecstatic at seeing him, but his lack of acknowledgment disturbed her. She had hoped he would say something, but not a word from him broke the silence. He stared only at his bound hands before him as they made their way forcibly forward. It was not like her friend to be bottled up like this. Had the gobioids done something terrible to him for him to remain silent for so long?

Finally she could not stand it any longer. "What's wrong, Steve? Did the reptiles do something screwy to you or what? You know you can tell me," Brandy urged softly, concern for her friend's well being ringing loudly in her quiet words. It was not like him to shun her. They had always shared everything, that is what had made their friendship so strong over the years.

"This is all my fault," Steve mumbled out miserably in a hoarse whisper.

"What on earth are you talking about," Brandy asked, staring at her friend as if he were mad. "What on earth is your fault?"

"All of this that has happened. Us being captured, Chameleon and his mad plans, Carina being taken."

"I can't say it has been a picnic, but how is all of it your fault?"

"I should never have rushed out of that bush and placed you in all of the danger that has befallen us. We should have just kept walking to your house and we would be there having fun right now."

Brandy looked intently at her friend and then threw her head back and laughed merrily at Steve's words. He snapped his head in her direction, frowning angrily.

"This isn't very funny! What the hell is your problem? Have you finally cracked or something? Here I am trying to tell you how sorry I am that we are in this mess and all you can do is laugh about it. Damn it, Brandy, sometimes you really piss me off."

"I'm sorry," Brandy began, stifling her amusement. "You should hear yourself. You sound like such a gloomer. You didn't get us into this mess. We got us into this mess. I didn't have to follow you into the clearing and help smack our goonie friends around. I didn't even have to come looking for you. I could have easily stayed behind and minded my own business. But I didn't, and you want to know why?"

"Because your crazy about me?" Steve offered with a small weary smile filled with relief.

"Yeah sure," Brandy said, grinning, and rolling her eyes. "Because I wanted the thrill of the adventure just as much as you did. I wanted to see what was going on with these creatures, too. You weren't the only one hit by Cupid at first sight by an elf you know," she added conspiratorially in a hushed whispered.

"You mean Forrest . . ."

"Shut up you goof, or he'll hear you," Brandy hissed with a sly grin, glancing over her shoulder at the brooding elf.

"Seriously Brandy, I am really sorry about all of this. I figured we would spend your birthday at your house watching old movies and eating too much junk food until we were sick. I never dreamed that we would end up like this."

"Like what?" Brandy smiled affectionately at her lifelong friend. She shook her head and bumped her shoulder into his.

"Like salamanders in a glass bowl, or, or puppies on a leash."

"Who cares?" Brandy shrugged nonchalantly. "It is the adventure of a lifetime. If it was too easy then how much fun would be in that?"

After a few seconds Steve beamed in total agreement. "You are right, it is the adventure of a lifetime. Do you think it will have a happy ending?"

"That I couldn't tell you," Brandy murmured softly, remembering the ominous warning of Forrest.

"It was kind of fun though, wasn't it?"

"Was? It still is!" Brandy reached her bound hands over and touched Steve's warmly. "I don't plan on giving in yet. Promise me one thing?"

"Anything," Steve replied brightly. His friend's enthusiasm was rubbing off.

"If we do go out, let's do it with a bang."

"Absolutely," he agreed. "Better than New Years Eve at Times Square."

"Now that sounds pretty good."

Braakk swung around in his saddle and glared at the two humans. He could not hear their words, but the conversation definitely sounded cheerful. "Quiet, back there," he barked, sending a dark look at the two.

"We're only talking, Braakk," said Steve, looking squarely at the one who had inflicted most of the bruises that showed upon him. "We're not going anywhere."

"Not yet, anyway," Brandy snickered under her breath.

"Just stop the talking. Your speech is irritating to listen to," he grumbled disgustedly, turning back forward in his saddle.

"What a grouch," Brandy added loudly with an antagonizing grin, and a small shake of her head. She had no intention to listening to the gobioid.

"No kidding," Steve agreed.

"Well tell me all about it. What have you been doing for the past couple of days?" Brandy looked intently at her friend with an eager smile. She was anxious to find out what had happened to him and all that he had seen, and she was just as anxious to tell him all that had befallen herself.

Chapter Twelve

Brandy and Steve talked quietly and non-stop to themselves as they traveled slowly through the rough terrain of the trees. Eventually the trees were replaced by low shrubs and in time those too disappeared, leaving only patches of dry grass in front of them. The sight of what stood before them ceased their talking and caused them to look keenly in wonder and apprehension. Brandy shivered involuntarily. The dark shadows of the plain in front of her seemed to sneak their evil tendrils forward and embed themselves in her spine. Lightning snaked its way across the gray forbidding sky, and the air seemed to become much cooler the further they walked. She sensed the same evil here that she had felt when in Chameleon's castle. The horses also seemed to sense the evil that lurked before them, for they complained loudly and tugged against the agouti to which they were tethered, refusing to go on another step.

"We must be entering his lands," Steve whispered. "There is no turning back now."

Brandy nodded silently at his words. Deep in her heart she knew that he spoke the truth.

Braakk halted the group and dismounted his travel beast. All eyes watched him as he made his way towards the elves horses at the rear of the group.

"Are we going to eat them?" Coer asked, drooling in anticipation.

Brandy felt her stomach turn at the suggestion. She saw anger well into the faces of her elf friends at the gobioid's words. They were very close to their horse friends, and such a thought was considered unthinkable to them.

"No," Braakk informed his cohort. "They will only slow us down. We must reach the castle no later than tomorrow morning. I will spare their worthless lives, only because we have no time to deal with them," he said, releasing their reins and sending them back towards the woods and brush behind them.

"They have more worth than you shall ever possess," Forrest said darkly. The horses hesitated after a few paces and looked back to their riders. It was not their way to abandon those who cared for them.

"To the clan," Puppis ordered their faithful mounts in a loud clear voice. The animals neighed sharply in farewell, turned, and quickly set off at a fast pace away from their friends.

"At least they will be safe, that is more than I can say for us," Volan said gloomily as Braakk returned to his beast and began forward once again, but at a much faster pace.

"Do not worry child," Draco said comfortingly. "All will work out in the end."

"How can you say that?" Volan spat angrily into the dust at his feet, then just as instantly was sorry that he had lost his temper with Draco. "Forgive me, but no one knows where we are going. No one knows what Chameleon is up to except for us. Who will warn the clan?"

"He's right," Steve admitted sorrowfully. "Carina never made it back to your clan. Chameleon has her. Your people do not know what is happening."

"Taken? How? Where?" Puppis asked in fright. A confused frown wrinkling her forehead.

"One minute he was standing there and the next he was gone," explained Steve awkwardly.

"Who?" asked Brandy in bewilderment.

"Chameleon. He used dimension traveling," said Volan.

"He is strong," Draco began, then hesitated thoughtfully. "Yet, there must be limitations to his power or he would have taken all of you at the same time. There is hope that he can be defeated."

"How encouraging," Brandy said, sighing deeply. "Should we draw straws to see who is going to jump him first?" She tried to laugh lightheartedly. At the others non-responsive looks she continued with a smile. "Look you guys, it is like Draco said. It will work out in the end. We can't go anywhere unless we want to risk the life of another. I'm not willing to do that. On the other hand, I don't intend on dying just yet either. So tough it up and lets think of a way to get the better of this wizard. He must have a weakness somewhere."

"Brandy's right," Steve agreed. "Everyone has a weak spot. We will just have to find out what Chameleon's is."

"How do you intend on doing that?" asked Forrest curiously, for he was not ready to give up yet either.

"Watch and listen to his actions when we get there," Draco said, nodding favorably at the human's words.

"I hope you are right," Volan said, his words heavy with doubt.

Carina paced restlessly, wringing her hands at the agonizing silence that enveloped her. She once again looked helplessly about her prison. It was the epitome of luxury. Soft thick rugs covered the floor in many layers. Bright tapestries hung over the walls, and the room was furnished with large comfortable furniture. The bed was made with silk sheets and hand woven blankets that were softer than baby rabbits fur. The food and drink far surpassed anything that the cooks at her family home had ever made. She had been bathed in a large silver tub, and her ivory white hair had been scrubbed so that it now gleamed brightly in the candle lit room. Her tattered and dirty traveling clothes had been replaced by a simple, yet elegant, white gown that fell to the tops of her feet, which were shod in delicate white slippers. Indeed, she was a very well kept prisoner, but a prisoner none the less.

She desperately scanned the room for a way of escape, but could find none. There were no windows or adjoining rooms that she could detect. The only door, that led to the hall, had been covered with a hiding spell, and really was not too sure of its location as it changed every time someone entered. Unless Chameleon or one of his gobioid slaves were there to speak to her or bring something to her, the door was not even visible to sight. It blended in perfectly with the smooth stone wall. Carina sighed despondently at her predicament and flung herself into a large hand carved rocking chair. She sat there huddled, with her legs drawn closely to her body, for many long minutes wishing a gobioid slave would come to her room. Maybe she could overpower it or trick it and flee this cursed place.

As if reading her silent thoughts, Carina heard the faint scraping of a gobioid's clawed feet approaching her room down the stone hallway. Frantically she looked about, searching for an appropriate hiding place. Where?

"Think, Carina, think," she urged herself desperately in a soft voice, hearing the clicking that meant the door would reappear in seconds and swing inward, exposing her to whoever would be entering.

"The bed," she whispered triumphantly, rushing to the majestic piece of furniture. Just as the clicking stopped, she flung herself effortlessly under the bed and pulled the blankets partially down the side to conceal herself from view. She held her breath as she peeked out beneath the soft material and watched the door swing open. A pair of large clawed feet shuffled into the room and walked to a table that sat to the left side of the chamber.

"Some refreshments for you . . . ," the creature began in its hoarse voice, then abruptly halted in confusion. "Princess?" it asked again, peering dumbfoundedly around the room. It saw nothing. How could this be?

Carina stifled the urge to gag as the pungent creature waddled over to her hiding place. She wished her heart would not beat so loudly within her chest, for she felt it would give her away for sure. She saw the bed sag with the weight of the gobioid as it leaned on the structure and patted its massive paw around on the cushions and coverings. Please don't look underneath, she begged in silence.

"Princess?" the gobioid snorted again, agitation and fear of its master creeping into its voice. The creature took one more long look about the room, then turned and headed back for the door.

Do not close it! Please, do not close it, Carina silently pleaded from her hiding place. Just leave it open and go for help, she urged at the back of the gobioid. A relieved sigh escaped her tired lungs and a wide smile spread across her face when she saw that the gobioid had done just that. He had left the door wide open and had hurried down the hall, mumbling in despair.

When she could no longer hear his voice, Carina quickly crawled from her hiding place and rushed to the door. Cautiously she peered around the frame and was relieved to see nothing. Securely pulling her skirt up above her feet, she bolted down the hall in the opposite direction that the gobioid had taken. When she reached the end, the corridor split to the left and right. She hesitated, not knowing which heading to take. Finally she settled on the left and carefully began making her way down the hall, as quietly as possible, but every step she took in her soft slippers seemed to echo loudly off of the damp and dimly lit walls that surrounded her.

She walked for what seemed an eternity, when abruptly the hall ended and Carina found herself at the top of a long narrow flight of stairs. Hesitating, she was not sure what to do. Finally, she reasoned that at least the stairs went down. Timidly she began descending the steps, pressing her back closely to the cold stones of the wall, trying to become one with its damp surface, and at the same time peering cautiously at what lay far below her. It was a large chamber. The only thing that she could make out a roaring fire pit that took up much of the center of the room. She continued her downward trail, and noticed that other things in the chamber began to take shape before her. There was a long marble table and some sort of large crystal that hung in the air.

Carina stared intently at the crystal. It glimmered brightly in the light of the fire. She stared intently at the suspended jewel, realizing that there was something within the depths of the stone. She gasped in terror when she beheld what was in its heart. It was Lyra, the Keeper of Spring. So the dream that Brandy had told them about was real. The human had indeed been brought to Chameleon's liar through a sleep trance.

Carina hastily made her way to the floor of the chamber and rushed over to stand before Lyra. Tears filled her eyes, and ran uncontrollably down her cheeks at the sight of her beloved Lyra imprisoned so.

"Do not cry, my child." The sound of Lyra's voice filtered through the crystal to Carina's ears and in her mind. "I am not harmed."

Carina stared trough her tears at Lyra's comforting gray eyes and smile. "How did Chameleon do this to you?" she whimpered like a child.

"I have been too careless and ignorant about the evil power that my child Chameleon has obtained from the dark forces of our land."

"How can you call Chameleon one of your children? He is nothing but evil. He cares not for who he harms. He cares only for himself."

"All elves of this world will always be my children, even if they do stray from what is right," Lyra said gently.

"He did more than just stray," Carina said, sniffing loudly and wiping her tears away with both hands. "He has completely betrayed and abandoned his people and his heritage."

"He made his choice, my child. Just as you yourself has done. That I could not do for him, nor can I for you. We are all given life and gifts, how we choose to use them are made solely by the individual."

Carina sighed. She did not want to be pacified about Chameleon's choice. He would always be evil to her, nothing could change that from her mind. For now he did not seem to be anywhere close by. She had to do something. "How can I free you from your prison, Lyra?" she asked, running her hands lightly over the smooth surface of the gleaming crystal. She glanced about the large chamber, yet saw nothing that she would be able to hold and try to shatter the crystal. "If only I had a sword or club," she whispered almost to herself.

"You can not, dear one." Lyra smiled sadly. "As I am bound here, there will be only one chance that I may be freed. It is also at that same moment of my freedom that I may be bound here for all of eternity. That is why it is imperative that you leave this place."

"I do not understand. Dear Lyra, I can not leave you to be doomed in this prison for all of eternity."

"And I can not let you sacrifice your young life for mine, for the consequences will be the same. You have much power within you, you must trust deeply in yourself. That will enable you to flee this place and prepare all of the elfin clans for what will come from the darkness."

"There must be something I can do for you?"

"There is not, my child. You must leave and bring together the other clans, just as your ancestor did so many years ago. Now leave me, child," Lyra said in a gentle, yet very urgent and motherly tone.

"I will not. I have to do something. I just can not leave you like this," Carina wailed persistently in frustration. She leaned her hot cheek against the coolness of the crystal, wishing for a solution.

"Oh, but there is something you can do, my dear princess," a dark voice from behind her said.

It was many hours later when Braakk finally stopped his agouti and swung from the saddle. "We will let the prisoners rest for a short while," he announced to the other gobioids.

Thankfully Brandy sank to her knees and rubbed her tired leg muscles. The ground was cold, damp and gave off a peculiar odor, almost like the smell of dead plants decaying.

"No wondered those animals stink," she said, wrinkling her nose in disgust and glancing at her captures and the agouti.

"This whole place smells," Steve agreed.

"What part of the day do you think it is?" Puppis asked, looking upward. The sky was so thick and gray that one could not tell where the position of the sun was.

"I am not sure, but I think it is past the mid part of the day," Volan said thoughtfully. "We have been walking for quite some time."

"I do not see how we will make it to Chameleon's lair by tomorrow," Puppis said. "You can not even see anything out there except for flat ground."

Brandy nodded her agreement with Puppis. All that she could see was the flat dead looking earth that surrounded them. She shivered as another cold blast of wind swirled around them. It had gotten colder and colder since they had entered Chameleon's dark domain, and none of them were dressed for much colder temperatures.

"They could make us walk all night," Steve ventured sarcastically.

"They could," Forrest agreed, "but I am not."

"Then you will pay first," Braakk began, shuffling up and hearing the elf's comment. He took a water flask and threw it to Draco, who passed it unopened to Volan. Volan in turn passed it around, until it once again reached Draco. He defiantly threw it back to the gobioid, ignoring the stare that the creature gave him. Forrest began struggling to his feet to face his ugly opponent, but a lightly placed hand on his sleeve halted his advancement.

"Remember what you told me," Brandy said softly, with a gentle smile.

Forrest returned her smile and dropped back down to his seat. "This time I will. Only this time, for you."

"Thanks, because I'm not ready to save you yet."

"Neither am I," he said, giving her a grin that was almost boyish.

"What are you two babbling about?" Steve asked, not understanding what the gist of the conversation was about.

"It's a private joke," Brandy assured her friend with a pat on the shoulder.

"And a very wise one at that," a voice from behind them said.

All heads whirled at the voice. It was Chameleon, grinning very pleased to himself. He stood masterfully over them as they all stared dumbfoundedly at him. What was he doing here, popping up from nowhere?

"Where is Princess Carina?" Forrest demanded with a glare at the elf.

"She is being very well taken care of by my servants. I assure you she wants for nothing." Chameleon grinned, strolling to the spot where they all sat huddled on the damp earth.

"Except her freedom," Steve spat at the evil mage.

"I should have thought that your constant punishments since we last parted would have slowed your tongue some what, but I see that it has not."

"I'm human, remember? We have a hard time absorbing what is told to us by stupid beings," Steve retorted.

Chameleon smiled slowly and ignored Steve's taunting words. He turned his attention to Brandy who sat staring defiantly at him. "Your bruises are healing nicely, my lovely mate," he purred, resting his cold hand on Brandy's tresses.

"Your mate?" Steve asked incredulously as the others gaped at the dark elf's words.

"I thought I told you not to touch me," she grimaced through clenched teeth, pulling her head beyond his reach, and ignoring her friend's comment.

"Soon you will not be able to pull away from my touch," Chameleon warned with a glint in his eye. "You had best learn to like it."

"Don't bet on it," Brandy said lowly.

The dark elf laughed, and continued on to the others. "Volan, Puppis, and Forrest. You are such faithful pets to the princess. I think I will bring you as a little prize for her. Then you will become my entertainment," he said coldly. Before they could utter any response he focused his gaze on Draco. "And then there is Draco. The keeper of this rag tag group. You have done well, and you are very wise in the knowledge of the elders. You, I will keep alive until the prophecy has come to pass, and then I will allow you to witness the fall of all the elfin clans as it was meant to be. As it should have been long ago."

"You talk bravely for an elf," Draco stated evenly at his foe, watching his words sink in. "An elf just like myself."

"I am no longer a mere elf, I have surpassed your existence long ago."

"You still look like an elf to me," observed Volan, his reckless grin once again filtering across his battered and bruised face.

Without another word, save a dark glare at Volan's impudence, Chameleon swung from the group on the ground and turned his attention on the gobioids. Braakk quickly rushed to his master and flung himself on the ground before him.

"Up!" Chameleon barked. "You are moving much to slowly, you will never reach the castle by morn."

"We will travel all night, High One. The prisoners will not rest," Braakk promised, cringing at the hard edge that his master's voice held.

"That will not be enough. You still would not reach the castle before the dawn of Spring let alone in the morning. You will take the dragon bridge."

"The dragon bridge?" Braakk asked fearfully.

"Do you question my judgment?" Chameleon roared, flames of anger lighting his coal black eyes.

"No master, not at all," Braakk said, cowering back a few paces at the mage's outburst.

"Then do it. You have nothing to fear from those simple reptiles. They can harm none that I send into that dimension."

"Yes, master." The three gobioids nodded eagerly in unison, gathering their food and equipment quickly back into their pouches and holders.

Chameleon faced the humans and elves once again. Then hesitated as if he were listening to something that was being carried by the blowing wind. A mocking smile lit on his pale face. "I must leave now," he announced. "Your princess needs my attention." With that his form wavered for a few seconds, then disappeared from sight.

"What is the dragon bridge?" Brandy whispered to the grinning elves around her.

"A weak spot," Volan and Puppis answered in unison, glancing at a smirking Draco.

CHAPTER THIRTEEN

Carina whirled at the voice. She knew who was there before she even faced him. It was Chameleon, the loathsome creature who had imprisoned Lyra in the gleaming crystal before her.

"How could you?" Carina spat at the smug mage, pointing behind her to the suspended stone.

"How could I what?" he asked innocently.

"You horrid monster," she swore in a hiss, advancing at him with hate filled eyes. "If I had the power I would burn you to a cinder where you stand so that you would become nothing but dust."

"My, my." The dark elf laughed in amusement at Carina's outburst of emotion. "You are not the same demure princess that I first brought here."

Carina fumed at his attitude. "What have you done to the Keeper of Spring? She must be released at once," she demanded.

"Or else you will do what?" Chameleon drawled, smirking contemptuously as he strolled closer to the princess, his footsteps echoing hollowly off the cold floor.

Carina clenched and unclenched her fists at her side. She wanted to the rip the smile from this elf's face. She had never felt such a rage building in her in all of her life. She had always been taught to be peaceful and to find an amiable solution to any problem that may arise, and yet at this moment, that was the last solution that she wanted.

She wanted to possess the power that Chameleon had, use it against him, and fling him off of his feet.

Yes, she thought to herself again with a satisfied smile, she wanted to see this elf before her hurled from his feet and sliding across the smooth stone floor. That indeed would make her very happy. Strangely, and without any effort on her part, she felt her mind take control of her very thoughts and shape them into a powerful ball of energy. The energy grew brighter and brighter in her mind and seemed to explode behind her eyes. With simplicity, she made the image of Chameleon's body fly into the air and slide across the floor. When the vision cleared her mind, she felt very weak. The strength in her legs left her, and she dropped tiredly to her knees, her head spinning wildly making her stomach queasy.

"Well done," Lyra's voice penetrated the haze that covered her mind.

"What happened," Carina stammered, shaking her head slowly to clear her vision. What she saw astounded her. Chameleon lay on his back on the other side of the large hall. He rose groggily to his feet, rubbing his coal black hair with his hand.

"Very impressive," he said with an angry snarl. "I had no idea that you had the ability for such forceful uses of power. Be assured it will not happen again for you shall not find me so unprepared."

Carina did not know what to say. She stared dumbly at the elf who stalked in her direction then stood furiously over her. She felt sure that he would likely strike her dead, but no repercussions came from him. Roughly he grabbed her by her arm and jerked her forcibly to her feet, not caring about the biting grip on her soft flesh. Then without saying a word he dragged her back to her room and threw her unceremoniously inside, slamming the door behind him, and making it vanish into the stone of the wall.

The princess trembled, and pulled her arms closely around herself. She was not cold, and for some reason she no longer held the fear of Chameleon that she once had. She trembled in excitement. She had done something that no other elf in her clan could do. She had actually moved another object, and not just any object, but Chameleon, the dark elf himself. She laid down flat on the soft thick carpets that covered her floor, running her hands through their lushness, and laughed hysterically at the ceiling. Her first powerful display of magic and she had directed it at the one who seemed all powerful. She let the calmness of the empty room reclaim her again as she continued to gaze upward.

"Yes," she said aloud to herself, feeling the reassurance of her words. "Lyra was right, I can feel power in me. But, you are wrong Chameleon, I will catch you off guard again."

The gobioids herded the prisoners together and set off at a slow pace. They talked nervously amongst themselves, but their words were not silent to those who followed behind.

"Do you think that we will be safe passing across the bridge?" Coer whined pitifully at Braakk.

"Of course," he answered, trying to believe his own words. "The master said we would be safe and that is all that must be said about the matter."

"I hope you are right," said the smallest gobioid, "because I do not feel very reassured by the master's words."

Coer stared at his companion and Braakk swung his glare hard at him. "You should never say such things, Srayv. The master hears all."

"Then we are all doomed," Srayv informed his comrades, looking from one to the other. "For all of us doubt his word in this matter, whether we say it out loud or not."

"What is it with this dragon bridge?" Steve asked in a hushed voice when the gobioids had ceased their grumbling.

"We only thought that it was a legend," Puppis began. "We never really believed that it existed."

"Most of us thought it was a, a, fairy tale," Forrest said, smiling lightheartedly at Brandy in the use of her own words.

"It must be the truth," Volan said. He grinned as his thoughts were comforted at the prospect of his life not coming to an abrupt end. "Then there is hope for us after all."

"Tell us about it, Draco," Puppis urged the silent, thoughtful elder.

Draco cleared his throat quietly, then began his story in a soft voice so that the gobioids could not hear his words. "The tale dates back to not long after the united clans first defeated the dark forces of Lacerta. Many of the dragons that had come forth from the dark were not all bad. The guivres for instance did not pose any real threat to the elfin clans, so Lyra made agreements with them. They had control of the large waterways in the dark cold months and we have them back in the warm bright ones. Then there were the large dragons. The heraldic dragons. They were immense, fierce and could spew fire great distances from their fanged, snouted mouths. They did not like being under the control of anyone, even those who had brought them forth, so some of them broke free from Lacerta's grasp and came forward from the boundaries of this dark sullen area."

"They didn't eat elves did they?" Brandy asked with a grimace, remembering her close encounter with the guivre.

"No, just the opposite. They offered their aide to the elfin clans in hunting down any remaining gobioids or dark elves that may be lurking in the wood or surrounding areas."

"So they went to the winning side," Steve said as he shrugged. "Humans have been doing that for a long, long time. You stay loyal to one until the other becomes stronger and then back again."

"No, not precisely. We never actually joined forces," Draco corrected. "They just did not like being commanded or enslaved."

"What happened then?" Puppis asked, when Draco had remained silent.

"For many long years all was the same. The elves never had problems from Lacerta, the changes of the seasons happened, and the dragons kept to themselves. Then Lyra came to the elves and informed them that the heraldic dragons could no longer be found."

"They just vanished?" asked Brandy, thoroughly captivated by the story.

"At first the elves thought so, then they picked up the faint trail left by some careless gobioids. It led back to the darkness of Lacerta's realm. It seemed that she had taken them back to her side as an ally, but later it was learned, through the capture of a gobioid, that the dragons had been indeed lured back. Only they were not working with Lacerta and her dark elves, they were imprisoned in some kind of dimensional state the gobioid called the dragon bridge."

"And that was the last time that the heraldic dragons were seen?" Puppis asked in wonder.

"To my knowledge, yes," Draco answered with a somber nod.

"I have to admit, that is a pretty cool story," Steve began a bit reluctantly, "but what has it got to do with a weak spot?"

"Remember some of those classes you slept through in school?" Brandy said with a grin, tapping playfully on Steve's head. "What does the constellation Draco mean?"

Steve's face frowned as he struggled to understand what his friend was getting at.

"Dragon," she answer slowly, hoping it would sink in.

"So what?" Steve shrugged.

"He has the ability of dragon speech," Forrest answered. "Not only can he talk with them, but he understands all that they say to him."

"And he can influence them with his will," Volan added impressively.

Steve nodded as the light of understanding flew across his face. "Now, that is some neat magic."

"It seems like the perfect solution," Volan said cheerfully.

"Yes," Puppis agreed eagerly. "Not only will we get them to help us, but we can also use them to warn the clans about what will occur if we fail to stop Chameleon and Lacerta."

"Excellent idea, Puppis," praised Forrest with a smile, making the younger girl elf beam happily at his compliment. "The dragons will be able to fly to the different clans and they will be ready for the gobioids."

"Are there others who can communicate with the dragons like Draco?" Brandy asked.

"We have not had much contact with some of the clans to the far north, but every group that I have ever encountered has always had at least a handful of telepaths. Though telepaths cannot talk directly to the dragons like Draco, they can get information from other animals around them."

"You mean if they have someone like Carina who can talk to the birds and relay the words back to the others?" Steve asked, thinking wistfully of the captured princess.

"Yes, but do not worry. With the dragons we will have her back in no time," Volan said reassuringly.

"There are some problems though," Draco added, sighing with concern.

"What? What could be wrong?" Volan asked, his smile instantly fading.

"Chameleon said that the dragons would not be able to harm us. He must have them under some sort of enforcement spell. I might not be able to communicate with them if they are so heavily ensnared."

The group looked blankly at their elder. He was the one who had told them all along not to lose hope, yet here he was doubting if they would be able to overcome the terrible odds that had been set before them. Forrest smiled wistfully at Brandy, trying to ease the frightened tension that formed around her eyes, but it was Volan who grabbed Puppis's worried, bound hands.

"Come on you gloomy and doubting group," he said cheerfully. "It will work out in the end, just watch and see. There are six of us and only three of our scaly pals up there. Who do you think the dragons will like to eat first? Us or the ones who have imprisoned them for the past thousand of years?"

"I like your thinking." Steve grinned and nodded appreciatively at the elf. "Crunch and munch."

"Are you prepared to face the consequences if we fail?" Draco asked.

"I am," Puppis answered without hesitation.

"Count me in," Steve said in acknowledgement of Puppis.

"Me too," said Brandy wistfully. "I don't have anything to lose." Except my life, she thought silently.

"What about you, Draco?" Forrest asked his silent elder.

Draco's seasoned, weathered face broke into a wide smile. "I have been ready to take on these vermin since we first spotted them."

CHAPTER FOURTEEN

The agouti that halted before them interrupted the quiet talking and planning of the humans and elves.

"We have reached our destination," Braakk informed his prisoners over his broad shoulder. He dismounted his travel beast and led it a few paces forward.

The elves and the humans strained to see what the gobioids were heading for. Coer and Srayv obediently followed Braakk, though their steps were not very eager to do so. Finally the captives saw what was so apprehensive to the creatures that held them bound.

A door shaped box of hovering light, not much larger than Braakk's body, shimmered brightly in the gloomy grayness that surrounded them. Every color imaginable twinkled like gemstones in the depths of the doorway. They could not see through it, to what was on the other side, but knew that it might change the course of their destination, or hoped so at any rate.

Braakk hesitated at the gleaming entrance, then turned to Coer. "Untie the agouti and let them travel back to the castle at their own pace."

Coer eyed his superior with uncertainty. "Do you suggest that we free our own beasts as well as the extras?"

"Yes. We are not sure how the dragons will take our presence, and having to deal with the actions of the agouti as well as our prisoners will be too much trouble. They will return to the castle even without us to guide them, they always do."

"You just do not want to walk. You have grown lazy from riding too much." Srayv snickered at a scowling Coer.

"One day I will pull your fangs right from your ugly mouth," Coer threatened his even more amused companion. He pulled his club from a pack tied to the agouti and pawed through his personal bags before releasing his grip on the creature, who wasted no time racing from its rider and joining the others ahead of him.

"Enough of that," Braakk barked at the two gobioids. "We proceed now." He turned his back on them and stepped into the glowing doorway. Coer and Srayv pushed Volan and Puppis through next, then Forrest and Draco, and finally Steve and Brandy before they too followed.

Brandy was instantly overwhelmed by the brilliance of her surroundings. She could see nothing but the flashing of the lights around her. She opened her mouth and called out Steve's name, but the sound that escaped from her lips did not even reach her own ears. She reached her bound hands out next to her and felt the soft fabric of her friends shirt, and knew that he was still with her. He moved closer to her, and although she could not see him, she knew that he too was puzzled by what was happening to them.

They shuffled forward slowly, not wanting to be trampled from behind by the two gobioids that followed them, if they were to stop. Then just as abruptly as they had entered the sparkling doorway, they left it. Brandy blinked her eyes several times, trying to erase the lingering flashes of light in her vision, and was even more amazed at what she saw. She didn't really know what to expect, but this certainly wasn't it. They were no longer surrounded by blinking colors, they were now in what she could only describe as the murkiest swamp she had ever seen.

They stood dumbfounded on a soggy piece of ground, that sucked impatiently at their heavy feet. On both sides of the path was thick, smelly water, with steam rising out of it. Bubbles hissed as they broke the muddy green surface like oatmeal boiling in a pot. Dense vegetation grew all around them. The plants, and shrubs, and bushes all seemed impassible by foot. The only clear cut way to go was forward on the muddy footpath.

Braakk and a doubtful Coer took the lead, leaving Srayv to close up the rear. Hesitantly and precariously the small group made its way on the slippery path. Steve and Brandy fell almost immediately in the slick muck that covered their path, for they were not as surefooted as their elf friends.

"Stay close to me, I will try to steady your steps," Forrest offered protectively, awkwardly pulling Brandy to her feet with his bound hands.

"Use this on your binds," Brandy whispered into his ear as she took her time steadying herself on her feet. She glanced fleetingly at Srayv, hoping he had not seen her action. She placed a smooth thin piece of rock in Forrest's hands and covered his fingers carefully over the artifact, for its edge was as sharp as a razor blade. She had felt it as soon as she had fallen in the mire and had wasted no time in retrieving the valuable stone.

"You are incredible, sometimes," he whispered. The elf smiled admiringly at the grinning human girl next to him.

"Only sometimes?" Brandy asked impishly, batting her long dark lashes at him playful banter.

"Yes, only sometimes," he replied, stifling the urge to laugh out loud. In a matter of a few paces he managed to rub the stone almost completely through the leather that held his wrists. One pull of his arms would snap the bindings all together. He secretively showed Brandy what he had done, and silently urged her to do the same. When she was finished with her task, he took the stone from her and indicated to Draco what they had done. With an appreciative twist of his lips, the elder elf did the same and passed it along to the others. Steve was the last to loosen his bonds. When he succeeded in nearly shearing the leather, he deftly tucked the stone into the pocket of his jeans.

"Now we wait for a chance," he mouthed quietly. Everyone nodded in anxious agreement.

Every step that they took forward increased the fatigue that gnawed at their tired limbs. They constantly looked to the gobioids for any sign of weakening, but they showed nothing except for constant and vigilant awareness of their surroundings. Their evident fear of their environment and master kept them alert.

Finally Brandy could go no further. She couldn't remember the last time she had gotten any decent sleep, and she was so thirsty that the green water all around them was beginning to look appetizing. She stopped instantly and fell to the ground in a heap. Forrest and Draco, who were following close, tripped over her form, landing heavily in the mud.

"I'm tired, and I want to rest," she informed the gobioids who looked blankly at her.

"Me too," Puppis stated, joining Brandy on the wet earth. She leaned against Volan, who knelt beside her and wrapped reassuring hands about her arm.

"Get up you weak animals," Coer snarled contemptuously at the prisoners below him.

"I would take a look in a mirror before I started calling someone an animal," Steve informed the gobioid, stepping into its path and blocking it from the others as it approached.

"You wish to challenge me?" Coer wheezed in amused laughter.

"Anytime," prodded Steve.

Coer looked to Braakk. The long tiresome trek had made him irritated. He had had his fill of dealing with these puny, weak humans and elves. He had longed for the opportunity to silence this particular human, but at the moment Braakk gave the orders.

"This human has grown to be a worse nuisance than a stinging bug. Deal with him, and bind him, then let his friends drag him in the mud. If not, leave him here to rot. I tire of his loud mouth and boasting ways," Braakk said carelessly. He pulled the plug from his drinking skin and poured the contents down his dry throat. One less prisoner to deal with would be for the better. He had wished that Chameleon would have let him dispose of them sooner, instead of hauling them along.

Coer licked his fangs in anticipation as he flung his bags to the ground. He hefted his large club in his left hand and advanced tauntingly at the human who stood unmoving before him. "You are making this entirely too easy, slug," slurred Coer.

"Slug? Well, that's a lot better than I can say for you. Take your best shot, if you think you can," Steve said in an inviting tone. Brandy and the others sat silent and motionless on the mud. All were ready to pounce on the others when Steve made his move. None had realized that their chance to fight was going to be given to them so soon, but they weren't going to waste the opportunity. So they waited poised, and prepared to snap their already loosened bounds and join into the fray with Steve.

Coer swung his club at the human male who merely grinned at the gobioid's feeble attempt, and quickly stepped back out of the weapons path.

"Is that the best you can do?" goaded Steve, shaking his head in scorn.

"Insolent wretch," growled Coer angrily.

Srayv laughed loudly at Coer's missed swing. "Not as slow as you thought."

"Shut up, or you are next," the angry gobioid threatened his amused comrade.

"You are getting fat and lazy," prodded Srayv with more chuckles. "You can not even hit a worthless human."

"Care to try again," invited Steve, preparing himself for an onrush by the enraged gobioid. He was not disappointed, for that was exactly how Coer reacted. His missed swing coupled by the teasing of his comrade prompted the gobioid into a careless assault on the human. He rushed forward, screaming like he didn't have any sense left, when he realized too late that the human had snapped his binds easily and now stood before him with his hands ready to meet his charge.

"How?" Coer stammered incoherently, dropping his club slightly before impact, and staring dumbly at the now free human before him.

"That was a big mistake," said Steve as the confused gobioid reached him. He swiftly grabbed the wrist that held the club and twisted backward it with all his might. With a sharp turn, he heard the bone in the creature's arm snap loudly as it broke. Coer instantly dropped his club, buckled to his knees, and cried out as pain rippled up his arm.

"Stop this immediately," Braakk order loudly, backing toward his pack to reach his weapons. He had stepped closer to the scuffle when he saw that the human had broken his bonds, but now realized that they were being set up by the rag-tag band of prisoners.

"That is far enough," grumbled Draco in his deep voice. He and Forrest had easily snapped the leather that bound them and rushed at the largest gobioid. Forrest confronted him fully while Draco rushed passed him to heft his massive double sided axe from the pack that Braakk stowed it in, no doubt intending on keeping it as a souvenir.

Srayv also raced back to his weapons, but was cut short by the two females and Volan. Brandy and Puppis were on their feet in a flash, any signs of fatigue vanishing even faster than their movements. They pounced on the retreating gobioid like cats on the chase of a fleeing mouse. The three of them fell to the ground in a flurry of arms and legs. When their struggling ceased, it was Srayv who pleaded pitifully to the females. Brandy laid sprawled across his legs and held one of his arms immobile. Puppis held his other arm and pressed his snouted face into the thick, dank mud.

"Very well done." Volan grinned with open admiration at the two mud covered girls that held onto the submissive gobioid.

"Shut up with the compliments, and bind this creature," scolded Puppis.

"Anything for you," Volan replied with a sweeping bow. He pulled a long piece of leather from one of Srayv's packs and easily bound the unresisting gobioid, who lay moaning in despair at what had befallen his comrades, and especially himself.

"Don't forget this one," Steve indicated the cowering form of Coer, who rubbed and cradled his broken limb and mumbled miserably to himself like some beaten animal.

"How could I forget him. I have such fond memories of our past time spent together," said Volan sarcastically, pointing to the bruises that covered his face, neck, and arms. He dug through the gobioid's other pouches and pulled another long tether from its depths, which he flung to Steve, who in turn roughly tied his captive, failing to show any consideration of his injury.

"What are we going to do with them now?" Brandy asked, trying to wipe the mud from her hands on her already muddy pants. What I wouldn't give for a bath, she thought to herself.

"We could throw them in the water and watch them sink," Steve suggested with a wicked grin, which was easily matched and agreed to by Volan.

"Let us just leave them here, get Carina, and go home," said Puppis almost pleadingly. She desperately wanted to be gone from this place and back to her comfortable home. She missed her family terribly, and this search for the human had not turned out to be the simple and fun excursion that she thought it would be in the beginning.

"We will need one of them to make it through the castle," Forrest began in thoughtfully. "The others will just be added baggage."

"I think we have something else to consider at this moment, children, besides the fate of the gobioids," Draco said in a quiet voice. All eyes turned in his direction and followed his pointed finger into the deep, green, thick brush. A pair of very large yellow eyes, set widely apart, blinked keenly at them from behind the bushes.

"Draco, is it a dragon,? Puppis stammered out in a mixture of awe and fear.

"Yes, child," he answered easily, knowing instantly what stood hidden behind the thick foliage.

The fear Brandy felt when being chased by the guivre returned in a horrifying rush. She wanted to flee from the view of those large knowing eyes. She closed her own eyes tightly, hoping that when she opened them, she would be back in her bright red truck traveling happily down her narrow dusty road, Not in the middle of a huge smelly swamp staring at a massive reptile that she knew could eat her in a snap of its fanged jaws. Slowly she lifted her lashes and focused on what she saw. It wasn't her dear dirty road, it was still those orbed shaped eyes, staring intently into her own.

The bushes that the dragon concealed itself behind bent and crumpled with the weight of its long, taloned foot as it emerged from the greenery, displaying the shocking largeness of it size.

Puppis drew in a sharp breath and quickly huddled closely to Volan for reassurance. Steve openly admired the size and grace in which the great dragon moved. Forrest, for once, seemed actually overwhelmed at the sight of that which had filled his childhood, in the stories that he had been told. Draco seemed almost humble before the creature whose namesake he bore. However, Brandy was neither overwhelmed nor impressed. She was terrified. She realized as the dragon came into full view that the guivre had been nothing at all compared to this beast that stood regally on two powerful back legs. It made any of the elephants, that she had ever seen at zoos, small in comparison. Its front legs were much shorter than the back, but they looked just as handy and forceful. Its plate covered body glistened luminously, despite the grayness of the light, in many hues of green that she had never seen before. Its small wings were iridescent, like a pearly seashells from the bottom of the ocean. And worst of all, its eyes continued to gaze from her to Steve and back, in constant motion.

"Does it want to eat us?" Brandy asked, her voice trembling in fear, yet unable to tear her gaze from the dragon's probing eyes.

Draco chuckled deeply at her question.

"I wasn't trying to make a joke," she hissed, momentarily taking her eyes off of the dragon and shooting a glare at the elder elf.

"I am sorry, child," he apologized. "The dragon is only curious about you and Steve. I would venture to guess that it has never before seen a human in this realm."

"Oh," Brandy muttered somewhat taken aback. The last thing she figured from this giant was that it would be curious about her. She only pictured herself as a very small snack for the beast.

"Well we've never seen a dragon before either," Steve began with a grin and a wink at Brandy. "Not in this realm or any other for that matter. This guy definitely has an advantage over us. It is slightly bigger than we are."

The dragon turned its large knowing eyes to Draco and tilted it's long snout in his direction. Draco looked intently at the giant as if he were listening to a conversation.

"What's he doing?" Brandy whispered loudly to her companions.

"The dragon was telling me that it has no intention of eating us, if that is what you are afraid of," Draco answered her question.

"That is good to know," Volan admitted with a nervous laugh of his own.

"This is Crimm," Draco introduced, indicating the dragon. He then pointed to Forrest, Volan, Puppis, Brandy and Steve, and told each of their names to the dragon, who nodded to each of them in turn.

"Can he understand what we are saying?" asked Puppis, releasing her grip on Volan's arm and stepping a few paces closer to the mighty creature before them.

"Yes, but he can not speak our tongue. He is able to communicate with me through mind speech," answered Draco.

"What does he think about the gobioids?" Steve asked curiously. He wondered if they were somehow distantly related, for they were both some type of reptile.

Before Draco could say anything, Crimm inhaled deeply, turned his head toward the slimy water and let loose a loud burning stream of flame, searing everything that it touched.

Steve laughed loudly at the dragon's display. "Well, I would say that about covers it."

Coer cringed deeper into the mud at the dragon's flame. Srayv said nothing, but his eyes betrayed the fear that he felt. Braakk, on the other hand, stood defiantly.

"Our master said that we could not be harmed by these creatures," he stated confidently to his comrades.

"Crimm relays that Braakk is correct. Lacerta has them bound in this realm, and they cannot hurt any who obey and follow her or her minions," Draco informed his companions.

"The dragons may not hurt them, but I still think we owe them something," Volan said menacingly to Coer.

"And Chameleon doesn't seem that worried about them either," Brandy added, aiming her comment at the gobioids themselves.

"You may think you have control now," sneered Braakk defiantly, "but without one of us, you will not be able to leave the dragon bridge."

"What does he mean by that?" Puppis asked in dismay as the reality of what he said settled in. "How will we be able to get back to the clan?"

Draco held us his hand to silence the rush of concerned questions that flooded him. "According to the dragon, the portals of the bridge can only be opened by Lacerta or one in her control."

"What does that mean then?" Puppis asked, fearing that they would be trapped forever.

"It means," Forrest replied, looking at the gobioids, "that they have another use to us now."

CHAPTER FIFTEEN

The sound of heavy footsteps crashing through the dense foliage attracted the attention of everyone; humans, elves, and gobioids alike. The ground shook under the onslaught of massive feet striking the ground.

"What on earth is that?" Brandy asked, eyes wide with alert. She could feel the rumble that the steps gave off to the very center of her heart. She clutched Forrest's hand tightly to keep from falling from her feet.

"Earthquake," Steve half guessed uneasily, planting his feet firmly in the squishy mud, trying to remain upright.

As abruptly as the shaking had begun it ended, and silence overtook all around them. Coer and Srayv sat closely in the muck while Braakk stood uneasily next to them. They had never experienced anything like what had just happened, and being bound would make it impossible to move quickly and find shelter from whatever had caused the commotion. Chameleon, whom they had so faithfully served, had surely abandoned them to some horribly unknown fate.

"Do you know what has caused the ground to rumble so angrily?" Draco asked Crimm, who seemed totally unaffected by what had occurred.

"What is it?" Puppis asked the elder elf when a smile broke across his tired features at what the dragon had said to him in his head.

"Crimm said that there is nothing to fear. The noise was produced by his family. When he spotted us, he contacted the rest of his family, or clan as we would refer to it. They too are just as anxious to see us as I, or we, are to see them."

Just as Draco had finished speaking, another dragon, the color of the setting sun, emerged from the surrounding brush. Then slowly a pair of deep green eyes peered timidly from the leaves that it hid behind, nearly concealing the massive bulk of its glimmering yellow body. Finally, two much smaller dragons, the size of one of the travelers, both of them blue black in color, emerged from the tall marsh plants that had previously hid them.

"This," Draco informed them regally, "is Suun. The kits are her children. The elder dragon is Garn."

"How adorable," Puppis gasped in delight as one of the smaller dragons came curiously up to her and timidly reached a small taloned claw out, gingerly touching her flame colored hair.

"Oh sure, they look cute and cuddly now, but they still have teeth," Brandy grumbled, backing away from the other small dragon who came over to inspect her. She released her grip on Forrest and kept her distance from the creature, but looked intently into its sensitive and intelligent blue eyes. It had understood her fear of it as soon as she had spoken, and as if out of respect, the blue-black dragon remained away from her, keeping a good deal of space between them.

"Do not be so silly, they have no intention of harming us, or they already would have," Puppis lightly scolded her human friend. She gently rubbed the ridged brow of the dragon who made soft giggling noises in return, and flapping its dark green wings happily.

"What are their names?" she asked Draco, who was still overwhelmed by the mighty beasts that had materialized from the dense brush.

"Your playful friend is Sith, and Brandy's new admirer is Soth. He finds you quite intriguing, child." Draco smiled his fatherly smile at Brandy. "Give him a chance, he promises that he will cause you no harm."

"I don't now," Brandy began dubiously. Her run in with the guivre still bothered her immensely. After all, wasn't this dragon related to him. Guivres were water bound dragons, and this was a dragon, only he had legs and small wings. Big deal, not much of a difference in her book.

"If he doesn't mind too much, I think I will keep my distance all the same," Brandy stated, walking a few more paces away from the dragon.

"I hope nobody accuses me of not wanting to try anything new from now on," teased Forrest with a twinkle of amusement in his gold, green gem like eyes. He had securely bound the three gobioids together in a sort of makeshift circle to keep them from trying to escape while the humans and other elves were all curious and fascinated about the arrival of the dragons. Having done so, Forrest stood closely to Brandy, shielding her protectively with his warm presence. He oddly liked his new role as guardian of this human.

"This is a little different than trying an onion," Brandy scoffed back, gently elbowing Forrest in the middle for making fun of her. "Onions don't breath fire or try to eat you. These do."

"Will they help us?" Volan impatiently spoke the question that they all held ready to ask.

Suun halted in her close inspection of Steve. She had been intrigued with the human, for unlike the female of his race, he was not afraid of her, and she could openly sense that. He had a different scent than what the elves gave off, and his mind seemed to be making a great deal of intelligent assumptions about her. He did not blink or look way when she gazed deeply into his eyes searching his thoughts. He said with his mind that he knew what she was doing, for he could feel her presence, but wished that they could communicate together. They were about to have that opportunity, for she felt as though she had nothing to fear from this group of travelers.

"Help you with what, small one?" Suun asked in a soft velvety voice. Her tones slipped through the air like gently notes of a happy melody.

Crimm swung his mighty green head in her direction. "Are you sure this is wise, letting them know of your ability of their speech?" he asked in the dragon's silent language of telepathy.

"You have ventured into the mind of the elder elf, you know as well as I that they pose no threat to us. They have come to us by the forceful means of Lacerta and Chameleon, but I believe that this may change," Suun answered the largest of the dragons, and he who was their leader.

"What of the Dark Queen and her pesky mage?" Garn broke in, tearing his fascinated gaze from the small band before him. He was the oldest of the dragons and vaguely remembered the last time he had encountered an elf. They were a very honest and open race, but that was long ago before Lacerta had imprisoned him and his kind.

"She can do no more harm to us than she has already done." Suun answered. "We were many in number at one time, and look at us now. We are reduced to a handful. What more can she do to us?"

"Think of the two little ones," Crimm indicated to Sith and Soth, who easily floated close to their elders with their small powerful wings.

"I sense no bad intentions from the pretty elf girl," Sith said, giggling in delight at the new arrivals. "I like how she scratched my head. It tickles."

"And though she is afraid of us, the human girl holds no harm in her heart for us," added Soth, swatting his brother playfully with his long tail.

"The decision is yours to make, Crimm," offered Suun reverently. "We will follow what you say."

"Yes," agreed Garn. "We can easily slip back into the marshes and they will follow us no longer. Then we shall never learn why they came."

"Let us hear them out," Crimm said slowly after a moments thought. He too was curious to find out why the elves had been made prisoners of the gobioids and on were their way to the castle.

The elves and humans gaped in amazement, first at Suun for speaking, and now at the apparent silent conversation that was taking place between them. Their questioning gazes turned toward Draco for guided answers.

"I did not know dragons could speak elfin?" Puppis whispered to Draco.

"Neither did I, child. Neither did I, but I suppose on this great land of ours anything is possible."

"What do you think we can help you with, little one?" Suun crooned again, smiling encouragingly at Volan.

Volan stammered, not being able to make any words flow from his jumbled tongue. He looked desperately to Draco, hoping he would intercede and talk with those that he held his name for.

Forrest quickly stepped forward and bowed elegantly to the regal beasts before him.

"We would like to humbly ask your help in warning our clans of impending danger that Chameleon and the gobioids intend to inflict upon them."

"Yes," Draco continued with all the feeling that he could. "The clans of the elves know nothing of this attack, and the losses to our kin would be innumerable, maybe complete."

"You ask quite a lot from us," Suun replied slowly. "You must understand that we may not leave the confines of this dimension. We have been imprisoned here by the Dark Queen. Sadly, only she may release us."

"So can one of the gobioids. As they are under her power, they can open the doors of this bridge at either end," Volan blurted out, suddenly finding his voice again in order to speak to the large, yet gentle, creature before him.

"We hold no control over these loathsome creatures. They are protected by Lacerta and her mage, and we may not touch them in any way," replied Suun, cutting her yellow eyes in the direction of the huddled gobioids.

"We can," Steve ventured. It wouldn't hurt his feelings in the least bit to beat these creatures into submission.

"Yes," Draco agreed. "Perhaps we could persuade them into cooperating."

"Before we can agree to help you in any way, you must explain to us why you have come here, and of what purpose Chameleon and the Dark Queen have for you," the thought words of Crimm settled into Draco's mind.

The elder elf turned toward his companions and told them of Crimm's request. "I must ask you, Brandy and Steve, to open your minds and let the dragons read your thoughts," he said to the two humans. "Start at the very beginning when you first crossed the barrier. Then the rest of us will fill in any of the detail that may be overlooked."

Steve nodded readily, but Brandy was not all that sure that she wanted a large reptile running ramped through her memories and thoughts. It was weird and plain wrong. Draco seemed to instantly sense her discomfort.

"Do not worry, child," he said pulling her into a fatherly hug. "They will do nothing to harm us, they need to know that we are being honest with them. They also need to see that Lyra is truly imprisoned, and you are the only one who has seen her in her suspended state of the crystal."

"Um, I have a lot of private things up here," Brandy whispered for only Draco to hear, tapping at her head with her forefinger.

"They promise to only look at what you show them about what has occurred thus far," Draco reassured her. "I too have sensed their intentions, they mean us no harm at all."

Brandy took a deep breath, slowly counting to ten and letting it out. "Okay," she said finally. "I trust you Draco, and for you I will do this. And for the clans. And for my friends. I would not want to think that my entire family were on the brink of destruction."

"Thank you, child."

Brandy turned to face Crimm. He peered deeply into her large mahogany brown eyes. She didn't try to shut him out as the pictures of all that had befallen her ran through her mind's eye as if it were a motion picture. Traveling down her dirt road with Steve in her truck, seeing the horned creature running in front of her vehicle, the crash, helping the elves, watching Steve being dragged into the brush, the attack of the guivre, being in Chameleon's castle, the fight with the gobioid, the revelation that Forrest made about her fate, and finally the fear she felt when first seeing Crimm himself. Then within a few seconds it was all over. She was blinking her eyes and shaking herself back into reality. She felt funny and out of breath, as if she had run a long distance in a very short time. She then watched as Crimm stared intently at her friend.

"Wow, that was weird!" Steve laughed, running his hand trough his dirty tangled hair after it was over.

"I know," agreed Brandy. "It was like seeing yourself do something and not even being there."

They watched the dragons quietly confer together at what Crimm had seen. They wondered what would happen if they weren't believed, or if the dragons decided that they did not want to help them. What would happen to the elves? The dawn of Spring was only a day away. How could they possibly warn the elves in time?

"How did Lacerta manage to capture Lyra?" Crimm asked Draco, eying the elder elf closely for the validity of his answer.

"We know not," Draco said, shaking his weathered face tiredly.

"He speaks the truth," Garn said to Crimm. "They all speak the truth, there is no doubt of that."

"Yes," agreed Crimm. "There is no doubt of their honesty. They are like children lost in a horrible storm. That in which they have spent their whole lives believing, is proving to be vulnerable. They are having a difficult time dealing with the truth of it."

"You see that their faith in Lyra has not diminished, even though she has been taken captive," ventured Suun, trying her best to influence Crimm. She knew not why, but she wanted to help these small beings. Maybe it was because she longed to be free again to roam over the lands like before, so long ago.

"We should help them if we can," broke in Sith, impatiently shifting from foot to foot at the constant talk of the grown ups.

Crimm shot the young dragon a warning look, for him to mind his manners, but Soth was ready to take up his brother's defense against the elder.

"I am with Sith. This old swamp is boring. We have never seen the outside lands like you guys have. We want to help them even if you decide not to."

Suun smiled at the youngsters, remembering her youth. How alike dragon kits tended to be, no matter the span of time. "Little ones, you know that we must all abide by the decision of Crimm," she said easily, not wanting to scold the eager children.

"Aww, come on. We never have any fun," Soth complained loudly, letting his thoughts get away from him to the point that Draco had picked them up and looked curiously at the young dragon, and then wonder heavily what exactly it was that the dragons were discussing.

"Careful," warned Crimm, reminding himself to discipline the little dragon later.

"Soth's right," Sith prodded, ignoring the reprimanding look from Crimm. "We have never had the chance to see what is out there. We were hatched here in the swamp."

"All of us have shown you with thought pictures what it was like outside the bridge," Crimm countered the kit who was swatting his tail impatiently on the ground at some unseen foe.

"That is different. You have shown us fresh clean water and how you bathed and swam in it. Neither Sith nor I have ever experienced that sensation."

"Soth's right," Sith agreed, jumping back into the conversation. "It is like eating a mud lily and then trying to tell someone else what it was like. Dull, really dull."

"The children have a point," interceded Garn with a small grin. He realized that Crimm was close to losing his temper with the young kits, and that would do none of them any good at this point.

"All right," Crimm agreed, with a note of exasperated annoyance in his thoughts. "If their plan seems stable we will help them. I must admit, I do miss the smell of fresh air, and all of the intriguing scents that floated upon it." he added reluctantly.

"Yippee!" shrieked both Sith and Soth at the same time, the exuberance of their delightful thoughts scaring Draco from his deep broodings.

"What happened?" Puppis asked anxiously, seeing her friend jump and watching the small dragons bouncing around joyfully.

"We have agreed to help you," Suun answered before Draco could say anything.

"We must know your plan first," Crimm's thoughts broke into Draco's mind.

It was Draco's turn to use thought speech, for he did not want the gobioids to be aware of their plans. "Volan and myself will accompany you back to the first door of the bridge. We will then, shall we say, convince Coer and Srayv to lead you back into the open lands. When you get outside you will still be in Lacerta's realm, but I believe that once you are not completely surrounded by her spell, as you are here, you shall be able to flee from her domain."

"Yes," Crimm nodded thoughtfully. "I believe you are correct in this assumption."

"What of the others?" asked Garn.

"I wanted them to get some rest and wait for us to return, but they insisted that time was of the essence, so they will travel toward the castle and try to find a way to leave the door open for us."

"A good plan, maybe not fool proof, but a good plan none the less," acknowledged Crimm. "If we are all in favor, I believe we shall give it a try, for we have too long been in this place."

At the others enthusiastic nods of approval, Crimm took the arm shake of friendship that Draco offered.

"Then let us be off," the elder elf said so that all could understand.

CHAPTER SIXTEEN

"Hurry back to us," Puppis implored Volan and Draco as they set off, pushing a very unwilling Coer and Srayv in front of them with axe and sword.

"And be careful," Brandy added. She had grown very fond of all of her new friends in such a very short period of time, but was especially attached to Draco because of his fatherly concern that he had time and time again displayed toward her. She had missed that easily given concern that he offered since losing her own father.

"Do not worry about us," Volan replied, waving back with his boyish grin. "It is these two who need all the help they can get," he continued, grinning wickedly with a wink.

"We had better get moving too," Forrest said as the dragons, two elves, and two gobioids wandered further and further from view in the dense brush.

Brandy and Puppis quietly nodded their agreement and picked up a few of the bags that the gobioids had once carried, slinging them over their shoulders.

"Come on, Braakk," Steve began, pulling the large uncooperative gobioid to his feet from the mud. "I'm afraid you're going to have to walk, no pamper treatment here."

"I am not going anywhere," Braakk said tonelessly, dropping back down into the murky earth.

"You're not?" Steve eyed him curiously.

"Why should I? You do intend on eliminating me once we are through the door, do you not?" he asked point blank.

"Well, actually I haven't given it much thought," Steve said. In fact the thought had run across his mind a time or two, but he didn't think that he would actually do it unless Braakk were to become some sort of major threat to his well being.

"You lie poorly for a human," Braakk said with a slight snort of a laugh.

"Thanks, I think," Steve replied with a small chuckle. He left Braakk sitting in the mud and pulled the others together in a small huddle. "That is considering how much experience you have had with humans."

"What are we going to do now?" Brandy asked. "Lizard head over there won't budge."

"We have to convince him that we won't do him in," Steve said, rolling his eyes and shaking his head.

Puppis stifled a laugh. "Are you sure you want to?" she asked the grinning human.

"We can not let him free when we reach the castle to warn Chameleon that we are there," Forrest reminded them.

"We can just tie him up, gag him, and leave him in a corner somewhere," suggested Steve.

"And hope that one of his ugly friends don't find him. That would definitely let the cat out of the bag," Brandy said to her dearest friend. Confused looks crossed the faces of her elfin friends, but they remained silent.

"Look, I know it's a chance but we really don't have too much of a choice," said Steve after a moments hesitation. "Plus, I don't think I could actually do him in."

"Steve is right," Forrest finally agreed. "We will have to give the gobioid our word that he will not be harmed, or I see no other way of crossing the door into the castle. Plus, we re running out of time."

"Do you think he will believe us?" asked Brandy doubtfully. She knew plenty of people who would readily give their word and then break it without a second thought.

"Yes, of course," Puppis replied without hesitation. "Even the gobioids are well aware of the word oath of an elf. For us, to break our word is worse than taking the life of another. He knows if we make such a promise to him, we will not go back on it."

"Then let's do it," Steve said. The group broke their soft spoken huddle and walked back over to the disgruntled gobioid who sat huddled in the mud, trying to listen to their discreet conversation.

"Braakk, as much I wish to repay you for what you have done to us, I will not. If you will lead us through the door at the end of the bridge into the castle, I promise you with my word oath not to harm you at all," Forrest vowed solemnly through clenched teeth.

The gobioid struggled to his feet and looked closely at the elf before him. He did not want to be tricked by this scrawny creature, that would be a foolish thing to do. He turned his head and eyed the female elf.

"What of you," he barked gruffly. "Do you also offer you word oath?"

"Readily," Puppis answered simply, wrinkling her nose at his bad breath that snaked out from his mouth. "You have my word oath."

"What about you humans," Braakk squinted at Brandy and Steve. "Much of your words are so foreign to me. How do I know if you word is as truth binding as it is for these other two?"

"Since you have never met one of us humans before, all I can say is you are going to have to trust us when we tell you that we will not harm you," Steve informed his former captor.

Brandy said nothing, but merely nodded her agreement to Steve's words when the gobioid shifted his glance in her direction.

"Then I will lead you," Braakk grumbled mostly to himself. "I do not really trust you, especially you human male, but I do not wish to end my days here in this smelly swamp."

That's a hoot, Brandy thought as she smiled to herself when they started trudging forward again through the slippery mud trail. He smells far worse than this place does.

Volan took one last glance behind him at the bright red hair of Puppis. They had been friends since they were children, they had shared many things from simple conversations to intimate nights during the celebrations of their clan, and until this supposedly simple search for the human, Steve, he had never felt as close to her as he did now. He felt an overwhelming need to protect her, even though he knew that she was an accomplished hunter as well as a master of the bow.

In all the years that they had been sharing things, he had never once mention what she meant to him, other than the importance of her friendship. He decided that if they were to survive this perilous expedition to its end, then he would find some way to let her know of his true feelings that seemed to be coming more and more to the surface. The only problem would be what to say, and if saying it would ruin the friendship that they already had.

"Just tell how you feel," Suun said quietly, so that the others would not hear them.

Volan looked up, startled, at the dragon. He had been deeply wrapped in his own thoughts, but he did not think that they were so obvious. Almost feather like, Suun wrapped the end of her long whip like tail about Volan's shoulders, giving him a little squeezing hug like a mother would her own child.

"You might be surprised by how she feels in return." Suun smiled reassuringly at the small elf beside her, revealing a wide row of pearly smooth teeth, gleaming brightly against her yellow skin.

Volan mulled the prospect over in his mind for a few seconds. "You think so?" he asked tilting his blonde mane upward.

Suun chuckled lightheartedly at her small companion. "We dragons are not so different from your people. We search out the one who becomes our closest friend, only in turn to be our mate for life. It is a very happy way."

"It does sound like a sensible approach," Volan said, nodding in agreement at the dragon's words. Falling silent again, he wondered what had happened to Suun's mate or if she had even had one, but thought better of it.

It took a surprisingly short time to reach the original door that the elves and gobioids had first crossed through. It appeared before them out of the gloom of the swamp, a bright shimmering space, blinking with a thousand colors.

"We can not begin to thank you enough for helping us warn our kin," Draco began, as they stopped in front of the door. Sith and Soth bounced eagerly around the others, ready to cross through the twinkling hues of the door, but knew they had to wait for one of the gobioids to go first.

"It is we who thank you," nodded Garn appreciatively at the elder elf, who translated his thoughts to Volan. He thought that the days to fly freely in the open skies were to be gone forever when they had been trapped by the Dark Queen, but these small people were about to make it a reality for him.

"Will you be able to find our clans that are scattered all about?" Volan asked Suun, who was trying to calm the young blue dragons down.

"It has been many hundreds of years since we have seen the blue of the sky, but our senses are still just as keen as well as our memory. We will find the clans that we remember, then depend upon our senses and that of our family to help us find the others," the brilliant yellow dragon promised.

"Other family?" Draco swung his attention from the gobioids to Suun. What in the heavens was she talking about. He thought all of the great dragons were gone, except for this small handful.

"Oh yes," Garn reaffirmed Suun's statement. "There were a few dragons who were skeptical about the call of Lacerta so many years ago. Even though we pleaded with them to return with us, they refused. They had grown to like the quiet ways of being far from she whom we had once served."

"We should have listened to them," Crimm acknowledged grimly, shaking his dark green head slowly.

"We were all so young then," Suun patted her old dear friend gently with one of her short fore claws. "We did not know what the boundaries of treachery and deception that were waiting for us". "Yes," Crimm began slowly, "but what a price we have paid for our foolish inexperience. We were once ten times the number we are now," the dragon said to Volan and Draco, settling himself back on his powerful, long kelly green tail."

"What happened to your family?" Draco asked hesitantly when Crimm did not elaborate further.

"When we were lured back here and found that we were imprisoned, many tried going through the doors unsuccessfully. They turned to ash as soon as they touched the glimmering lights. It was a horrible sight, still many tried until we finally lost hope of ever passing through that way." Crimm took a deep breath, but did not continue, as if remember the past had become too painful.

"Then we noticed that others began disappearing," Garn took up the tale, speaking softly. "First, its was in groups of twos and threes, then it dwindled down to one at a time. At first we did not know what was happening. We thought excitedly that some had found a means of escape, and searched all about the confines of this prison hoping that we too would find where they had gone."

"Sadly, that was not what had happened," Crimm continued, his voice clearing and stronger than before. "Before the time that Lacerta had put a protection spell on these creatures." he said, pointing an accusing claw at Coer who visibly shivered in fright, "A gobioid came into our dimension, thinking himself safe. We tortured him unmercifully until he finally told us what had happened to our missing family. Lacerta had been taking them to the castle and using them as a sacrifice."

"A sacrifice," Volan echoed the green dragon's words with shock after Draco had finished telling him all that the dragons had said.

"Yes," Suun tilted her sunny head sadly. "A dragon's blood is very powerful in the making of magic, for it was magic which made us in the long ago very beginning."

"Since then we have been powerless against the Dark Queen, and our numbers have slowly diminished, leaving only us five," Crimm finished sadly, remembering those who he had once known. "We had all but given up hope for the future of the kits."

"That is all to change now, old friend," Suun spoke, so that Volan could understand. "Because of our new friends we are about to be free, and the two little ones will know freedom."

"You speak very true indeed," Crimm replied, rising to his hind legs.

"Then you had best be on your way before the patience of the young ones run out," Draco said, smiling at the giant reptiles, who moved with unbelievable grace and bearing.

"Up!" Volan commanded sharply to the two gobioids who had remained huddled dejectedly in the mud from the moment they had stopped.

Without hesitation they jumped to their feet, not sure of their fates anymore. The only thing for certain was that Chameleon had abandoned them, they were at the mercy of the elves, and worse, the dragons.

"You go first, Coer," Volan ordered, nearly shoving the unresisting gobioid through the glimmering thickness of the door.

Sith and Soth did not wait for permission to pass through the lights. Unafraid of anything that might happen to them, they blindly bounded through the opening, claws clenched together, squealing in delight. Suun reached out instinctively to grab them before they went through, suddenly afraid that they would not be able to pass, but she did not reach them in time. The youngsters shot through the opening completely unharmed.

"Good-bye small ones," she murmured, smiling to Volan and Draco with a tear in her luminous eyes as she too passed from sight in the doorway.

"Thank you," Garn thought simply to Draco as he vanished from sight.

"You had best hurry," Volan said to Crimm when the green dragon did not follow his kin through the lights.

Draco wrinkled his brow dissatisfied at what Crimm had thought to him, but nodded to the dragon and pushed a surprised and confused Srayv through the door of the bridge. "Hope that we never meet again," he threatened gruffly to the bewildered gobioid.

"What is going on?" Volan asked, not understanding what had just happened. He would have thought that Crimm would have been just as eager to escape his prison as were the others.

"Crimm says that he will be coming back with us to the castle," Draco replied, preparing to head back the way that they had come earlier.

"What will the other dragons think?" Volan asked in wonder at the odd decision that the dragon had made.

"They already knew of my decision," Crimm assured the elder elf. "Tell your young friend not to fret over my choice. It was a practical one. If you are to be able to cross the other door with your friends, then you must reach them when they reach it."

"How will that be possible?" began Draco with his thought, and was quickly answer when Crimm easily floated above the ground with the power of his small, yet resourceful wings. They glowed warmly in the dull colored air, like giant sea pearls waiting to be plucked from a shell.

"You see," Crimm stated, smiling in pleased satisfaction at the wonder that played on the faces below him. "These are not just for good looks, they work."

"Incredible," Volan breathed in a whisper. He knew that dragons could fly, but he had never seen one do so. By the

Mother of Spring herself, he had never seen a dragon until a few hours ago, and now he was witnessing one in flight. If he were to live out this adventure, he would surely have tales to tell his children about for many long winters to come.

Crimm gracefully returned to the muddy ground and lowered his massive bulk down, stretching his long neck and heavy head fully out on the earth.

"What does he want us to do?" Volan asked uncertainly.

"Ride," Crimm answered Draco's unspoken question simply.

"He wants us to ride," Draco repeated, chuckling in amazement at the stunned expression on the face of his friend.

"Umm, Draco, if you have not noticed, this is a little different than riding a horse. I mean," Volan stumbled awkwardly for words. "Heavens, I do not know what I mean," he said with a sigh, throwing his hands up in the air in confusion.

Draco chuckled and clapped Volan on the back. "Crimm says we can ride most comfortably just behind his neck on his shoulders."

"Sure, whatever you say," Volan replied dubiously, following Draco to the prone figure of the giant reptile.

"Would you like me to ride up front?" Draco asked, laughing merrily at his companion. "I thought you youngsters were supposed to be the adventurous types."

"Go ahead, old man, laugh at me," Volan grumbled, climbing onto Crimm's back behind the joking Draco. "You will not be laughing when we fall off and get our heads stuck in the mud, and then suffocate to death."

His uncertainty only made Draco laugh even harder. The elder elf had hoped his whole life that he would be able to meet that in which he was named for. He had not been disappointed at all. These beasts were even more regal that he could have ever hoped. Additionally, to be able to communicate with one was an even bigger thrill. He knew that if he did not survive this quest to free Lyra, he would not go to the heavens feeling that his life had been unfulfilled.

Draco bravely leaned to the side of Crimm's thickly muscled neck to get a better view. His shifting of position brought forth a curse from Volan and an increasing grip that the younger elf had on his elder. Draco chuckled quietly to himself and relished the view of below. Everything was in miniature. The bushes, the trees, and even the muddy little path that they had followed, and from their height, the swamp did not seem so foreboding or sinister. It took on a peaceful and beautiful texture. The colors of each different plant blending in perfectly with the one next to it.

So wrapped up in the enjoyment of his flight, that Draco did not even realized that Volan had been talking loudly into his ear.

"Do you see them?" Volan yelled loudly at Draco's back. "Look, just up ahead on the path."

Draco followed Volan's outstretched finger. It was the others. Puppis, Steve, Forrest, and Brandy, leading a dumbfounded Braakk. They all stared numbly up at the sky, squinting to be sure what they saw was real.

Volan laughed for the first time on their short flight and waved wildly at the others, nearly losing his balance and falling from the back of Crimm.

"This is great," he yelled, laughing to Draco, his fear finally escaping him and exuberance taking over.

CHAPTER SEVENTEEN

Puppis rushed over and hugged Volan tightly as he clamored off the gleaming plate covered back of Crimm.

"Volan, heavens preserve us, are you all right?" Puppis asked, her voice full of distress. She held her friend at arms length, looking him up and down with concern filled eyes, searching for any signs of damage.

The male elf laughed with excitement. "Do not fret, Pup. That was the most thrilling thing I have ever done. Well, almost," he added, with a spirited wink.

The red headed elf, sighed in relief. Here she had been terrified for the life of her friend, and he was having a wonderful time. "Were you frightened at all?" she asked in curious wonder at what the sensation of soaring over the earth would be like.

"Not at all," he began with a nonchalant wave of his hand, and then caught himself when he noticed the look of mock surprise on Draco's face. "Well, maybe just a little bit at first, but then it was incredible. You can see everything. You would not believe how big this place is, you can see almost forever up there."

"Just so long as you are safe." Puppis smiled, hugging Volan closely again.

"Crimm would like to know if you would like to take a ride?" Draco asked Puppis.

She looked at the giant dragon who seemed to be inviting her with a nod of its head. She bit her lip in indecision, partly out of uncertainty, partly out of fear. "I do not think so. I am a little tired," she answered slowly. "Maybe when all of this is over," she added quickly so as not to hurt Crimm's feelings at his polite and generous offer.

"I think you are right, child," Draco responded. "I think we could all do with a little rest before we try to tackle the castle. What do you think, Forrest?"

"I think you're absolutely right," Forrest readily agreed, trying unsuccessfully to stifle a yawn at the suggestion of sleep. He turned and looked at Steve, who had already settled himself against a thick soft clump of bushes.

"No complaints here," Steve offered with a laugh. "I'm getting kind of used to sleeping on the ground."

"You?" Brandy teased in mock surprise with raised eyebrows. "Mister I'm So Uncomfortable all the time?"

"What can I say, your couch is lumpy to sleep on?" he quipped back, remembering many nights that he had spent on her old sofa instead taking the long ride back to his apartment.

"Gripe, gripe, gripe," Brandy teased as she laughed, rolling her eyes skyward.

"Yeah, yeah," Steve replied, shutting his eyes tightly, and laying still, rolled up in a tight ball with arms tucked under his head.

"I think he is already asleep," Puppis whispered with a giggle.

"He has been through an extraordinary ordeal. We all have," Draco comment. "I think we should all turn in."

"We should set up a watch schedule," Forrest said tiredly. He did not want to stand watch at that very moment, but he knew that they could not be too careful. They were closer than ever to Chameleon.

Crimm cocked his head at Draco, sending a swift message to the elder elf. "Crimm says that he will build a fire to warm us and keep watch the whole time we sleep. He said that we children need our rest," Draco added with a grin as he settled down to try and get some sleep. It had been a long time since someone had called him child, as he constantly did to others.

Puppis and Volan drifted quickly off to sleep wrapped securely in each others arms. Brandy laid a short distance from Steve and found that she had a hard time falling asleep even though she was past the point of exhaustion. She feared Chameleon would be there when she closed her eyes, she didn't know if she could deal with that again.

A short time later Forrest knelt quietly beside her. "May I join you?" he asked with a half smile, once again using words that she had used on him.

Brandy returned the sentiment and gave him a small nod, pointing to the empty space beside her. He laid down on his back and folded his hands beneath his head, staring upward.

"I figured you would already have drifted off," Forrest began casually, as if searching for something to talk about.

"I have a hard time sleeping here in this land."

He turned his gaze quizzically in her direction. "Why? You must be fatigued?"

"Your buddy, Chameleon, keeps popping into my dreams," Brandy replied wryly.

"What is a 'buddy'?" Forrest echoed the odd word.

"A friend or pal."

"Then, Chameleon is not what I would call a 'buddy'," Forrest returned sarcastically.

"I know," Brandy said, with a tired laugh. "I was only teasing you. It's kind of a sarcastic play on words. We humans do it a lot to joke around."

"Oh," Forrest said slightly taken aback at her odd humor, then became quiet, returning his gaze upward. After a long silence, he looked back at the human girl and studied her profile intently. There was no doubt about her loveliness, even though an ugly bruise marred her face and she was covered with mud. He remembered how her hair had looked the first time he had seen her. It glistened with bright red streaks from the firelight. Her eyes had blazed in anger when they had crossed words, and she did not fear him at all. The remembrance caused a happy smile to spread across his tired, dirty features.

"What are you grinning about?" Brandy asked without turning in his direction.

"How . . . ," he began in a shocked tone. He thought her eyes had been closed.

She peeked out from under her thick lashes and smiled impishly at him. "Some things don't have to be very obvious to be known."

Forrest felt his cheeks warming at being caught staring, so he instantly changed the topic. "Let me ask you something? Do humans not sleep on a bed?"

"What are you talking about?" Brandy laughed questioningly in total confusion.

"Steve said that he slept on your couch. Is that what you spend your nights on?"

Brandy covered her face with her arms to conceal her amusement. This was too much. If she didn't know better, she was beginning to think that Forrest was jealous of Steve.

"What is so funny?" Forrest asked indignantly.

"You are."

"What? You are an exasperating human girl," he replied angrily, turning away from her and staring back at the blank sky, wishing he had said nothing.

"I'm sorry, really" Brandy apologized trying to stifle her smiles. She reached out to take the elf's hand and give it a gentle squeeze. "If you remember, I told you the first time that we met, Steve and I are very close friends. There is no romantic or physical relationship between us. Sure, he stays at my house lots of times. I sleep in my bed and he sleeps on the couch. That's like a long chair and bed put together. He's like my brother, nothing else."

Forrest wrinkled his brow thinking on the words that Brandy told him. "So as a friend you two are not intimate with each other?"

"Good heavens, no," Brandy replied impulsively. Boy, this guy is thick headed sometimes, she thought to herself. "Why, do you?"

Forrest was taken aback by her forward question. "Many in our clan, who are very close friends, have relations without being bound together for life."

"Do you have close friends that you have relations with, too?" Brandy pressed slyly, enjoying the embarrassed look that was covering Forrest's face once again.

"No . . . ," he began slowly, but was quickly cut off.

"So, you have a mate already?"

"No." More confusion, and now slight irritation.

Brandy smiled and opened her mouth to make another comment, when Forrest placed his finger tips lightly on her lips.

"You humans talk too much," he whispered, wriggling closer to her and wrapping his arms comfortingly around her slender frame.

"So I've been told." She smiled contentedly, closing her eyes and resting her head against his strong chest, sleep overtaking her almost instantly.

Carina laid on the luxuriously soft sheets of her bed, and stared at the white ceiling in her dark room. All the candles, save one, had been extinguished by the gobioid servants who tended to her, and she had been informed that it was time to sleep. Yet sleep was the last thing on her mind. Her body was alive with excitement and revelation. She had not seen nor heard from Chameleon since their meeting in the large underground room. She had expected him to come bursting into her room at any moment after she had been dragged back, but he never appeared. This had given her ample time for thought, and many thoughts had surfaced.

Why had she never been able to use such forces of power before now? Could it have been a coming of age type of surge, or was it always there and she did not know it? Carina thought over what had happened several times in her mind. The only thing that made any sense was the fact that Chameleon had made her furiously mad. She had never wanted to inflict hurt on anyone the way she had wanted to do it to him at that moment. It went against everything that she had ever been taught or believed in. She did not want to hurt things, for all that was about them were gifts, not to be taken advantage of.

Chameleon was different. He was a plague to elves all over their lands. He had denounced that he was even elfin any longer, but yet, Lyra had stilled called him one of her children.

"Just as Lyra had called me one of her children," Carina said softly to herself, listening to the sound of her voice echo off the stone walls and drift into nothingness.

She took a deep breath and slowly let it out. For some reason, she did not feel the consuming hate that she had once felt for Chameleon. She still despised what he had done to Lyra, but the burning hate was gone. Perhaps it was because, even though she was his prisoner with her life hanging in the balance, the Mother of Spring did not blame Chameleon. She still held the love and caring for him as she would any of her elfin children.

"Perhaps that is what she is trying to teach me," Carina pondered. Slowly she sat up in bed and stared about the gloomy dark room. Planting her small feet on the cold damp floor, she stood and padded over to the table that held a candelabra. In it were six candle sticks, partly melted, but still holding plenty of potential life.

Carina looked sharply at them. "Light, come on, light," she urged them to no avail. With a disgusted sigh, she slumped her shoulders in defeat. Turning her back on the candles, she headed back for her large bed, deciding to give sleep another try.

"Do not give up, child. Try again. See what you want and pull it from the inside of your being."

Carina whirled at the sound. It had not really been a voice, but more like a whisper floating on the wind. More than that, she knew the voice easily. It had been Lyra. Tears welled into Carina's sky colored eyes. Tears of hope, fear, and desperation. Tears that threatened to sap all of her strength should they get the better of her.

With a deep determined breath, Carina straightened her shoulders and marched back to the candle holder. This time she fixed her gaze strongly on the object before her. She pictured it fully in her mind, seeing and feeling every inch of it, every detail, down to the last little glob of melted wax. Then she took the picture and made it come to life.

She envision the tiny flames dancing with life on top of their wax coated wicks. She felt the meager, yet friendly warmth that they gave off. She saw the way their light chased away the foreboding gloom of the room.

She felt her heart pound wildly in her chest and saw the image before her swim in confusion. She closed her eyes tightly, for the span of a heartbeat, then opened them. Her candles were lit. All six of them glowed happily before her as if thanking her for giving them the freedom to burn.

The princess groped weakly for the small hand carved chair by the table and sank gratefully onto it, her knees feeling frail after exerting so much power from within to light the candles. Her drained feeling did not last for long. The sight of what she had done, quickly gave her even more energy, and she looked about the room to see what else she could experiment on.

Lyra smiled contentedly from within the confines of her crystal cocoon. Yes, she thought peacefully, you are doing excellently. You have learned quickly that power may be obtained from means other than hate. This will help you in your struggle against my sister and my lost child.

Lyra ceased suddenly in her thoughts as she sensed that they were being listened to.

'You gloat loudly, my sister,' a silent voice entered Lyra's mind. 'Beware, your little one is learning too little, too late.'

'Perhaps, perhaps not,' Lyra thought cautiously back.

CHAPTER EIGHTEEN

Chameleon halted in front of the tall heavy door. He hesitated before knocking to gain entrance. He had been here in the castle of Lacerta, the Dark Queen, for many, many long years. He had heard her call come clearly to him, often in the dark nights of his youth, as if she were only paces away instead of far to the south of his clan.

When he finally acknowledged her summons and had first arrived, eager to learn all of the spells of magic that were promised, he had found a beautiful and willing teacher. Though she was still weak, both mentally and physically, from her first confrontation with the elves and Lyra, she a was tireless academician. She filled his days with the tedious task of remembering spell after endless spell, until he could recite them without hesitation or having to pause and think it over.

She also occupied his nights as well. She was an insatiable lover, and would call or come to him nearly every evening. Chameleon was an attractive male, for many elf maidens had told him so, and he thought himself quite experienced for his age, but Lacerta had shown him things that he would never had imagined. She took him to the heights of pleasure that he had never known could exist.

Then, after the five years of his studies ended, all of it changed. After he had master all of the things that she could teach him, and he was given control of the castle and the gobioids, his Queen dismissed him. She no longer called him to her chambers in the dark of night, and no longer slipped silently into his bed, waking him from sleep. They never saw one another in the huge shadowy estate, except when she needed his assistance in bringing one of the pesky dragons to her black tower so that she could drain its living essence to increase her own power. Not only had she taught him everything that he could have ever imagined about the arts of magic, but she had also changed him. She had shattered the soft spot inside of him. She had taken advantage of the weak side of him, the side that still cared about another living thing, the side that honestly wanted to shelter and protect Lacerta from the horrible things that she may have to face. She had taken that small bit of kindness from him and turned it into a lifeless cold spot. A place that was so cold, it burned. A burning that had made him bitter and full of hate, scorn and loathing for those beneath himself.

Slowly, Chameleon raised his strong pale hand to rap on the thick wooden door that was ornately decorated with hand crafted brass. Before his flesh could touch the timber, the door slid smoothly open.

"Enter," a silky voice from within called. It was the voice of beauty laced with venom.

Chameleon did as he was instructed. He had not been summoned to these dark chambers in many a long week, months, and even years. He advanced into the night black room a half a dozen paces, the door swinging tightly closed behind him. He did not turn or flinch. His Queen was testing him, and he knew it. He could not see at all in the inkiness of the room, but his senses were alive. He knew that Lacerta was close, he could faintly smell the sweet scent that she washed her hair with, but more importantly, he could sense her strength. It had grown considerably in the past months.

Suddenly the torches on the walls flared into life, revealing all the room had sought to hide. Chameleon squinted his eyes for a moment, trying to adjust them to the abrupt appearance of the light. It was as he had remembered. The walls were covered with charts and symbols, some of which he still did not know the full meaning of. Two large tables were littered with new and experimental spells. Books were carelessly discarded everywhere. Cobwebs hung in abundance, and fat furry creatures wandered lazily and unafraid about the room. In the corner was a huge stone fireplace that look as though it had not been lit in ages. Off to the left was the passage to Lacerta's tower room. He could detect the bony remnants of the Queens last dragon victim, laying ominously in the pale moonlight that filtered through the small window of the tower.

Turning his eyes to the right of the room, he watched as the golden door to Lacerta's inner chambers lightly slide open. Chameleon remained where he was, not daring to take the liberty of entering his mistress' chamber unbidden.

He did not wait long.

"Chameleon, my mage," Lacerta purred, cat like from the depths of her chamber. "Come to me."

The elf did as he was bade, and entered the spice scented alcove. It was dimly lit from a few scattered candles, but his dark eyes had no trouble adjusting quickly to the dimness of the room, showing him what he already knew would be there. A few large trunks overflowing with black and gray clothing. A washing stand, holding a golden basin, surrounded by bottles of fragrances. Fur rugs were scattered without design about the cold stone floor, and an impressive feather stuffed bed heaped with silk sheets and pillows.

"My Queen," he said lightly, his eyes glancing over the figure of Lacerta sprawled seductively on the bed. She wore only a flimsy gauze black shift. Her large breasts rising and falling steadily with each breath. She was slim of leg and waist, but full figured elsewhere. Her long silvery hair flowed like water about her, and her white pale skin glowed like pearl in the faint candlelight.

"So formal, my lonely mage," teased Lacerta. She peered invitingly at him with heavy gray eyes.

Chameleon said nothing, but watched his mistress closely. She was toying with him, and he saw it openly. Since she had dismissed him years early, he had spent all of his free time learning all that he could from the great library that the castle held. He was no longer the naive pupil that he once was.

"You are lonely, are you not?" she asked, reaching out a delicate hand to draw him down next to her on the bed, by the sleeve of his robe.

"I have much to occupy me within the castle, Mistress," Chameleon began tonelessly. "The dawn of Spring is only a day away, and there is much to prepare."

"That is not what I mean," Lacerta crooned, brushing her full pale pink lips against Chameleon's tightly clenched cheek.

"What do you mean?" feigned Chameleon, looking deeply into his Queen's gray unfeeling eyes. The smile upon her lips never reached her eyes.

Lacerta laid back against a mountain of pillows and tapped her fingernails absently together.

"You have brought the human girl here," she said, not as a question, but as a statement of fact. "Twice."

Chameleon shrugged his shoulders, ignoring the ugly annoyance that was stealing across Lacerta's pale and lovely face. "She amuses me. She has a very strong spirit, and should prove to be worthy entertainment."

"I see." Lacerta nodded quietly, the darkness spreading. "And what if I do not permit her presence."

A thin amused smile twisted at Chameleon's lips. "If you do not permit her presence," he echoed wryly.

"This is my domain," the Queen hissed, sitting up sharply. Her gown fell from one shoulder, exposing almost all of her breast, but she made no move to fix the garment. "I am in mastery here, it would do you well to remember that."

"I have never forgotten, my Queen," Chameleon whispered, leaning close to Lacerta's intoxicatingly scented form. "But, I wonder if you remember how we once kept one another amused during the night."

"That, my mage," she said with a throaty laugh, her anger ebbing suddenly, "one could never forget."

Many hours later, Chameleon held Lacerta's soft naked form close to his own beneath the silky sheets. Absently he stroked her long silver hair, and stared deeply into the dark of the room. The candles had long since extinguished themselves by burning all the way down, but the darkness did not keep Chameleon from seeing. His mage sight showed him everything as if it were day.

"What thoughts keep you from resting, my mage," Lacerta asked softly with sleepiness, sensing his thoughts were turbulent.

"I am thinking of our plans for the dawn of Spring. Destiny is close at hand, mistress," he reminded her.

"Yes, and it shall be glorious. My sister and her meddlesome elves will pay dearly for what they have done to me," Lacerta vowed, grinning into the dark, her weariness vanishing immediately. "Banishing me to this forsaken place. I admit I like the darkness, but that does not mean that I would not like to roam freely as she does, or did," she added with a snicker.

"The elves," Chameleon murmured almost to himself. His thoughts drifted briefly back to his youth when he had lived among the elves. He had no parents, they had been killed, while hunting, when he was still a babe, and he had been raised by an ancient widow, who kept a strict reign on all he had done. When she passed on he had decided to remain on his own, in solitude, instead of going to live with another family. Those few years, before he had answered Lacerta's call, had been almost fun. He did as he chose, came and went as he pleased, and answered to no one. Yet, even surrounded by others of his kind he was lonely. No one understood what he longed for and what he knew waited for him out somewhere other than the clan. When he had told the elders about his plans to leave and find the voice that had been calling him, they refused to let him go. They told him if he did so then he would be banished from the clan, for they claimed that only darkness and evil called. He had left anyway, and now his home was here in the castle.

"Do you have misgivings for leaving your kind?" the form close to Chameleon's asked, peering with glowing gray eyes into his own.

"No," he said, shaking his head firmly. "The elves expelled me. They look at me with more hate, than they even do you."

"My sister still claims you as one of her own," Lacerta commented, overhearing what Lyra had told the elfin girl.

"She is a fool," Chameleon sneered. "She was easily captured and held because she believed that you had changed and wanted to end the bickering that has followed you both for almost all of time."

"Yes, one would have thought she would have known better. That has always been her fault," sighed Lacerta tiredly, shaking her head. "My dear, dear sister thinks that everyone is so good. You are right, my mage, she is a fool. Only this time, she shall not overcome me, and I will have control of all the lands. Then the elves will pay slowly for the defeat that they caused me so long ago, and so will Lyra," she mumbled as she finally slipped into an effortless sleep. Thinking only of the victory that was soon at hand.

Chameleon grew silent as his queens breathing became slow and regular. He let his thoughts wander to Carina. She had been easy to capture, almost too easy. He had wanted some sport involved, but then again he should not complain. He had her and that was what was important.

Her display of sudden power in the lower chamber did concern him though, he thought to himself, with a frown marring his handsome features. She had caught him completely off guard. That had never happened to him before. The strength that she had shown was indeed impressive. Too bad he would not have time to try and turn her to use that newfound power for himself and his Queen. Mostly himself. Well, that was not going to happen, Princess Carina had a purpose, and that purpose was soon to come and pass.

Wearily, Chameleon closed his coal black eyes and tried to relax. The image of the human girl floated up to greet him. The sight made him grin in anticipation. She too had a purpose, and that was to be with him. Even his Queen would not be able stop that, he vowed. He had grown used to having what he wanted, and he wanted the human girl.

Chameleon opened his eyes with a start. Something had touched at his mind, warning him, even though he was deep in sleep. How long had he slept, he wondered. The room was no longer bathed in black darkness, it was dimly lit in gray. It was morning.

"Bane," Chameleon cursed angrily under his breath. He had much to accomplish, and sleeping was something he could do without for days if need be.

He looked down at Lacerta, who was still nestled close to him in the tangle of ebony sheets. Her face almost looked youthfully innocent. It held a small peaceful and contented smile. A smile that could have brought out that tenderness that Chameleon had once felt for his Queen, but that was before. His heart no longer held any place for tenderness. That, he had learned carefully, was only for fools.

He easily released himself from Lacerta's grasp. She mumbled soft words that he could not understand, but did not wake. Chameleon fetched his clothes that had been carelessly discarded earlier and hastily dressed himself. Something was happening just outside the castle. In the direction of the dragon bridge, he decided quickly after listening intently to the air for a moment.

As he left Lacerta's chambers he pulled his heavy robe over himself and rushed down the seemingly endless corridor that led to the main level of the castle.

"Where do you wish your breakfast this morning, master?" a squatty gobioid asked humbly as the dark elf moved through the halls to his own living quarters.

Chameleon impatiently dismissed him with a wave of his hand without bothering to answer the bothersome reptile. He was too busy to deal with anything so menial, like a meal, at the present. Something was happening. He was not sure what, but he knew that something was not right. He could feel it nagging at him.

When he reached his set of rooms, he burst through the main door, not concerning himself with the task of closing it. He ran his eyes across the many tables that filled his study. He was very tidy and the room reflected it. Books lined shelves, that covered every wall, in perfect order, by size and title. His tables were covered in equal order, some held potions, others held charts and papers. Oil globes hung suspended from the ceiling and flared into life as Chameleon impatiently snapped his fingers.

A large gray rat peered fearfully at his master from behind an ancient stone vase that took up most of the space of a corner.

"Light," Chameleon ordered, shooting a glance at the dark cold fireplace. Flames sprang upward, easily chasing the chill from the damp stone room. He roamed restlessly about the room, turning over papers, and pushing things all about his work tables.

"What Master seek," the rat squeaked nearly noiselessly from its hiding place.

"The mirror," Chameleon roared loudly.

"Mirror," squeaked the rat, his shiny bead like eyes darting nervously around.

Chameleon narrowed his dark gaze at the small trembling animal. He had given the rodent the ability of speech as a sort of amusement which had come in handy quite a few times when he needed an extra pair of eyes about the castle. Although at other times it only made him want to squash the bothersome creature. This was one of those times.

"Tar," the elf began, trying to control his temper that threatened to explode. "Have you seen the mirror?"

"Pretty mirror," Tar chattered fearfully, bobbing his head up and down. "Pretty mirror, show Tar."

"Where is it?" Chameleon seethed slowly, reaching for the annoying rodent.

The rat scurried across the room, out of his master's reach, and passed through the entrance of Chameleon's sleeping alcove. The elf followed and watched the rodent make his way over the thick blood red carpet. Tar stopped at the foot of the large bed, and pointed its tiny foot under the red woven blankets that hung over the edge.

"Pretty mirror, Tar look," the animal squeaked weakly, hoping his master would not retaliate too severely against him.

Chameleon suppressed a grin as he retrieved the mirror from under the bed. It was not too large an object, and its surface was smooth and shiny. It was encircled with dried dragon claws and teeth. He lowered himself in a sturdy chair made of tanned red dragon hide. The dark elf pushed back his sleep tangled hair and peered deeply into the mirror. It did not show his reflection, but instead began flickering with glowing colors.

"Xell amsc zin," he whispered in deep concentration at the blank face of the mirror. Suddenly the colors swirled wildly and an image took shape.

Chameleon smiled happily at what he saw. He rose from his seat and placed the mirror back in its holder which stood on a black carved table. He picked up a silver comb and ran it through his hair, smoothing the dark strands back into place. He took off his heavy robe, and draped it off the back of his chair, replacing it with a light weight cape that shimmered even though it was dark hued.

"No more mirror, Tar," Chameleon warned the trembling rodent as he made his way out of the room, his cape flaring wing like behind him.

CHAPTER NINETEEN

Chameleon hurried down the hall and away from his chambers. He was somewhat amused and, at the same time, somewhat annoyed at what he had seen in his mirror. The ragged band of elves and humans were coming to the castle. Somehow they had overcome the gobioids who were bringing them to him, and they now were presumptuously attempting to gain access into the castle by themselves.

He smiled cynically. Well, let them try. He was going to have a little reception waiting for them. He descended a few levels deeper into the castle, and came upon the rooms that the gobioid warriors occupied. They were very crowded and smelled of filth, but that was how the creatures preferred to be.

Chameleon wrinkled his nose in disgust as he waved his hand in front of the heavy steel door, and it easy opened before him. The humming of noise quickly diminished when the dark elf entered the rancid quarters of the gobioids. They all ceased whatever activities they had been doing and turned their reptilian, yellow eyes in his direction.

Chameleon surveyed the warriors in loathing distaste. They slept on the floor, like wild animals, using only a thin blanket as protection against the chilling cold that seeped through the thick stone walls. He had no idea about their personal hygiene, but seriously doubted if they ever bathed. They would eat anything that could not run from them, which caused the rats that roamed the estate to keep their distance from this area of the castle.

"My Lord Chameleon," a harsh voice rasped, wheezing heavily with each syllable. "To what do we honor this visit?"

Chameleon turned his steely gaze on an immense and husky gobioid that spoke. He was easily twice the size of any of the other creatures who stood dumbly around, and he was much more articulate than many of his kin. The gobioid sauntered out of a separate room from what the others shared. Female gobioids, barely dressed, lounged all about the large creature's private chamber, and giggled grotesquely whenever they looked his direction.

"I want some of your men to go into the dragon bridge, just outside the lowest level of the castle. There are intruders," Chameleon ordered flatly, not liking the bold and almost defiant glare that the gobioid's eye held.

"As you wish, my lord." The gobioid bowed in false sincerity at the elf's words, causing a wave of snickers to ripple through the others.

"Do you mock me?" the dark elf hissed raising a black eyebrow in the gobioid's direction and flinging a glance at the room of creatures, silencing them instantly.

"No, my lord," said the large gobioid with veiled remorse in his tone. "What type of intruders are bold enough to dare invade us?" he added, quickly changing the flow of the conversation in his own favor.

"There are four elves and two humans. Eliminate them all except for the female human. She is to be unharmed. I want no mistake about that," Chameleon warned, the silent threat from his features told him that the gobioid easily understood.

"As you wish." The large creature nodded. "Anything else?"

"Yes," Chameleon drawled, nodding slowly and tapping his chin with a long slender finger. "There is a gobioid with them, Braakk, he has become a traitor. Eliminate him as well."

"Braakk?" the gobioid replied, grinning in surprise. "He has always been trouble. He shall be the first to fall," promised the warrior.

"Excellent." Chameleon smiled as he turned and left the reeking chamber. He well knew of the discontent that lay between Braakk and the gobioid captain, Grikk. Many of the other gobioids seemed to prefer Braakk over Grikk, and that had not boded favorable for Braakk in his competitor's opinion.

"Yes," the elf said, chuckling lightly to himself while making his way back to Lacerta's tower chambers, "things are going very well indeed."

Forrest was awake, but did not open his eyes. He laid perfectly still. He could feel Brandy's body very close to his own. She was still asleep, for her breathing was light and regular, but his senses were alive with alert. Someone or something was moving about the camp. Slowly he opened his eyes so that only a crack of pale gray sight filtered through. With a sigh, he grinned and opened his eyes fully. It was only Crimm. The large red dragon was shuffling around the campfire. Forrest propped himself wearily up on his elbows, trying to get a better view of the reptile and his movements.

"What's up?" Brandy murmured sleepily, rubbing her eyes so that she could see what Forrest was looking at with so much interest.

"Nothing," Forrest said slowly, glancing quickly into the sky trying to figure out what Brandy meant by that, then decided it must be another of her odd statements. "I am curious to see what Crimm is doing."

"He made us something to eat," Draco called to them from the other side of the fire. "Come over and have some, it is quite good."

"What is it?" Steve yawned loudly, crawling from his balled up position on the ground. "Man, am I ever stiff. I don't think I moved a muscle all night," he groaned, stretching his arms over his head.

"I do not think any of us did," Puppis said, trying unsuccessfully to stifle a yawn.

Volan pulled her to her feet and hugged her warmly. "I for one am glad you did not," he whispered quietly into her bright hair.

"Me too," she said, winking recklessly back.

Steve walked numbly over to where Brandy and Forrest sat by the fire and squatted down between them. "If I didn't know any better," he began, conspiratorially draping his arms about both of their shoulders and glancing toward Volan and Puppis, "I would be willing to bet that there is something going on between those two."

"I think you're right," Brandy replied with a giggle, nibbling on her meal simlantaneously. It was some type of fish wrapped in many different kinds of leaves and somehow steamed until tender. Most of all, it was delicious.

"They have been close friends for many years," Forrest informed them, with a casual grin in Brandy's direction that she didn't miss. With a small smile, and a slight reddening of the cheeks, she turned her attention back to the fire.

Steve glanced curiously at Brandy and then smiled widely. He understood perfectly how she felt. It was the same for him every time he thought of Carina.

"And, you know, if I really didn't know any better," he began in a teasing voice, looking from Brandy to Forrest with a knowing nod, "I would bet almost anything that there is something going on between you two."

Forrest shrugged and looked away. Brandy blushed profusely and swatted her best friend on the arm, but Draco laughed loudly at the youngsters. "I think you are right," he echoed the human girl's earlier words with a fatherly chuckle.

"What is going on?" Puppis echoed as she and Volan sat down about the small fire, eager to have a meal.

"Nothing," Brandy grumbled irritably, knocking Steve's arm off of her shoulder and pushing him to the ground. "Twit!" she whispered in a hiss at him.

Steve shook his head and laughed. "My, my, aren't we touchy this morning," he said with a chuckle as he tried to prop himself up on his elbows. "Better find you some coffee quick."

Finally she could hold back no longer. Brandy laughed with her dear friend. "You are a horrible goofball, Steven Rixx." She smiled, stuffing her mouth with more of the delicious fish. "You will pay dearly for this, so watch out," she warned shaking a finger at him.

"I'm so scared," he retorted back, but at Brandy's dark look he decided to back off. "You know I was only kidding, don't you?" he asked with a hurt puppy type of look.

"Sure," Brandy replied, trying to suppress her amusement by rolling her eyes and shaking her head.

The elves watched the two before them in wonder.

"What are you talking about?" Puppis asked in confusion. "Are you angry with one another?"

Steve and Brandy laughed aloud. "No!" they both exclaimed at the same time, then fell into laughter again.

Forrest stared at the two humans for a moment. The bond they shared was very close, he could not deny that. He wondered, with a slight touch of envy, how nice it would be to have someone that close to share things with. He wanted to grow close with Brandy, but at the same time was too afraid to do so. His feeling about her future had not changed, as much as he had hoped that it would. It had been the opposite. The closer they got to the castle, the stronger the feeling was about her impending doom. He wished that he could make it go away, or even take her place, but he knew that was impossible. For unfortunately, his premonitions were never wrong.

"Hello, Forrest, you awake in there?" Brandy's cheerful voice cut through his dark brooding and caused a sheepish grin to cross his face.

"I am sorry. I was just thinking," he mumbled awkwardly.

"That is a dangerous pastime, my friend," Steve warned with a smile.

"Yeah." Brandy giggled. "And Steve knows all about that."

The others laughed merrily as Steve stuck his tongue out at his friend. "Well, I can see how appreciated I am here," he pouted, trying not to crack up, and rose to his feet. "I think I'll go give Braakk something to eat."

"Let him go hungry, he deserves nothing more," Volan said, shooting a dark look over at the sullen and bound gobioid.

"Normally I would agree, but I sort of owe him the favor," Steve replied. He grabbed a couple pieces of the wrapped fish from near the fire and went over to the gobioid.

"You must be hungry too," Steve offered hesitantly to Braakk. He sat down in front of the gobioid and slightly loosened the creature's binds. Braakk had inflicted a lot of pain on Steve, but Steve had always been one to repay any debt or service that had been given to him. So he felt as though he owed the gobioid the kindness of at least one meal.

Braakk did not move. He stared absently at the food before him. He was hungry, but he did not understand the intentions of the human.

As if sensing his thoughts, Steve pushed the fish closer to the unmoving gobioid. "I didn't do anything funky to the food. It's not poisoned. You showed me the courtesy of bringing me food when you had me captive, and now, you could say, I am returning the favor."

Braakk lifted his yellow eyes and curiously studied the human. "Even after the way that we, and I, have treated you?" he asked dubiously.

"Yeah," Steve answered simply with a shrug.

"You humans are most unusual," Braakk stated, reaching for the wrapped fish. He devoured the entire contents in less than a few bites. After wiping his snouted face, he gave a satisfied belch.

"My thanks," he snorted out clumsily.

"Don't mention it. Sorry I didn't have a spoon."

A small grin twisted at Braakk face. "It is alright. I do not use one very often," he added with a hoarse chuckle.

Steve retied Braakk's hands and rose to leave. "Thanks for leading us back across the bridge," he said quietly with a sincere nod.

Braakk made no reply, save for a small grunt and returned his complete attention to something on the ground that Steve could not see.

"Crimm says that we should leave, it is still a bit of a walk to the castle," Draco informed them when Steve had returned to the group.

"I was about ready for another nap." Volan yawned loudly, rubbing his contented stomach. "I guess it will have to wait."

The small band picked up the bags that they had confiscated from the gobioids and prepared to leave. The bags contained pouches of fresh water, an array of hand sized knives, and some other objects that they could not identify. They threw the things that they did not recognize into the fire, and watched in bewilderment as they turned to blue smoke and faded from sight.

"Some of Chameleon's magic," Forrest grumbled, dumping a bag of green water onto the fire, extinguishing it.

They had each recovered their weapons, and had them securely strapped to their person, knowing that their uses would be needed in the castle. Draco effortlessly flung his mighty axe over his shoulder and led the weary and dirty group forward. They followed Braakk, who obediently and wordlessly trailed behind the giant dragon, Crimm.

Brandy reached over and tightly squeezed Steve's hand. "This is it," she whispered apprehensively to her friend.

Steve said nothing in return, only nodding his head in solemn agreement.

Carina slowly opened her long lashes. She struggled into a sitting position, rubbing her puffy tired eyes, and yawning noisily. She lifted her hands over her head and stretched for a long while. Then flopping back on the thick comfortable pillows, she carefully surveyed her surroundings. She was still imprisoned in Chameleon's castle. She had hoped that when she awoke she would be back in her chambers at her father's home. She missed him terribly, and all the others in the clan. She wondered if they even sensed that something was amiss.

Carina shook her head sadly. The dawn of Spring was almost upon them. She was about to be sacrificed to fulfill some old prophecy that the Dark Queen, Lacerta had placed upon the elves. The princess sighed deeply. She would gladly give up her life so that one she loved would be saved, but to be trapped, and sacrificed was a different matter all together. Also, not being able to do anything to warn her family and her clan of the impending danger was more than she could stand.

Her heart ached in despair. She wished desperately that her newly found powers could somehow help her, but she knew not how to make that happened. Suddenly, she heard the faint clicking sound on her wall. The door materialized and a gobioid shuffled into her room, placing a silver tray of food on the small table by the wall.

"Your meal," the creature rasped courteously, keeping a close eye on the captive princess. He readily knew the fate of his kindred that had let the princess escape the day earlier. He had died slowly and very painfully from the sounds of the screams that had rent his body. The gobioid shivered in remembrance, but their master had made sure that all knew of the consequences if the princess were to escape her chambers again.

Carina sat up on the side of her bed. She opened her mouth to speak to the creature that had brought her food, but the gobioid darted quickly back out the door, locking it securely. She watched sadly as the image of the door faded from view and large stone once again took its place. She shook her head despondently, lowering her face to her hands. She closed her eyes tightly, trying to keep the tears that wanted to fall, held back. It did not work. Slowly, one by one, they escaped through her firmly clenched lashes. She had thought that her new power would be her chance to escape from this luxury prison, but it had not happened. She had tried all night to make the door appear on the wall the way she had been able to make the candle light. Yet, time and time again, nothing had happened.

'Carina, my dear child, do not cry so,' a soft caring voice whispered through the princess' mind.

Carina snapped her head up and stared wildly about. Someone had spoken to her. Where were they? Hesitantly she rose from her bed and walked to the center of the room. Wiping the tears from her eyes and face, she blinked several times, clearing her blurred vision.

"Who is there?" she called out tentatively.

'It is I, child,' the voice said again, only this time Carina knew the voice. It was Lyra.

"Oh, Lyra, where are you?" Carina wailed in relief and despair. "Have you freed yourself?"

'No child,' Lyra said gently. 'I am still held as before.'

"Then how are we speaking?" stammered Carina, twirling in slow circles, looking at every corner of the room.

'Your constant use of your power has opened up many new channels in you. You are not only becoming more proficient in your use of power, but also in your ability to accept the flow of power.'

"So, the more I use my ability, the more I will be able to do?" Carina asked slowly, trying to understand all that Lyra was telling her.

'Yes, child. Unfortunately, time is very short. My time is close at hand, and I am afraid so is yours,' Lyra said, a hint of wistfulness creeping into her usually confident tone.

"There must be some way to stop this," Carina countered, feeling stronger knowing that she and Lyra could at least communicate together. She paced the room trying to think of a solution.

She stopped her pacing and placed a slender finger on her lips in thought. "Do you know how you can be released?" she asked after a moment.

'My sister was quick to gloat when she imprisoned me. She claims only the sacrifice of one life for another will break the crystal. A price that she knows I would never allow another to do for me.'

"Then why am I different. Why will I be the one whose blood will keep you bound forever?" Carina asked in confusion.

'Because my sweet child, you are innocent in the ways of her darkness. She knows you would willingly give yourself up for me.'

"I would, dear Lyra, if it meant your freedom," the princess stated matter-of-factly and without hesitation.

'That is why she must use you,' Lyra said softly. 'You have a virtuous and pure soul, and you have much untrained power. She can use and harness that power to try and destroy me.'

"I do not understand," Carina said slowly, beginning to pace again. "Draco told us that the prophecy called for the first female descendant of my line to be sacrificed. Why is that? How did Lacerta know that I would have such power?"

Lyra smiled inwardly at Carina's simpleness of the situation. 'Female elves have always been very powerful, and your sire of so long ago was the elf who held much magic. His magic was passed down through the ages and has resurfaced through you. I sensed it easily when you were born, as I am sure my sister did also.'

"So she has been waiting for me all this time," Carina said, more as a statement than a question.

'Yes, my child, it would seem so.'

Carina took a deep breath and sat back down on the edge of the bed. Then a thought came to her. "We may have hope yet," she said optimistically.

'What is that, child?' Lyra asked curiously.

"There are still the elves and humans that I traveled with. I believe they will come."

'Yes, child,' Lyra agreed without hesitation. 'I also believe they will come.'

Chapter Twenty

"That is far enough," a very large gobioid commanded imperiously, suddenly appearing before the band of weary, but well armed, rescuers.

"Grikk," Braakk mumbled spitefully under his breath. He would almost rather be held prisoner than to be rescued by this worthless piece of misshapen gobioid. They had long been rivals for the leadership position of the gobioid warriors. Braakk had never openly challenged Grikk for the title, because of Grikk's obvious size and powerul superiority, even though many of the gobioids had urged him to do so. Now he wished that he had.

The group pulled their weapons free and ready for use. Puppis and Brandy broke off to the side and readied their bows. Puppis swiftly laid a long straight arrow against the string and pulled it tight, while Brandy carefully notched a short arrow on her crossbow. Draco gave his massive axe a few test swings in front of him, and Forrest and Volan both held long swords casually, yet fully alert at their sides. Steve gripped two long bladed knives tightly, one in each hand.

"I hadn't realized we were going to have a welcoming party," Steve commented wryly over his shoulder to the others. "You should have told us that your friends were going to be here to greet us," he remarked to the scowling gobioid.

"These are no friends of mine," Braakk hissed under his breath so that only Steve understood his words. The human male squinted at him curiously, as if he didn't understand

Braakk's meaning. "Do all humans get along?" the gobioid asked simply.

Steve shook his head no, but said nothing. He didn't have time to try and figure out what was going on. The gobioids had advanced closer to them, not showing any signs of fear from the group. To make matters even worse, Crimm had gotten out of the way and was hovering in the air over them. He was enspelled so that he could not help, and help was what they desperately needed. The lead gobioid was huge. He easily towered over all those in their group and was well muscled to boot. There were eleven other gobioids, behind the leader, and they were dressed in some type of leather armor, heavier than what Braakk wore. They all brandished either long swords or wicked looking clubs with the ends embedded with spiked steel.

The lead gobioid held up his hand and halted the advance of his warriors when they were about a dozen paces in front of the rag tag band. Lazily he lowered his sword tip into the muddy earth and leaned confidently against its large gem encrusted pommel.

"These are indeed dire straights that you have fallen into, Braakk," the mountainous reptile chuckled with no humor in his voice. "It seems that you have indeed become a traitor to our cause."

"What do you mean by that, Grikk?" Braakk all but spat in hateful fury at the larger gobioid.

"I would call it consorting with the enemy," Grikk shot back, pointing an accusing finger at his foe. "You have been tried and I find you guilty of all charges," he stated flatly.

Braakk laughed, shrugging his large shoulders. "You find me guilty? Who gave you the power to do anything other than follow orders?"

"That is the funny part about it, Braakk. I am following orders. You have been cited a betrayer, and a risk to us all," Grikk gloated, watching the realization of his words sinking in.

"By who," Braakk demanded, instantly angry. He tugged at his binds, wishing them off of him so that he could break Grikk's knees and toss him into the thick murky water.

"Master Chameleon, who else."

Braakk froze. Either Grikk was lying or their master had indeed branded him. He squinted his yellow eyes at those who accompanied Grikk. None were what he would call a friend. He understood what was happening now. He was to be eliminated, and by saying he had aided the elves and humans would make it easy to pacify those who were loyal to him. His Master Chameleon must have indeed ordered it, or Grikk could easily be found out.

Steve also easily grasped what was happening before them. For some reason Braakk had fallen from grace, and he was going to be vanquished, just as they were going to be. Then a thought struck him. Maybe not. He leaned close to Forrest and whispered quietly to him.

"We should free Braakk," he said quickly in a hushed tone. "He knows that they will kill him, maybe he will fight. If not for us then at least for himself. Either way we have a little more help with those other gobioids."

"What about afterwards?" Forrest glanced at the human.

"If we are still alive, we will worry about it then. If not," Steve trailed off with a shrug. "Will it really matter?"

Forrest nodded in agreement. He pulled a sharp heavy knife from his waist belt and handed it to Steve, who hastily accepted it after tucking one of his own knives away. "Give him this," he said. "He should at least have a fighting chance against these rogues."

Steve grinned and turned toward Braakk. He held the knife before him and grabbed one of Braakk's arms.

"Are you to do me in before these vermin have the chance?" the gobioid asked spitefully.

"Not today," Steve replied with a chuckle. He slashed the leather binds that held the reptiles wrists and tossed them to the ground. He flipped the knife in his hand and held it to Braakk, hilt first.

"What is this?" Braakk asked in confusion, not touching the weapon.

Steve shook his head in amusement at the gobioid. "Do you want to just lay down and die, or do you want to have a chance? Take it and fight."

A grin of understanding spread slowly across Braakk's face. He took the blade firmly in his scaly claw. "You humans are definitely curious. This I will enjoy," he stated, turning his gaze toward Grikk and the others.

"If I am accused of aiding these pitifully puny humans and elves, then I might as well commit the crime," Braakk announced in a loud challenging voice for all the gobioid to hear.

Grikk grinned, very pleased with what was occurring. He held no doubt that he and his men would easily overtake the band before them, but the added pleasure of eliminating the only one who had ever grumbled or showed signs of wanting to overthrow him, would be an extra bonus.

"Prepare to die slowly and painfully," Grikk shouted boisterously. He lifted his large blade from the ground and held it high above his head. The other gobioids, behind him, shouted in harsh voices and began rushing forward.

Forrest, Volan, Draco, and Steve held their ground, with weapons ready. Braakk raced recklessly forward, engaging Grikk in head long battle. The others steered clear of the two large gobioids. For theirs was a private fight. Puppis and Brandy drew the first victims down. Puppis released an arrow with her bow first, catching a gobioid full in the chest. The powerfully shot arrow pierced his armor and sent the creature bellowing to his knees, none of his comrades stopping to aide him, only rushing over his fallen form.

Brandy's first try missed it mark badly. She was terrified of the rushing onslaught of the creatures. Going one on one was bad enough, but have yourself outnumbered two to one was even worse.

"Steady, Brandy," Puppis caution her. "We have few arrows between us, make them all count."

"Sorry," she mumbled awkwardly. She knew that Puppis was right. Much was at stake. She was not only fighting for her own self, but for the lives of all the others as well. Quickly she set another arrow on the tee of the crossbow and took aim. A gobioid was only a couple of paces away from Steve, and her friend was already trying to keep one of the creatures at bay. She took a deep breath and let it out slowly. Pulling the trigger, she followed the expeditious arrow as it flew effortlessly through the air, hitting exactly where Brandy had aimed. The gobioid fell to the ground in an instant, dead on contact, the arrow protruding horribly from the side of his head.

Steve sighed thankfully when the approaching gobioid dropped to the ground and didn't move. The one that he was desperately trying to fend off was proving to be difficult. He found himself at a great disadvantage. The gobioid was armed with a heavy club, and he only had his two knives. His advantage was his quickness, and that was the only thing that was keeping the gobioid from bashing in his head. Steve nimbly jumped back and forth, darting his knives out and causing gashes to appear on the gobioid, but at the same time enraging the creature further.

Draco easily dispensed with two of the gobioids, who rushed at him, with two mighty swings of his axe. They fell to the ground as if they had been wheat in the field at harvesting time. The third gobioid who approached him, with an incredibly long sword, was much more cautious of the elder elf and his double sided weapon. The gobioid parried quickly, despite its bulky weight, and inflicted many nicks and cuts on the elf. Draco held his ground. He gritted his teeth and pitted all of his strength against the gobioid, determined not to fall.

Volan engaged two of the gobioids with his sword. He was a good fighter, but he had only practiced against others in his clan or tree trunks that could not run from him. He had practically never encountered a foe that was very experienced, and having two before him was proving to be quite a different and difficult task. It was all he could do to hold his ground. He made no advances against the gobioids, and they had only caused minor wounds to him. The girls had managed to injure one of the creatures in the leg with an arrow slowing it somewhat, but it had not brought the gobioid down.

Forrest swung his great sword effortlessly. The first gobioid that rushed at him, lost his weapon arm in a blink. The creature howled crazily and flung his unarmed body at the elf. Forrest side-stepped the gobioid and it crashed into the mud. The elf quickly ended the noise from the creature with a single stroke of his blade. The other gobioid grinned recklessly at the elf.

"You are good," he hissed in consent, "but I am better," he boasted.

"Then let us see," Forrest invited evenly.

The gobioid sprang forward with amazing speed, catching Forrest off guard. He lurched back to avoid a sweeping blow from the creatures sword, and stumbled on a rock. Falling to his back, he deftly rolled to one side just as the gobioid's blade whizzed across the space that he had occupied only seconds before. Forrest rolled back to his feet, his body and sword covered with thick mud, and crouched ready for the gobioid. As the creature lifted his blade to attack again, the elf shot out, with the speed of a striking snake, and sliced the gobioid across the mid-section. A grunt escaped the gobioid's mouth as he looked to the seeping wound.,

"Well aimed elf, only you will have to do better than that," the gobioid slurred, chuckling darkly, not noticing the pain.

Forrest said nothing, only waiting for the gobioid to advance on him again. And as before, when the gobioid lifted his arm for a massive swing, the elf sprang into action and inflicted another horrible gash on the creature, close to the first one. This time the gobioid did not smirk. His sword arm dropped and he clutched desperately at the wound with his free hand. He yelled loudly and charged at the elf, not taking any heed at all.

Forrest evaded the sudden rush of the gobioid. The creature sailed past the dodging elf, and as he did so, Forrest brought his arcing weapon down in a disabling blow, severing the creature's sword arm. The gobioid howled in rage and pain. Mud covered his body as he struggled to regain his footing.

Forrest waited patiently. He knew the end was near for the gobioid, even if it did not. The reptilian warrior charged at the dark haired elf, much slower this time. Forrest stood ready, and as soon as the creature was within range he lifted his sword and swept it across the filthy form of the gobioid.

The gobioid sunk to the ground and stared keenly at the tired and worn elf. "Well met," he croaked in a feeble, yet harsh breath. He then closed his eyes and moved no more.

Puppis and Brandy watched the movement all around them from their somewhat safer vantage point. Repeatedly the females released volleys of arrows at the gobioids. Many of them missed their marks, for the actions of the creatures as well as their friends were erratic and unpredictable. Their biggest fear was not being set upon by one of the gobioids, but of accidentally wounding one of their friends.

"So you are the stinging bugs that are causing so much interference," an ugly grayish green gobioid drawled as he lumbered up to them at an incredibly rapid rate of speed.

Brandy gasped as she took in the sight of the creature. Neither of the girls had noticed his approach until it was too late. He was much taller than either herself or Puppis and the sheer bulk of him was overwhelming. His arms and legs were thicker than trees. He laughed coarsely, not fearing either of the females or the bows that they held. He carried a long heavy club with steel spikes sticking out of it from the grip all the way to the end tip.

Brandy fumbled to place an arrow on her crossbow. Puppis quickly placed and drew an arrow on her bow string. She pulled it fully and fired at the approaching gobioid. The sharp stick went cleanly through the gobioid's thick arm.

He slowed his progression for a moment and glanced down at the protruding annoyance. With a small sarcastic laugh, he snatched the arrow from his arm and flung it to the muddy earth as if it were no more than a loose string coming off of his clothing.

"Was that supposed to hurt," he cackled in full amusement.

Puppis stared in fear. Within an instant the gobioid was on her. He swung his club cruelly at her head, intending on killing her with one pass. At the last moment, Puppis regained control of her senses and flung her bow up on front of her, deflecting the blow of the club, but at the same time destroying her weapon of defense. Brandy finally succeeded in placing an arrow on her crossbow with shaky hands. She quickly raised it and released the small missile at the gobioid. It struck the creatures solid shoulder with a thud. The impact slowed the gobioid's advance long enough for Puppis to scramble away from the creature.

The creature grinned and snorted in contempt at the arrow that had been placed in his shoulder. "That was not very nice," he hissed at the two females.

"Oh, shit," Brandy muttered, looking around her. "I think we're in trouble now," she stated matter of factly, realizing that they didn't have any arrows left.

"Not quite yet," Puppis answered quietly. She reached into her boot and pulled out a small knife. Its slender blade glimmered brightly in the dull grayness that surrounded them. The handle was made of some type of translucent red stone. The elf female deftly tossed the blade in her hand, catching it by the hilt. She flipped the small weapon at the approaching gobioid with amazing ease and speed. The small knife arced gracefully through the air, cutting the distance in the span of a heart beat. Within a blink of the eye, the blade struck home, planting itself firmly in the gobioid's forehead. The creature's yellow eyes rolled upward as he fell on his back, flat upon the squishy, muddy earth.

"Wow!" Brandy gasped in total amazement. "You have got to teach me how to do that," she said, staring at the fallen form of the gobioid.

"Maybe I will, if my hands ever quit shaking," said the elf girl, laughing nervously, not wanting to look at her handy work.

"That was really cool," Brandy praised her friend, wrapping an arm about the elf girl's shoulder and hugging her close.

"Thanks, but what of the others?" Puppis asked in a trembling voice, looking past the fallen gobioid to what had befallen her friends. "Volan," she whispered in fear at what she saw. Her friend was battling two gobioids and he was not faring well. He was covered with numerous small cuts that stained his clothing and skin red.

"Let's go," Brandy said, grabbing Puppis by the arm and tugging her toward Volan and his two attackers.

As they rushed recklessly forward, Puppis called to her friend. "What are we going to do?"

"Double team him," Brandy said, smiling wickedly. "I'll jump on his back and you grab his legs. Then we'll knock him to the ground."

"Then what will we do?" Puppis stared wide eyed at the plan.

"Then he's toast," Brandy said, pulling the knife that she carried from her waistband. She clutched it tightly in her sweaty palms. A few paces before the females reached one of Volan's assaulters Brandy let out and unearthly shrill. Puppis followed closely behind with one of her own, only louder. They sounded like a couple of huge hunting cats jumping on unsuspecting prey. The effect was exactly what Brandy had hoped for. All the fighters momentarily halted what they were doing and stared at the two filthy females. Brandy sailed through the air and landed on the back of the gobioid. Simultaneously, Puppis dove at the legs of the creature. The impact sent the gobioid crashing to the ground. His weapon flew from his grasp and rolled well out of his reach. Puppis struggled to hold onto the creature's powerful legs. Brandy put her full weight on top of the creature's chest and raised her knife threateningly over the gobioid's face.

"Just chill right now," she warned callously, gasping in breaths of air, trying to calm her racing heart.

The gobioid looked curiously at her, not understanding what she had just told him, but he had not missed the tone of her voice. He grunted loudly, but did not fight back.

The moments distraction proved to be the turning point of the fight. Volan quickly recovered from seeing Puppis and Brandy jump on the gobioid. He took advantage of the other creature's dumbfounded look at what had happened to his comrade. In a flash of Volan's sword, his opponent lay unmoving on the ground. Volan sank to his knees, gratefully enjoying the coolness of the mud beneath him.

Puppis raced to her friend in concern. "Are you alright?" she asked in a strangled whispered. Tears flooded her eyes, and streamed muddy trails down her dirty cheeks. All she saw was the cuts and blood that criss-crossed Volan's skin.

"I am now," Volan sighed heavily, hugging the frail elf girl close to him.

Steve sprang forward, like a flash, when the gobioid in front of his turned his head to glance at the commotion. When he did, Steve shoved both of his knives into the creature's midsection. The gobioid fell to his knees, and was mercifully eliminated in a blink by a swing of Forrest's sword.

"Thanks," Steve sighed wearily to the elf, pushing his sweat spattered and mud encrusted hair from his flushed face.

"Do not mention it," Forrest returned.

Draco also took advantage of the commotion, when the gobioid he was battling chanced a glance at the sudden noise. The elder elf's heavy axe licked out and sliced cleanly through the arm of the gobioid.

The creature dropped his weapon and hugged the damaged limb close to his body. He saw that he was the only one left standing against the elves and humans. The creature stood uncertainly for a moment, not sure what to do, but a moment was all it took. He turned his back on his fallen peers and raced back to the opening of the dragon bridge.

"Stop him," Puppis yelled to Draco. "He will warn Chameleon."

The elder elf nodded his silently. He lifted the axe and gave it a mighty heave. The weapon sailed end over end through the air, but finally reached its victim. The gobioid staggered for a few paces when the axe struck him fully in the back, stretching desperately for the glimmering door that he knew he would not reach.

"That was great." Brandy turned her head and beamed with admiration at Draco. "How do you guys do that?" she asked, but when she did, she felt herself being lifted from the gobioid. The creature grabbed her by her shirt front and flung her away from him. He then jumped to his feet and raced away from the band of fighters into the thick bushes and out of sight.

Brandy laid dazed in the murk. Her head ached and her vision swam. Steve and Forrest rushed to her side, crouching closely to her.

"Brandy, are you dead?" Steve asked in a worried tone, shaking his friend gently by the shoulders.

"Not yet," she gasped painfully, trying to regain her breath. "You know, I think I'm ready to get off this ride now. I'm out of tickets."

"I know exactly what you mean," Steve answered, nodding to his friend. His heart ached at the sight of her. She was dirty, bruised and in terrible pain. Yet she kept going on, because she believed in these elves and all that they stood to lose.

"What about Braakk?" Brandy croaked, suddenly remembering the gobioid.

The others looked about at her question. They spotted the two large gobioids not far from them. They had long since abandoned or lost their weapons to one another, and now fought hand to hand. Both of the creatures were covered with heavy wounds, and thick green blood.

The elves and humans approached the fighting pair cautiously. Braakk caught sight of them and yelled hoarsely. "Stay back," he warned. "This I will finish on my own."

The group said nothing, only nodding, understanding the gobioids want for revenge.

Braakk wrapped his powerful hands around Grikk's throat and squeezed with all his might. His strength was nearly spent, but he knew that Grikk was close to death. Grikk struggled fiercely in Braakk's grasp, but could not loosen the hold.

"You are finished," Braakk said triumphantly as Grikk's body went limp. He pushed the gobioid's body to the mud, and looked spitefully upon it. A second later he too fell to the wet earth, unable to hold up his large form any longer.

"Steve," Braakk barely managed to call out the human's name.

Steve knelt beside the fallen gobioid. "That was a good fight, Braakk," he said to the creature.

"My thanks to you," Braakk wheezed. "My time is almost gone. My blood flows freely, as does my life, and there is nothing that will stop it. You must help me rise."

"But . . . ," the human began and was cut off by a feeble wave of the gobioid.

"Quiet," Braakk ordered with a weak smile. "You have done me an honor by letting me defeat my true enemy. Let me repay you a favor by leading you through the bridge. I have met my destiny, now is the time for yours."

CHAPTER TWENTY-ONE

Puppis finished wrapping the wounds that marred Volan's form about the same time that Brandy had completed seeing to Draco. Neither of their injuries had been severe, but they bled, so tending to was a must. The females had shredded the bottoms of their long tunics and used the clean inside part as bandages.

"I think we are about ready to go," Brandy announced, smiling proudly at Draco, who nodded approval at her handiwork.

"Nicely done, child," Draco complimented. "We must leave, time is drifting swiftly."

"Yes," agreed Forrest readily. "We are quickly running out of time to accomplish what we must." They all stood, prepared to leave their small resting area, and looked expectantly at the gobioid who had suddenly become a great asset to them. Braakk leaned heavily on Steve's shoulders, using the human to help support him as he hobbled painfully forward. His victory over Grikk had been very satisfying. It did not matter that he would pay with his own life. What mattered was that he had been able to prove that he was the better warrior in the end.

He paused just before the twinkling lights of the gleaming door. A fit of severe coughing overtook him and he crumpled to his knees, even though the human held a tight grip on him. The choking ceased quickly, but it had weakened him considerably more. Blood, from his numerous wounds, began flowing more freely. His vision swam with uncertainty, and he felt the black grip on death creeping closer upon him.

"Do you think you can continue?" Steve asked hesitantly. He wanted very much to cross the door, but he also realized that the gobioid was near death. Despite what Braakk had done to him, Steve still felt a sense of compassion toward the dying creature. He realized that if Braakk had refused to help them, they would have never defeated the gobioids.

"I will make it," Braakk returned feebly. "You must repay the final debt that I owe to Chameleon. He has unjustly condemned me," the gobioid trailed off weakly, struggling to regain his footing and consciousness.

"We shall try," Draco spoke up deeply. He gripped Braakk firmly by his other arm and, with the help of Steve, lifted the battered gobioid to his feet.

"That is all I ask." Braakk nodded appreciatively to the elder elf, one seasoned veteran to another.

"What of the other gobioid, the one who escaped?" Puppis asked with worry, glancing back to the thick foliage.

"Did Crimm see where he went?" Brandy chirped in her added question, following the elf girl's look.

"There is no need to seek him out or be concerned about him," Braakk said in a strained whisper, trying to make his voice heard to all. "He will not return to the castle or his fate will be worse than mine. He has failed in his mission and he knows that. He would rather perish here than in the hands of Chameleon, or worse, the Dark Queen herself."

"I hope you are right," Volan replied, nodding grimly.

The group lined up in silence behind the gobioid. Steve and Draco released their grip on the creature, and Braakk swayed uncertainly on his unstable legs. Then slowly and carefully he walked forward and disappeared into the glowing light. Steve and Draco followed closely behind, in turn trailed by Forrest, Brandy, Volan, Puppis, and finally Crimm. They emerged within a blink on the other side of the door. All that surrounded them was blackness. None could see a thing. Not an outline, or a shadow of anything was visible.

"Where are we?" Brandy whispered as softly as possible into the stillness that threatened to smother them. She could feel something watching them, she was sure of it. It was the same feeling she used to get as a child when she would convince herself that some specter or horrible monster was in her closet at night when she went to bed and turned out the bed lamp.

Before anyone could answer, the room sprang into light. Torches, that were lined very closely together, suddenly flared into life. They blazed brightly, causing all to squint their eyes and shield them from the sudden blinding effect.

"Welcome," a silvery voice floated invitingly. "I have been waiting for some time to meet you."

Chameleon easily took the steps two at a time. His energy had been renewed with the thought of the pesky band of humans and elves being done away with. He reached the door to Lacerta's tower chamber in a short period of time. He did not knock before entering, only waved his hand and let the door open at his bidding.

Lacerta's outer work chamber was dimly lit with the early morning grayness. The fat creatures that had bravely walked about in the dark hours the night before, now scurried for cover in the natural glow that bathed the room. The golden door that separated the work chamber from Lacerta's private alcove was opened slightly in an unspoken invitation. After a moments hesitation, Chameleon went to the entrance and slipped silently through.

His Queen's room was not illuminated by the pale light of outside, for her heavy dark shades that covered the windows permitted nothing to pass. The mage's eyes quickly adjusted to the darkness that enveloped the room. His gaze swept to Lacerta's large bed. She still laid, gently tangled, within the soft confines of the sheets. Her silver hair flowed all about her, her pale skin gleamed an invitation in the dimness that surrounded every corner of the room.

"Come closer, Chameleon," Lacerta purred in a near whisper, without moving, from the depths of her slumber.

"Did I disturb you, my Queen," the dark elf began reverently, approaching the bed and stopping at its edge.

"So formal, are we," said a chuckling Lacerta deeply. She lifted her head elegantly and studied the mage close. "You have news for me?" she asked with a raised eyebrow, already knowing the answer.

"Yes," Chameleon halted for a moment, taking one last look at his Queen's peaceful and lovely features. His news would surely change her mood for the worse.

"What is it?"

"There has been a slight problem," Chameleon began, emphatically stressing the word 'problem'.

Lacerta's eyes narrowed severely at her mages tone. She sat up straight in the bed, not bothering to cover the sudden nakedness that her action caused. "What problem?" she hissed slowly.

"The gobioid's no longer control the prisoners in the dragon bridge."

"What?" Lacerta roared in anger. The breathtaking beauty of her face was becoming a horrible mask of rage.

"The elves and humans must have overtaken them somehow. Gobioids are not very bright, it could happen," Chameleon said dryly, looking with admiration at his Queen's nude form.

Lacerta opened her mouth to say something, but snapped it shut. She flung back the covers from her bed, and made no move to catch them before they slid to the cold floor. She climbed from the bed and hastened across the room. Grabbing some black and silver garments, she quickly dressed, ignoring the tangled mass of hair that hung wildly down her back.

"There is something else," Chameleon said softly, not wanting to cause more rage from his Queen, but at the same time knew it was inevitable.

"What?" Lacerta snapped with cold irritability.

"Your pets, the dragons, have left the bridge."

Lacerta froze in her movements. She had needed the few who remained as a final source of extra power to make her plan work without fail.

"Yet, for some unknown reason," Chameleon continued smoothly, "the one you call Crimm did not leave."

"Excellent," the dark Queen exclaimed with a deep sigh. Things were not as bad as they had first appeared. "What have you done to recapture the renegades?"

"I sent Grikk and some of the other gobioids into the bridge to take care of them." The elf turned, so that his Queen could not read the thoughts that floated uncontrollably in his mind. He had taken care of those pesky elves once and for all. They would trouble him or his plans no longer.

"Very well." Lacerta nodded sharply. "Let us see how your kin is faring against my forces," she added, gibing her elf frigidly.

Chameleon cut his razor slit eyes at his Queen. Her face was the picture of beautiful calm once again, but her stare could not be mistaken. She was silently warning him that she held him responsible for what had occurred.

So be it, the elf thought to himself as he followed Lacerta into her tower room. He would have to watch his Queen closely, for he did not plan to fall like some simpering idiot gobioid.

Lacerta passed quickly through her work chamber and into her tower. She ascended a narrow flight of stone steps easily until she was nearly at the top of the peaked ceiling. The alcove they entered was very small. It barely accommodated the presence of the two people, for most of the space was taken up by a large mirror. The mirror's outer shell was made of an ancient black rock that no longer could be found anywhere in all the lands, but the surface of the mirror is what drew Chameleon's gaze. The surface glowed an eerie red, almost the color of flowing blood. The mirror hung freely in the air that surrounded it, nothing supporting its bulk or weight.

Lacerta stared deeply into the swirling red surface. Her hand gingerly stretched forward and touched the smooth glass face. The brushing contact with her fingertips sent shivers of power rushing from her into the flat vision, and with that touch, the vision altered quickly. Shapes and images began taking form before them. It was the gobioids, rushing down on the bedraggled band of elves and humans.

Chameleon and his Queen watched in fascination at the brute strength of the gobioids as they attacked with no hesitation or regard to their own safety. They mused silently in their own way at the skirmish that took place between Braakk and Grikk. Their gazes of fascination soon turned to amazement and then astonishment as the images played out before them, and finally to an end.

Chameleon said nothing. He boiled angrily on the inside. Those stupid creatures that Lacerta seemed so fond of could not ever take care of a tired dirty band of elves.

"It seems we are going to have visitors," Lacerta purred catlike, her eyes glinting at the prospect. Her serene features did nothing to betray the feelings that raged within her. She rubbed her fingertips thoughtfully together. "We must prepare to greet them," she added with a slight evil grin before descending the narrow steps, leaving the dark elf to silently follow.

The group stared in dumb fascination at what they saw. Lacerta, and Chameleon, stood only paces away, and the rest of the room was lined in a host of heavily armed gobioids.

"She looks almost like Lyra," Brandy gasped in a shocked whisper to Forrest who stood near her. Her hand flew to her mouth at once when she realized what she had said aloud.

"You humor me greatly, little one." Lacerta laughed merrily. "Although, you shall soon find that my sister and I are nothing alike." The elegantly dressed Queen advanced toward the human girl, surveying her with interest. She was nearly covered with dried mud. Her long hair was a mat of tangles and dirt. Her clothing was torn, and cuts and bruises showed through in many places, and yet her dark elf had been correct, this one possessed a very strong and vibrant spirit. Pity it would not do her any good in a short while.

"Your little human is not very attractive, my mage," she snickered almost inaudibly to Chameleon, who glowered visibly at her, yet remained silent.

Draco lifted his axe slightly and the others followed suit by bringing out their weapons once more. This only seemed to delight Lacerta further. She eyed the filthy and severely battered group with open amusement.

"You do not actually think that you will survive against us, do you?" she crooned merrily, waving her hands about the room at the heavily armed gobioids. The small band was easily outnumbered five to one.

"Perhaps not," Draco spoke up gruffly, without fear. "We shall not be slaughtered either."

"You misinterpret my actions all together, elder elf. I have no intentions of harming you. You will be made quite comfortable here," Lacerta promised with suave charm. "The choice is yours, of course."

Draco hesitated, not knowing whether he should trust the evil beauty that stood near him. Her flowing silver hair blended perfectly with her long shimmering silver gown. Her eyes beckoned to him, but his mind flared in warning. She could not be trusted. He tore his gaze from the sinking feeling that seemed to overwhelm his by looking at the Dark Queen, and glanced behind him at the others, hoping they would voice an opinion.

"If we die," Volan whispered to the group, "we will never be able to help Lyra. Staying alive is more important at the moment."

"He's right," Steve agreed. "Live to fight another day. Carina needs us alive also. We are no good to her dead." The others reluctantly and slowly nodded their agreement. They did not want to give up to Lacerta, but what choice did they really have.

Draco turned back to Lacerta. "We accept your hospitality," he said with false sincerity through clenched teeth, dropping his mighty axe to the stone floor. It thudded hollowly, and was soon joined by the other weapons dropped by hesitant hands.

"Excellent." Lacerta clasped her hands in delight. She smiled triumphantly at the small band. "You have made a very wise choice."

She turned her attention to the gobioids who stood close by. "Seize them!" she ordered, with an icy tone.

"What?" Forrest and Draco uttered at the same time. They tried to make a grab at their weapons that laid on the floor by their feet, but the gobioids were on them in a flash. The creatures roughly pulled their arms behind them and twisted them until the elves could struggle no more.

Puppis, Brandy, Volan, and Steve were corralled together and surrounded by the creatures. They made no moves to try and fight at the sheer number of opponents that faced them, but fumed silently instead.

Lacerta strolled lazily around them, smirking to herself, until she faced Crimm. The mighty dragon had remain still and quiet. He knew all to well what his outcome was going to be. No doubt he would meet the fate that had befallen his kin. He felt their lost and tortured souls floating all about him in the large castle. He wanted nothing more than to turn this silver beauty to ash, yet at the same time, could not. She held him totally within her power. A power that he must obey.

"My dear, dear Crimm." Lacerta smiled, reaching a delicate white hand out to stroke the dragon's long green snout. "It has been long since we have seen one another."

Crimm remained silent. He narrowed his orb shaped yellow eyes at Lacerta. He pulled his nose from her reach, and sent a helpless glance at the elves and humans. Their fates would not be much better than his own. Possibly worse, for their fate was uncertain.

"Do not ignore me, Crimm," Lacerta warned coolly. "It is very rude."

"What do you wish of me, my Queen?" Crimm thought blandly to her, turning his yellow gaze in her direction. His thoughts betrayed no fear.

"My, my we have changed, have we not?" Lacerta chuckled into the dragon's thoughts with her own dark ones. "You used to be so . . . mellow."

"That was long ago. Much has passed."

"Yes, it has," Lacerta thought, nodding thoughtfully and tapping a delicate finger against her flawless cheek. "All the same, I am glad you have decided to join your friends. Your presence will be most useful." She motioned to three of the gobioids, who stood off in a corner. They responded immediately as if they were puppets.

The creatures cautiously approached the dragon and wrapped a hand pounded golden chain about Crimm's thick long neck, at every moment prepared to subdue the creature if necessary.

However, Crimm made no moves to resist what was befalling him. He sensed the power of retaining that flowed through the chains almost as soon as he had entered the room. He had nowhere to flee, and accepted his fate with a sense of forlorn dejection. His destiny had been sealed.

"It is nice to see that you still have manners." Lacerta grinned slyly at the large submissive reptile.

She turned her back on the dragon and paced a slow circle back toward the front of the group. "Now that only leaves you, Braakk," she said in a slow calculating drawl at the battered gobioid who laid unmoving on the floor covered with filth and blood. The sight of him disgusted her, for he was a traitor.

Braakk blinked his heavy eyes several times, trying to clear away the fogginess that was threatening to overtake them. His Queen appeared to him to be nothing more than a shimmering silver blur. Her voice was that of a songbird, laced with the venom of a snake.

"Did Grikk take your tongue as well as your life?" Lacerta demanded harshly. She expected the gobioids to obey her in all things, and even though he was near death, this one had not.

"I hear you, O Queen," Braakk rasped out hoarsely with all the strength that remained within him. "I hear you and I defy anything that you request of me. I shall die free from those who sought to imprison me."

Lacerta eyed the gobioid uncertainly. None had ever dared speak to her in such a way before. She glanced at the gobioids about the room. They shifted nervously at Braakk's words, but said nothing. "You forget your place, Braakk," she warned the underling, the coldness of her threat lacing her tone.

"I have no place here any longer. Death claims me as I speak, and I proclaim with my last breath that I denounce you and your dark mage. This handful of elves and humans have shown me what honor is, and it is not in this place." Braakk gasped one more rough grating breath, his body shook briefly, and then he was still. His torturous end was over.

"Thank you, Braakk," Steve whispered lightly to the quiet form of the gobioid. He lifted his hand and touched his eyebrow in a brief salute.

"Honor to you," Puppis murmured to the fallen gobioid. Her sentiment was quickly echoed by Draco, Volan, and Forrest. The gobioid had fallen helping them. The elves would not forget that, even if they had been enemies.

"Have a safe trip," Brandy said loudly, daring her enemies with her eyes. She smiled weakly at the broken figure. She shook her head as a single tear of tired sadness escaped her.

Lacerta stared in disbelief at the group before her. She could not believe what she had just witnessed. These elves and humans had actually done honor to one that they were foes with. She shook her head in contempt and disgust. "You are weak and despicable creatures," she nearly shouted at them. "Take them to the cells at once," she ordered the gobioids, then turned and left the chamber in a silver flash, with Chameleon and the three gobioids leading an unresisting Crimm close behind.

The elves and humans looked at one another dejectedly, for once again, they were prisoners. Slowly, they followed the gobioids out of the room and down a dark corridor, deeper into the heart of the cold, lifeless castle.

CHAPTER TWENTY-TWO

"What do you think they have done with Crimm?" Brandy asked glumly after they had been sitting in dark silence for what seemed an eternity. The gobioids had taken them far down into the castle. The air was cold and stale, and moisture seemed to hang off of the walls. They had been unceremoniously thrown into a large dank cell that reeked of death. The gobioids hastily retraced their steps, as if even they did not like being in this part of the castle, and had fled back up the stairs and out of sight. The prisoners only source of light was a lone torch that had been left burning in a steel holder on the wall, and as they sat pondering their fates, its flickering life was fading fast.

"Who knows," Steve spat angrily at what had befallen them. "Lacerta probably ate him for dinner, for that matter."

"That is gross, Steve," Brandy said grimacing at her friend and placing a hand over her loud rumbling stomach. She had been hungry, but not any longer after Steve's outburst.

"Can you reach him, Draco?" Puppis asked quietly, from where she sat huddled closely to Volan for warmth and reassurance.

"I will try." The elder elf sighed wearily. For the first time on this quest, he was beginning to miss his warm fireplace and his wife's hot cooked meals. He adored his home life, but roaming had always been in his heart and blood.

He shut his eyes and let his mind wander out. Taking a deep breath, he completely relaxed his entire body. His mental self slipped effortlessly from his physical being. He looked at the youngsters crowded around him. They all had eager eyes fixed on his now vacant form. A smile crept across his fatigued features. They had all come so far, and for what, he wondered. Slowly he slipped through the bars and left the cell. He retraced his steps that he had taken down to this pit, until he was once again in the chamber that they had been recaptured in. He then found Crimm's footsteps on the damp floor. With his keen dragon sense, he could easily make out the trail that the mighty reptile had left behind as he had been led forward from the room. The trail wandered round and round the castle, finally settling itself in a large underground chamber.

Draco stood at the entrance of the large room, seeing everything easily from his vantage point. Crimm, still bound by the bright gold chain that hung loosely from his neck, was tethered near a large roaring fire pit. Chameleon and Lacerta stood near a smooth black table, talking loudly to one another, but their words did not reach his ears. Although he could see, he could hear nothing at all. The elder elf looked past the two who held him and his friends in a cell below, to a tremendous crystal that seemed to hang in the air, as if floating.

It is she, he thought to himself. Just as the human girl had describe. The Keeper of Spring, Mother to them all, Lyra was trapped within the confines of the glittering stone. This was indeed serious. How would they be able to escape from their cell, free Lyra, and help Carina at the same time? For once, Draco was at a loss for a plan. He hoped the children would not be.

Slowly and unhappily he retraced his steps, remembering each turn that he made, and returned to his still form in the cold, uninviting cell.

"Are you alright, Draco," a gentle touch from Puppis and her softly spoken words broke through the haze of his trance.

"Yes, child, quite all right," the tired elf responded with a feeble smile. "I have seen that in which you have, child." The elder elf turned his gaze toward Brandy. "Lyra is indeed imprisoned just as you told us. It is all as you said, the room, the table and her crystal tomb."

"So what do we do now?" Brandy asked all those around her. She was fresh out of ideas, but the thought of dying in this cell was more than she could stand. She wanted a chance.

Draco said nothing, only shook his head in slow resignation. Volan and Puppis looked at one another, tears of frustration flooded the elf girl's eyes, but she refused to let them fall.

"We need to find a way out," Forrest said, stating the obvious. He rose to his feet and pushed on the cold steel bars of the cell door. They were embedded into the thick stone wall of the castle and did not even rustle when he pressed his full weight upon it.

"That obviously isn't the way," Steve snapped irritably at the elf, instantly regretting his tone. Forrest wasn't the problem here, Chameleon, Lacerta and the gobioids were.

"Sorry," he mumbled miserably, running a hand through his tangled hair. "I'm just tired, hungry, dirty, and really pissed off," Steve tried to explain with a feeble shrug of his shoulders.

"Do not trouble yourself with apologies, my friend," offered Forrest, placing an understanding hand on the human's shoulder. "I think we can all correlate to how you feel."

"Thanks." Steve grinned sheepishly, still ashamed of his words.

"Don't worry," Brandy offered with a bright smile and a knowing nod, sounding a little more confident than she felt. "We'll think of something. We haven't come this far to fail now." At least I hope not, anyway, she added silently to herself.

Carina laid dozing in the comfortable cocoon of her bed. Slowly she opened her sky colored eyes and looked at the canopy over her. Someone or thing was in her room. She had not heard the door open, but she could definitely feel a presence. She was sure that she was no longer alone in the room. Gingerly she lifted her head and scanned the room.

"You!" she gasped in a solid mixture of alarm and fear at what she saw. The Dark Queen herself sat in silence in the chair next to her bed.

Lacerta chuckled mildly at the elf princess. "You act as if I am a monster, my dear child."

"You are," Carina accused the lovely, silver clad woman. "All that you have done is monstrous. How could you have imprisoned your own sister?"

"Those are very harsh words indeed, small one. Have I not treated you well enough?" Lacerta asked with a wave about the room, ignoring the question about Lyra. "You do not seem that uncomfortable."

"Comfort is nothing without freedom," whispered Carina.

"Freedom is it? That will be here soon enough," Lacerta purred.

"What does that mean?" Carina asked, narrowing her eyes suspiciously.

"The dawn of Spring is upon us. Only a few more turns of the hour hand and you will be free of that which binds you to this land."

"I will no let you touch me," vowed Carina belligerently, hate and anger beginning to brew within her.

Lacerta laughed aloud in pure amusement. "How I wish you would have been acquired for me sooner. I would have truly enjoyed taming that wild temper of yours, but, chatter is not the reason for my visit," Lacerta began, rising with a flourish from her seat and walking absently about the room. "I have things to show you, and we need to begin."

"I am not going anywhere," Carina stated defiantly, crossing her arms and legs tightly together. "Especially with you," she added with a stubborn glare.

"Yes you are," Lacerta said evenly, the cold calculating tone entering her simply spoken words. She stared intently at the elf maiden on the bed, using her power to force the girl forward.

Carina instantly felt what the Dark Queen was attempting to do. She opened her mind and let the raw untrained power flow from her own being. She quickly threw up a wall of energy to block the surge of power that came from Lacerta. The princess offered a small triumphant smile when she realized that she still controlled her own limbs and not the other way around.

An evil glint of rage stole in Lacerta's eyes. She clenched her perfect pale lips tightly together in fury. "You dare toy with me?" she roared fiercely.

Carina's small smile faded almost as quickly as it had begun. She scooted back against the headboard of the bed and held a fluffy pillow protectively in front of her like it were a heavy shield.

"I will show you what real power is," bellowed Lacerta, anger crackling around her like lightning. Her beautiful features twisting malignantly in hatred. She raised her hand and pointed her fore finger at the bed in which Carina huddled on. Flames erupted all about the shrinking princess, creeping closer to her with every heartbeat.

Carina's eyes flew open in fear, panic gripped at her insides. She pressed her back tightly against the wood behind her, trying to escape the deadly fire that crept slowly up on her, inch by inch eating away at the silky bed sheets. She could feel the heat that the orange flames gave off, and desperately wanted to jump from the burning linens but could not. She seemed trapped with no where to go.

Just as abruptly as they had begun, the flames ceased. It was as if they had never been. Carina carefully placed her fingertips on the spot that was only moments ago alive with fire. It was cool and smooth to the touch. The bed and its coverings showed no sign what so ever of having been alight. Had she imagined it?

The princess turned her fearful gaze toward Lacerta, who smirked in satisfied content. "Were they ever burning, or was it an illusion?" she asked in a timid voice.

"It was quite real," Lacerta gloated, the calm beauty back on her face. "If I had chosen, you would be cinder by now."

Carina swallowed dryly and hugged the pillow closer to her. She looked warily at the Dark Queen, almost expecting another onslaught of destruction.

"Shall we leave now?" Lacerta asked with a simple glimpse at the girl huddled on the bed, ignoring her pitifully frightened look. She turned, her silver gown rustling softly with each movement, and waved her hand at the wall making the door visible.

Carina did not answer, or argue back. Somewhat unsure, she climbed off the bed and quickly slid her feet into her slippers. She followed Lacerta from the room and down the dimly lit corridor, making sure that she did not get too close to her, but not too far back to miss anything that the Dark Queen may say to her. They walked silently for many long minutes until Carina heard a gentle breeze of music drifting by. After a brief moment of straining to listen, she realized that Lacerta had begun to hum. It was soft and compelling, yet totally foreign to her, and then she heard an unusual scampering sound. Her eyes search the dark shadows for an answer to what made the noise and easily found it.

Rats. Not small mice, like the ones who occupied the woods, but large, fat, ugly rats. They were drawn to the sound of Lacerta's voice. They seemed to almost dance in tune to the melody of her humming. Carina lifted the hem of her skirt to keep the rodents from getting tangled in it as they rushed by her to be close to the silver form of the Dark Queen.

The princess continued to keep her distance from the mass of flea infested creatures that jumped about the floor before her. Abruptly the humming stopped and so did Lacerta with her mass of rodents. They sat expectantly about her, looking up with beady black eyes. She turned and smiled sweetly in the torch light.

"Go down those steps. Your would be saviors are there," she informed Carina with an amused chuckle.

Carina skeptically looked down the dark steps that led below, but felt it wise to say nothing. Slowly she began descending the steep steps, keeping a hand placed against the wintry, slime covered wall for balance in the black darkness. Carefully she took each step, at any moment expecting something to grab her from any direction. Just as her eyes were adjusting to the inkiness of her surroundings, a torch flared into life near her head. She halted her progress, blinking several times to clear her vision, and continued cautiously on. When the light of the first torch would no longer reach into the gloom, another would mysteriously appear and light her way. It continued the same way until she reached the bottom of the stairs.

With a deep breath she released her hold on the wall and stepped forward. Instantly a torch illuminated the darkness before her. A loud gasp escaped her lips at what she saw. A small iron bound cell, and within the confines of that cell was her friends. Draco, Volan, Puppis, Forrest, Brandy and Steve. They were all, thankfully, still alive. Carina instantly noticed their tired features and ruined clothing. They were covered with dried mud, and all had several cuts and bruises, but they were still alive.

The flash of a torch lighting and a loud gasp caught the attention of all in the cell. Simultaneously they all turned in the direction of the sound.

"Carina?" Puppis choked out in disbelief. "Is it really you?"

"Yes," Carina said softly, not trusting her voice. Tears of joy sprang to her eyes and blurred her vision. She rushed to the cell and pulled desperately on the cold bars.

Steve was the first to recover. He went to the door and gingerly brushed the tears that escaped down the princesses face. "I am sorry," he began awkwardly. "I'm afraid I have failed in helping you," he stammered.

"No." Carina smiled weakly through her tears. "Just having you here makes hope possible." She reached her hand through the bars and lightly touched Steve's bruised cheek. "I just wish we had not been separated," she whispered for his ears only.

Steve grasped Carina's hand and held it tightly, wanting the reassurance to continue that he felt with her presence. He felt her warmth spreading over him like wildfire, defrosting the despondent chill that had covered him and buried itself within the depths of his bones.

"Are you well, child," Draco asked with fatherly concern as he approached.

"Have they hurt you?" Volan echoed.

"Did you manage to escape?" Forrest asked hopefully.

Carina smiled widely at the rush of question and the feeling of care that she received from each. "I am fine," she answered. "I am not harmed, and no," she said sadly, shaking her head. "I did not escape."

"How did you get here?" Brandy asked, knowing she wouldn't like the answer.

"Lacerta brought me here," she answered solemnly.

"Why?" asked Puppis, not believing it was out of kindness for her princess.

"I do not know," Carina said tears running hotly down her pale face. "Only that I am sure she knows how it pains me to see you all like this."

"Do not worry. That matters not, child," Draco said, patting the princesses arm. "It is enough that you are safe for the moment. We shall find a way out of this prison and come to you," he stated certainly. All around the elder elf nodded their agreement. They knew not how, but somehow, they knew they would.

"Have you seen Lyra?" Forrest asked Carina. He looked at her in wonder. She seemed to have aged in years in the short span of days that had passed since they had seen each other last. Her eyes held a source of wisdom and knowing that he had never noticed before.

"Yes, but more than that, we have spoken," Carina answered with unrestrained excitement in her voice that pushed away her grief.

"How?" Puppis blurted out, glancing past the princess for any sign of Lacerta.

"It is hard to explain. It is more than mind speech though. Since I have been here in the castle I have possessed a power that I never knew I held. I can do things that I thought were lost to all elves."

"The blood of your ancestors must run strongly through your veins," Draco offered with an insightful nod.

"You are correct elder elf," Lacerta's smooth voice filtered through the thick damp air. She walked with the grace of a timid deer down the stone steps, almost seeming to float. Her host of rats followed her compliantly, eager to be near their mistress. "You know much of the elfin history. I am surprised you did not see the power in your princess sooner, but that is of no matter now," she added with a small shrug of her shoulders.

"Release us," Forrest snarled angrily at the silver beauty emanated an aura of shimmering light about her. "You have no right to hold us like animals."

Lacerta's laughter tinkled merrily from her lips. "I do as I choose, and nothing else," she easily informed the elf before her. She looked intently at the enraged male. He was intriguing, much like an animal, wild and untamed.

"Perhaps I shall not eliminate you right away," she drawled slowly. "You are rather attractive, in a crude sort of way."

Forrest fumed, his face growing crimson, yet held his tongue. How dare she insinuate interest in him, he thought fiercely.

Lacerta clasped her hands together and turned her attention to Carina. "We must leave now, my dear. You have a very important engagement to keep."

Hesitantly, Carina pulled herself free from Steve's grip. Obediently she followed Lacerta back up the stairs, pausing to take one last look at those she left behind. Tears threatened to overtake her again at the look on the faces that she saw. Blinking heavily several times, she turned back to the silver form in front of her and walked forward silently.

CHAPTER TWENTY-THREE

Chameleon stood in the darkness, his eyes seeing everything that was passing before him. His Queen, Lacerta, led a very subdued and compliant Carina along the dark passages of the castle to the cell that held the others of her kind, and the two humans. An array of rats danced merrily all around the tall silver clad woman, intently listening to her soft humming. The dark elf narrowed his eyes at the scene. What was his Queen attempting to do, he wondered. What would come of her showing the princess where the other captives were?

He wrapped his light cloak around his arms and wove his concealing spell into the air about himself. This was one of the things that Lacerta had not taught him, but that he had found for himself while spending countless days and nights in the huge library, lined completely with ancient tomes and volumes of hidden knowledge. He had used this spell many times when wanting to gain information without being seen. He had even practiced the spell in the presence of his Queen without her knowledge, so he felt confident in his stalking of her now.

Chameleon waited patiently in the shadows, just above the steps, while Carina briefly talked with her kin. He knew well the reason for her visit now. Her spirit was slowly being broken by Lacerta to make her less of a threat. His Queen wanted to let the little princess know just how feeble her magic was against that of her own. It appeared that Lacerta had succeeded, for when they emerged back up from the cell below, Carina's face was pale and drawn, her confidence was visibly shaken. She hung her head in despair, and clasped her hands tightly before her, turning them white at the knuckles.

They passed easily by, not sensing his presence in any way, and vanished from sight down the dark uninviting corridor, followed by the rats.

The dark elf smiled to himself as he released the concealing spell. He shook his cloak back and let it ripple behind him as he descended the stone steps to the cell below. Torches sprang to life with each step that he took downward. When he reached the bottom, all eyes turned in his direction. Again a smile flickered across his lips at the impact his arrival had on those before him.

"What do you want?" Steve glared at the smirking elf outside of the cell. He wished that Chameleon would come closer so that he could rip him to shreds.

"No doubt to wound us deeper," grumbled Draco angrily. He longed for his axe to deal with the grinning mage.

"You injure me greatly with your tones," Chameleon feigned hurt poorly. "I am only here to see that you are still intact within our hospitality. I would not want the rats to find you too soon."

"What is the difference?" Puppis pointed out in a soft tired voice. "The end result is going to be the same, is it not?"

"Do not be such a pessimist," scolded the dark elf, pacing slowly back and forth before the cell. "I just may allow you to live to see the downfall of your kin."

"Do you not mean our kin," Draco reminded the bitter elf, with a raised eyebrow.

"No!" Chameleon snarled loudly. "Elves no longer mean anything to me. They have banished me, so now I banish them."

"Then, I would just as soon you kill me here and now," Volan said evenly, walking to stand at the front of the cell. "I would rather face death than watch those that I love suffer and die at the hand of one of their own."

"Do not tempt me," warned Chameleon in a dark tone.

"I was not trying to," Volan answered back quickly.

"What do you want?" Forrest asked, echoing the human male's earlier words, not phrasing his request as a question, but more of a demanding statement.

Chameleon anger was instantly replaced by amusement. He chuckled as he strolled with slow deliberate steps towards the cell. "You are very entertaining indeed, Forrest. You who are so sullen and mighty at the same time. Your emotions betray you like a running stream. I can see right through you to the core. I can see through all of you. You fear me, yet your hate of me will undoubtedly make you reckless if given the chance. It is a very interesting combination. I would almost be tempted to let you try and escape this cell if circumstances were different, but they are not. The prophecy of old will come to pass in the short span of a few hours. Believe me, I will make all of you painfully aware of it when it happens." The dark elf halted his steady stream of words to let their sharp edges sink in. He smiled to himself, and lifted his powerful hands in the air. The lock of the cell clicked and the door slowly drifted open. The occupants of the cell watched curiously, none making a move to exit.

"Come, Brandy," Chameleon said in an almost gentle way to the trembling human girl who was trying to make herself invisible from his view. "You do not belong here. It is time for you to meet your destiny."

"She's not going anywhere with you," Steve blurted out before Brandy could utter a word. He walked to the entrance of the cell and attempted to pass through, but when he did, he met with a wall of electrifying energy that lifted him from his feet and sent him sailing to the other end of the small cell. He hit the bars with a terrible thud and landed in a heap on the cold damp floor.

Brandy rushed to her friend and knelt beside him. Gently, she brushed his tangled hair from his face and found him to be conscious.

"That hurt," he groaned weakly, struggling to sit up.

"How dare you hurt my friend," she shouted at the dark elf outside of the cell, her fear of him diminishing and being replaced with anger. "You could have killed him."

"That was of his own doing." Chameleon shrugged without care. "Only you may pass from the cell, he was a fool to try and leave, for he was not given permission."

"You are the fool if you think that she is leaving with you," Forrest challenged, placing himself like a barricade between Brandy and the dark elf.

Chameleon shook his head slowly from side to side. "Do not try and stop what is unavoidable. Brandy is to be my mate, it has been decided." He laughed sharply. "By myself, of course." He narrowed his eyes sinisterly at Forrest. "Stand aside or be removed," he warned lowly.

"Make me."

"As you wish," the dark elf said without care. He pointed his left forefinger at the defiant elf and spoke quietly to himself.

Forrest grabbed at his throat as his eyes widened in surprise and alarm. Unseen hands were wrapped about his neck and squeezing the air effortlessly from him. He flung himself about the cell trying to release the deadly grasp. Volan and Draco rushed to his side and tried to offer assistance, but nothing was to be done for him. Forrest's vision began to spin as his need for oxygen increased. He tried to curse the mage with his last breath, but no sound would come. He fell to his knees, his skin growing paler with each passing moment.

Brandy watched in horror at what was happening. She knew what she must do. Any delay would cost Forrest with his life. She jumped to her feet and hastened to the cell door. Not bothering to hesitate, she shot through the opening to Chameleon.

"Please, release him," she begged, clutching at his arm, trying to pull it, and the powerful force that it held, from Forrest. "Please."

Chameleon lowered his arm, releasing the struggling elf, and looked into the flickering depths of the human girl's bottomless eyes. They were flooded with tears, but held a sparkle that called to him like a beacon deep in the starless night.

"Please," Brandy pleaded again. "I will go with you. I will do as you ask, but please don't harm my friends."

Chameleon hesitated, then completely closed off his channel of power. "This one time I will do this for you," he said for her ears only.

"Thank you," Brandy whispered sincerely, smearing the tears from her face with the back of her grimy hand.

"Brandy, don't," Steve called powerlessly from the cell. He did not have the strength to rise yet, but he could easily see what was happening. His friend was giving into the mage for them.

"I will be alright," Brandy said with a bold smile at those she was leaving behind in the cell. She watched the door shut and lock itself back. She felt Chameleon's light cape settle feather like over her shoulders and arms, and she saw the haunted look that flooded into Forrest's gem like eyes as he still gasped for breath. Her breathing came in a ragged gasp, for suddenly the air seemed very thick and heavy, and unbearable to breath. All before her began to swim. Then she saw nothing. Exhausted darkness overtook her, and her knees gave away.

"Brandy, you know that I love you," Forrest began in a serious tone.

Brandy gave him a wry smile and batted her lashes seductively at him. They were sitting under an ancient mushroom shaped oak tree. Its trunk was as big around as the arm span of five people. Its limbs were lush and full of dark green leaves. Birds chirped happily in its branches and serenaded them with soft notes. The wind blew peaceful breezes through the endless twists and turns of the tree's being. Brandy sighed contentedly and wrapped her arms tighter around Forrest. She had never felt so happy or at ease in her whole life.

Forrest looked deeply into the serene face of the human girl who laid on his lap. She was the most beautiful creature he had ever seen. Her shiny hair flowed recklessly over his legs. The curls danced playfully in the gentle puffs of air. He took his finger and lightly traced the line of her chin and jaw, letting it trail playfully down her curving throat.

"That tickles," Brandy giggled the words, wriggling into a sitting position, and half heartedly trying to crawl out of the elf's reach.

"There is no escape, my love." Forrest grinned in reply, pulling Brandy back onto his lap, showering her lips, cheeks, and throat with light, feathery kisses.

"Who's running?" Brandy murmured, running her fingers through the silky length of Forrest's black mane. She leaned her head back, letting Forrest explore every inch of her pale soft flesh with his sensuous lips.

"I think you may possess magic after all," Forrest breathed heavily into Brandy's thick swirling hair.

Brandy's laugher was velvet. "You haven't seen anything yet," she whispered, pressing her lips delicately to his.

"What are you doing with my mate!" a voice demanded with the fury of a thunder storm from behind them.

Forrest and Brandy were on their feet in an instant. Brandy squinted into the waning sun light at what she saw. It was Chameleon. His clothing were torn and ragged. An arrow protruded horribly from his chest, and his complexion was even paler than usual.

"Leave my mate alone," Chameleon hissed through clenched teeth at Forrest. "Touch her again and you die."

"No! No! No!" Brandy shrieked in despair. "This can't be happening. You're dead. I saw you die in the castle."

"I will never leave you. Not even death cannot separate us." Chameleon laughed wildly, his eyes gleaming wickedly. "I will always be with you."

"No!" Brandy yelled long and loud, over and over again.

"What bother pretty human girl," a squeaky voice shook Brandy from her all too vivid nightmare.

She sat up in a large bed with crimson sheets and coverings practically strangling her. She was covered with a thin layer of sweat, and her breathing was erratic. She looked frantically about the room, not recognizing her surroundings. "Why won't he leave me alone," she sobbed in anguish. Tears flooded her eyes and streamed down her flushed cheeks. She hugged her knees close to her body and rocked back and forth, trying desperately to soothe her frazzled nerves.

"Who not leave pretty human," the squeaky voice spoke again.

Brandy blinked away her tears and looked at the foot of the bed, seeing a rather large rat staring at her. She squirmed back a few inches on the bed, not wanting the rodent to come near her.

"Pretty human safe here. Tar protect," the fat rodent announced proudly, waving a small front paw at her in a gracious type of bow.

"Thank you," Brandy said, in a tearful voice, sniffing back her fears. "I think," she added to herself with a skeptical look at the talkative rodent. Another strange thing in this land to get used to.

"I Tar," the rat began, bouncing up the bed clothes to sit beside Brandy on a large fluffy pillow. "Who you?"

"I'm Brandy Wells"

"Nice know you, Brandy Wells," the rodent said. Tar grinned, sharp yellow teeth showing eagerly through his twitching whiskers in a pleased smile.

Brandy smiled indecisively at the rodent who talked and seemed genuinely pleased to make her acquaintance. She pushed back the bed covers, and for the first time realized that she was clean. Not only her body, but her hair as well. For the first time in many days, she was not covered with grime, dirt, and mud. It felt wonderful.

Her hair hung long and full, red highlights glimmering brightly in the deep brown depths of her tresses. Few of the bruises and scrapes that she had remained. She was dressed in a long shimmering green sleeping gown. Thin, braided straps ran over her shoulders and attached to the low cut front and form fitting body of the dress. The soft, silky material hugged her hips and flared out gracefully at the knees and ankles, to provide a swirling motion when she walked. Silk slippers, encrusted with shiny diamonds, rested on a tiny footstool by the edge of the bed. When Brandy placed them on her feet, she found them to be a perfect fit.

"Just like Cinderella," she mumbled sarcastically to herself, her sullen voice echoing hollowly off of the walls in the quiet room.

Brandy crossed the dimly lit room and stood before a long dressing mirror. She studied her image closely. She did indeed look very elegant in the luxurious gown, but the traces of fatigue could not be missed from around her eyes.

Carefully, she wandered about the confines of her prison. There was no doubt that she was in Chameleon's chamber. His dark clothing hung neatly in a wardrobe near the large bed. It's his bed, she told herself, that she had been sleeping in. She wondered if the dark elf himself had been the one who bathed and dressed her. She hoped not.

Brandy continued her survey of the sleeping chamber. The curtains, linens, and rugs were all the color of midnight and scarlet. With a grimace, she realized that it suited Chameleon perfectly. For his soul was as dark as night. She walked carefully to the door that led from the elf's chamber. Touching the door with timid fingers, Brandy found that it easily swung open. She stared into the dark deepness of beyond. Gathering all of her courage, she stepped forward into the room. When she did so, it flared into light by a suddenly blazing fire.

"Tar, like that trick," the rat stated in his squeaky voice, materializing out of nowhere at the human girl's heel.

Brandy jumped and clutched her trembling hands together. "Don't scare me like that, Tar," she scolded the cheerful rodent gently.

"Tar, sorry," the rat apologized, stroking Brandy's skirt bottom with small paws. "Please no mad at Tar."

In spite of her severe dislike of rodents, Brandy smiled down at the humble creature. "Don't worry, I'm not mad at you, Tar," she began with a slight grin. "You just startled me, that's all."

"Tar do no more," he promised, bobbing up and down, scurrying around Brandy's feet.

"What is this place?" Brandy asked in amazement at all that she saw. Hundreds of leather bound books lined many tall book cases. Several tables were covered with bubbling potions over small flames, and tubes that held things she did not recognize. Oil lamps hung from the ceiling, as did many different types of chains that seemed to be attached to nothing. Crystal bottles containing many different colors of inks and dyes were surrounded by gold and silver quills. Unusual charts and drawings were scattered about, and they too meant nothing at all to the confused human.

"This master's work place. Very important place," Tar said with a knowing air. "I watch master's work place," he added importantly.

"You have quite a bit of responsibility then," Brandy commented to the little rodent, who seemed eager for any conversation.

"Tar important," the rat agreed, grinning and standing of its hind legs, twitching his long scaly tail.

"Yes, you must be," Brandy returned gently. "It is very important work guarding a prisoner, such as myself."

Tar cocked his head and looked curiously at the human. "Pretty Brandy no prisoner," he stated matter of factly. "Pretty Brandy master's mate."

Brandy looked at the rodent, choosing her words carefully. "You mean I can leave this chamber if I would like?"

Tar shook his head firmly. "No, no. Pretty Brandy must stay here. Safer here. Tar take care pretty Brandy. Tar do all for pretty Brandy."

"Oh, I see," Brandy murmured softly. "Well thank you, Tar. That is very kind of you."

She turned and walked slowly back into the room. She wondered how she was going to escape from her new cell and get back to Steve and the others. How long had she slept for? It didn't feel as though it were for any length of time. She wondered what time is was. Perhaps morning had passed? Maybe it was already too late to do anything? No, she shook her head firmly. Chameleon would have come back to gloat if the dawn of Spring had already passed. She had to think of something.

The swirling mist of a mirror caught her attention. She walked to the black carved table and looked at the mirror. Its surface was smooth glass, but she could make out a faint spiral motion deep within its shiny depths. She reached her hand out to touch it, but was halted by Tar's voice.

"No touch," he squeaked an urgent warning. "Make master very mad."

"It's okay, Tar," she said, lifting the mirror from its holder. "See, nothing happened."

"Master yell at Tar. No touch, he say."

Brandy smiled at the fearful rodent and knelt down on the floor by the table. "Come here, Tar," she said gently to the rodent, patting the space beside her.

Tar scurried close to her and planted his front feet on her leg.

"You can look at it," Brandy said, offering Tar a chance to look at his reflection.

A twitchy grin immediately creased his furry face. "Pretty mirror. Tar see self."

"Tar is a very handsome rat," Brandy assured the rodent in a convincing tone.

"Not pretty like pretty Brandy," he chatted back.

"You are very kind, Sir Tar."

"Pretty Brandy kind. Show Tar mirror," Tar squeaked. "But what master say?" he added glancing back at the doorway.

"Didn't you tell me that I was your master's mate?" Brandy began, a plan suddenly forming in her mind.

"Yes," Tar bobbed eagerly.

"Then if I say it is okay to use something, it should be okay. Right?"

Tar thought silently for a moment. Mulling over what he had been told. "Yes, yes. Pretty Brandy right. Master say I do for you. I do for him too, so it is same," he squeaked in excitement at the new revelation.

"Then would you do a big favor for me?" Brandy asked, stroking Tar's small head with light fingertips.

"Anything pretty Brandy," Tar chatted eagerly, scurrying all about the room.

Brandy rose to her feet and went back into the work room, Tar close to her heels. Picking up one of the silver writing quills, she turned and faced Tar. "Do you know where the other human like me is being held with the elves?"

"Yes." Tar nodded, anxious to do make his mistress happy.

"Would you bring him this?" she asked in a pleading voice, holding out the quill.

Tar quickly took the quill from Brandy's hand and placed it between his strong jaws. Suddenly he stopped, dropped the quill to the floor, and faced his mistress. "You sure okay? Not make master angry?"

"No, of course not," Brandy assured the indecisive rodent with as much confidence as possible. "You are helping me aren't you? And Master Chameleon said that you can help me, right?" she added, hoping fervrently that Tar believed her.

"Pretty Brandy right," Tar squeaked, picking the quill back up in his teeth, and heading for a hole by the door. "Be back soon," he promised as he vanished from sight.

Brandy let out a relieved sigh. Now to get out of here herself, she thought.

CHAPTER TWENTY-FOUR

Tar scurried down the dark halls and the steep steps until he stood before the cell of sullen prisoners. He dropped the quill on the floor and stood on his hind legs, surveying the occupants in the cell. His sides heaved deeply with each breath that he took. He was very weary. His front legs and paws were sore from the long run, for he had not stopped once to rest. It had been worth the trip, the little rodent thought to himself. Pretty Brandy would be pleased that he served her so well.

Tar picked the quill back up and advanced to the barred door of the cell. The elf female turned in his direction and eyed him with open curiosity. The rodent waved a shy paw at her when she advanced in his direction.

"Hello there, little fellow," Puppis offered gently, crouching down by the door, looking with keen interest at the small creature who stared knowingly at her.

"Who are you talking to, Pup?" Volan asked his friend, giving her an odd look.

"A rat," she replied with a small laugh. "A most unusual rat at that. He has a silver writing quill in his mouth."

"Me no rat, me Tar," he announced importantly, dropping the quill and informing all the occupants in the cell, who now looked with open interest at him.

"Where did you come from, Tar?" Draco asked, intrigued by the rodents use of intelligent speech.

"Master Chameleon's chamber."

"Great," Steve moaned. "The torture has begun. Rats with quills to do us in, and who knows what else."

Tar paced about, twitching his whiskers, and looked at the human male. "You pretty Brandy friend?" he asked with an uncertain air. This human's tone was not pleasant.

Steve stared at the rat. "Where is Brandy? What has that monster done with her?" he almost shouted at the rodent, causing it to scurry back into the shadows.

"Great going, big mouth," scolded Puppis, swatting Steve on the arm the way she had seen Brandy do many times in the past.

Steve was taken aback by the elf girl's reaction. His face broke into a wide grin. "I guess I deserved that," he said with a chuckle.

"You had better apologize to the little one out there," Forrest suggested, pointing into the silent gloom. "It is obvious that he came here looking for you."

Steve took a deep breath of resignation and shrugged his shoulders as Forrest's words sunk in. "I'm sorry if I startled you Tar," he called out. "I didn't mean to."

"Really convincing," Volan muttered to his human friend.

"So I'm not used to talking to rats, okay."

"You not mad at Tar?" a squeaky voice called from the shadows.

"No, of course not," Puppis said encouragingly. "Come back out and tell us about Brandy."

Tar crept forward, carefully keeping an eye on the human and his sharp voice. "Pretty Brandy very nice to Tar. Talk to Tar. Pet Tar. Tar like pretty Brandy."

"So do we," Draco spoke in a gentle tone to the rodent.

Steve dropped to his knees and looked intently at Tar. "Sorry if I yelled, but Brandy is my closest friend. I was just worried about her."

"Pretty Brandy fine. Tar protect her," Tar replied inching closer to the cell again.

"What is the quill for, Tar?" Volan asked, unable to contain his inquisitiveness any longer.

"Present for human male," Tar stated brightly, remembering his errand. He picked up the quill and shoved it between the bars with his small capable paws. "Pretty Brandy send."

"That was very considerate of her," Steve replied, nodding appreciatively. "You must thank Brandy for me, since I am locked in here."

"Tar will do." Tar bounced around the cold stone floor. "Tar do good."

"Yes." Steve couldn't help but grin at the little rodent. "Tar did very good."

Forrest looked at the silver quill that Steve beamed at in his hand. He opened his mouth to asked that in which all his friends were about to ask, when Steve shook his head silently, keeping his question unasked.

"Tar leave now. Go back to pretty Brandy. Tar protect pretty Brandy," he stated again. Flipping his scaly tail, he turned to retreat back up the stairs.

"Wait, Tar," Steve called to the rodent. "I have something for you, too."

"For Tar?" he echoed, beady eyes wide with uncontained pleasure.

Steve dug deep into his tattered jeans pocket and withdrew the stone that they had used to escape form the gobioids. When Brandy saw it, she would know that he had gotten the quill that she had sent.

"This is for you," he said, placing it on the floor outside of the cell.

"Ooh. Very pretty," Tar gasped in uncontrolled joy, reaching for the dull stone. "Tar like very much." Tar placed the stone in his mouth, carefully closing his teeth against the sharp edge, and raced back into the darkness. The faint scraping sound of his claws could be heard briefly, rushing up the steps. Then there was silence.

"I tell you Forrest, Brandy is one clever girl. You had better not let her slip through your fingers." Steve grinned deviously, patting the confused and embarrassed elf on the shoulder.

"Are you going to tell us about the quill or not," Forrest shot back, a little more irritated than he had intended.

Steve laughed and shook his head in amusement. "If it wasn't so dark, I'd be willing bet our friend here is blushing," he said elbowing Draco, who grinned along with the others in the cell. It was painfully obvious to all the feeling Forrest harbored for the human. Obvious to all except himself, of course.

Finally, the scowling elf's face broke into a grin. "Okay, I give up. Now will you please tell us about the quill?"

"This, my friends, is a tool for the fine art of picking locks," Steve said with a flourish, placing the point of the quill into the lock on the front of the cell.

"Picking locks," Puppis echoed, trying to understand. "What is that?"

"Back where we live, in the human world, things are not very trusting. We have to put locks on everything that we own or it will be stolen. Brandy has a terrible habit of locking herself out of her house. I have become quite proficient over the years of fiddling with the lock to get her back in. She knew this would be just the thing to get through the lock on this door."

"Do you think it will work, child?" Draco asked, intrigued by the human's ability to free them with a mere writing quill.

"No problem." Steve grinned with a wink. He twisted the quill around in the hole until he heard a slight click. Leaning against the door it smoothly swung open. "The pen is mightier than the sword," he quoted, grinning and holding the quill up.

"Amazing, you did it," Volan commented. "This must be your magic."

"Will we be able to pass through?" Puppis asked, remembering what had happened to Steve earlier.

"There is only one way to find out," Forrest said. Before anyone could try and stop him, he walked through the opening, clenching his fists tightly by his sides, expecting the worst.

"I guess we can," Steve returned with a smile, and just as quickly shot through the opening, not wanting re-experience the pain of the blast he had taken.

"Where to now?" asked Volan, looking into the darkness up the stairs.

"Now we go and stop Lacerta," Draco said moving forward without fear of what stood ahead.

And get Carina, too, Steve thought with determined silence.

"It could take hours trying to find the chamber where the Keeper of Spring is being held," Puppis stated, following Volan closely in the dark stairway leading out of the cell area.

"No it should not," Draco countered. "I took care remembering all of the turns and twists of the corridor of the cursed place when following Crimm's path in my trance walk."

"Then we must make haste," Forrest commented in a low voice. "Our time is nearly up."

"That it is, child," Draco agreed, a hint anxious apprehension lacing his quietly spoken words. "Thankfully surprise will be on our side."

Tar squeezed his well fed mid-section through the hole beside the doorway. His beady eyes scanned the perimeter of the work room. Seeing no sign of his mistress, the rat proceeded to the sleeping chamber. There he found his mistress nervously pacing the carpeted floor.

"Tar back pretty Brandy," he loudly informed her in a happy high pitched voice.

Brandy halted in her pacing and turned, smiling down at the small rodent. "Did you see my friends? Are they well?"

Tar scurried over to Brandy, who knelt down beside him. "Friends okay in dark cell. Human friend talk loud scare Tar. Then human friend nice to Tar. Give Tar present," the rodent said excitedly, holding his smooth stone prize out for Brandy's inspection.

"How nice," Brandy murmured, relieved that Steve had indeed gotten the quill from Tar. Nothing had stopped her little rodent friend along the way and upset her plans. She knew that Steve should easily be able to pick the lock on the cell. He had been doing it on her house lock for years. Now she had to find a way to get out of her cell. How would that be possible? She glanced at Tar and he gave her the perfect answer. The little rodent stood on his back legs and rubbed his stomach.

"Tar hungry. Tar go find something to eat," he complained mildly, as if too lazy to hunt something down.

"You know," Brandy began, mimicking Tar by patting her own stomach. "I think I am rather hungry myself. Maybe you could open the door and show me the way to the kitchen, and I'll make both of us something to eat," she offered with an encouraging nod.

"Tar not open door. Master forbid. Master squash Tar if Tar open door," Tar squeaked, running circles of agitation on the thick carpet.

Brandy smiled and patted the nervous rodent. "I wouldn't want you to get hurt Tar, but surely Master Chameleon wouldn't want his mate to go hungry, would he?"

"No," he began, halting his uneasy prancing. He stood on his hind legs and tugged at his ears in frustration, not sure what to do. "Tar know," he exclaimed suddenly, jumping up and down. "Tar get ugly bumpy gobioid to get food. Be right back," he said, scurrying out of the room before Brandy could say anything to him or try to stop him.

"Great," Brandy mumbled out loud to herself. "Now I have to deal with a gobioid to get out of this cursed room." She threw her hands helplessly up in the air and resumed her restless pacing about Chameleon's chamber.

She looked closely at all of his personal items. His work tools, his spell books, and many objects the were foreign to her. She pulled open his wardrobe and poked casually through his clothing. Almost all of it was black with a few smatterings of red mixed in. There were robes, cloaks, and slim fitting pants, and a few pairs of black leather pull on boots. As she came to the end of the clothes that were hung, she chanced upon an unexpected shade of green. Hidden in the back of the wardrobe was a suit of tree green clothing, much like what the elves wore. Could it be that he still had feeling for his kin, despite what he said, she wondered.

Maybe there still was a speck of his youth left under the hard shell of evil that he tried so hard to portray.

Brandy carefully arranged the clothing back the way they had been and closed the door to the wardrobe. In spite of all her efforts, she had not found a weapon. Nothing that she could use against the gobioid, that is if Tar were able to convince one to come to the chamber.

The clicking sound of a key being inserted in a lock instantly convinced her that her little rodent friend had done just that. She rushed into the work room and slid under a table. The hem of her gown caught on the head of a nail protruding from the leg of the bench beside the table. Brandy grasped the gentle, delicate fabric and tugged on it. It wouldn't give. Frantically she glanced towards the door, it was beginning to open. She pulled at the skirt of her gown with both hands causing the material to split. She tumbled backward under the cramped space of the table and held her breath, hoping the gobioid hadn't heard her. She watched in agonizing terror as the creature shuffled slowly into the room, passing inches from her hiding space. It walked through the doorway into the sleeping chamber.

"Mistress?" the creature called out in a low voice.

Brandy scrambled from her hiding place and bolted for the door. Half way across the room a squeaky call caused her to halt in her progression to freedom.

"What pretty Brandy doing?" Tar chirped happily in a loud squeak. "Tar brought bumpy ugly gobioid with food."

"Hush," Brandy whispered loudly at the little rodent, but the damage had already been done. She glanced at the doorway connecting the two room of Chameleon's chamber and found herself staring at a tall mean looking gobioid. She spun back toward the hall doorway and ran as fast as she could.

"Trying to fly like a bird," the gobioid chuckled with a wheeze. With amazing swiftness the gobioid crossed the distance that separated himself and the human girl in the span of two heartbeats. He reached out with clawed hands and grasped her bare arm just as she was to cross the threshold.

"Let me go!" Brandy screeched in anger. She swung her free fist back and hit the offensive smelling gobioid on the snout.

"That was not very nice," the gobioid growled, roughly grabbing her free hand and twisting both of her arms behind her back, shoving her back toward the sleeping chamber.

Brandy lashed out at the gobioid with her feet. Each blow she delivered to the gobioid's limbs sent shivers of pain up her legs to the tops of her thighs, but she did not care. Her constant struggling had made it impossible for the gobioid to drag her any further. As he tried to fend off her kicking, her arms came loose from his grip. She lashed out with the fury of a cornered alley cat. She kicked, punched, scratched, and pulled whatever hair she could reach on the gobioid's balding head.

The creeature was taken aback by the ferocity of the snarling human girl. He pushed her away from him and raced back toward the door, intending on locking her in.

Brandy's adrenaline was pumping much too fast for her to give up now. She fought with an air of desperation, seeing her one chance before herself. She jumped on the back of the retreating gobioid, not letting him reach the door. The impact of her weight hitting him caused it to stumble in its footing and crash into one of the work tables. She rolled free, from the now enraged gobioid. It howled in pain as chemicals, from bubbling vials and tubes, fell on its exposed skin, melting it like wax on a burning candle.

Brandy tripped over the flailing leg of the gobioid, but struggled to crawl toward the open doorway.

"Not so fast," barked the gobioid, madness creeping into its eyes.

She felt the gobioid's cold claw gripped her ankle and pulled her back. She kicked backward with her free foot, feeling the creatures cheek bone crush with the impact. The gobioid screamed with rage and pain, but released his grip on Brandy's leg. She quickly jumped to her feet, but just as quickly the gobioid followed suit. Green blood streamed down his face from the horrible gash that her slippered foot had caused. With a low growl he lunged at the human girl.

Brandy side stepped at the moment of impact. The gobioid slammed his full weight into another of the work tables, smashing it to pieces and falling to the stone floor with it and its contents. Brandy pulled off one her slippers and threw it at one of the oil light globes that hung from the ceiling. The slipper shattered the thin glass of the globe, sending a fine shower of oil all about the work table. The oil erupted into searing flame almost as soon as it made contact with the chemicals that were spilled and mixed the two together. In rush, the room was almost completely enveloped in flame.

The gobioid screamed in terror and pain as the flames devoured his chemical soaked form. Brandy grimaced at the sight, her stomach lurching at the horrifying smell of burning flesh. She turned to flee from the chamber, but stopped. Where was Tar?

"Tar?" she called out above the crackling of the fire. "Where are you?"

"Pretty Brandy . . . Tar stuck."

Brandy swiveled her gaze, in the direction of Tar's squeak, to a corner. Tar was huddled in its depths trapped by a pile of blazing charts. She rushed to the corner and, with the help of a nearby book, pushed the burning charts far enough aside to get her hand on the small frightened rodent. Holding Tar close to her chest, Brandy turned and rushed from the blazing, smoke filled room.

When she finally reached the hall, she fell to her knees and gasped for fresh air. As the clean air reached her tired lungs, coughing overtook her. Her body racked with the painful chokes that the poisoned air of the chamber had inflicted upon her.

"Pretty Brandy okay?" Tar asked fearfully from Brandy's lap. He stroked her leg gently with singed front paws, hoping she was not harmed.

"I'll be fine," she panted, finally feeling the fresh air deep within her lungs. Tears from the gassy smoke streamed down her smut covered face. She took the hem of her now dirty and tattered gown and wiped her face.

"Are you alright, little friend?" she asked Tar, looking at his feet that had been mildly burned from the heat of the flames.

"Tar be fine if pretty Brandy fine," he squeaked bravely. "Friend Tar fine."

Brandy smiled brightly at the rodent. "You are very brave."

Tar grinned and glanced back at the room. "Master Chameleon be very mad when he see chamber."

Brandy laughed, patting the rodent's head. "You are probably right, Tar, and I really don't care. It wasn't very nice of him to lock me up in there."

Tar stared in disbelief at his mistresses word. Brandy only laughed again at his distressed look. "Come on. You need to show me the way to the big chamber with the hanging crystal."

She struggled to her feet, leaning against the wall for support for a moment, and then bent down and scooped the trembling rodent up into her arms.

"Master Chameleon be real mad," Tar quaked fearfully.

"Don't you worry, Tar. I'm going to take care of Mater Chameleon," Brandy promised the rat, feeling very confident. For some reason she was instantly aware that all was soon to come to an end.

In painful slowness, in order to avoid anymore confrontations with gobioids, they made their way down dark corridors and narrow stairways until they reached a dull damp hall. Brandy recognized the passageway immediately. It was the one that had been in her dreams. The dreams that had haunted her almost every time she had closed her eyes.

"You had better stay here," Brandy whispered to Tar, placing him gently on the ground. Without waiting for a response from the rodent, Brandy began creeping forward toward the bright light emanating from the end of the tunnel. Her stomach drew in tight knots, nervous sweat trickled down her back. She wiped her clammy palms on the smooth silk of her gown. Without realizing it, she had held her breath until she was at the opening of the massive chamber. What her eyes beheld made her bite her lip in alarm.

Puppis, Draco, and Volan were battling a large force of gobioids, barely keeping them at bay. Steve was engage with three others close to where Carina laid bound and barely moving on the black marble table. Her body twitched occasionally, but that was the only signs of consciousness that the princess showed. Lacerta stood between the table and the crystal that held Lyra chanting noiselessly with her eyes closed in concentration. Forrest had somehow managed to get by the gobioids and was trying to hack at the crystal with a sword. The steel of the weapon bounced ineffectively off of the shiny surface. Crimm was tethered by the gold chain near the roaring fire pit. His stately body was a crisscross of knife slashes.

Brandy scanned the room for signs of Chameleon. Finally she spotted him on the far side. He was yelling at more gobioids, who rushed into the chamber from the stairway, to eliminate the intruders.

She watched in terror as she saw the dark elf fix his gaze on Forrest and began a slow deliberate chant. She darted from her hiding place and raced across the room. She glanced back at Chameleon just as a blaze of orange crackling light flew from his fingertips towards Forrest's unprotected back.

"Forrest!" Brandy screamed as loud as she could. "Look out!"

Forrest turned in her direction, puzzled wonderment playing across his features. He opened his mouth to say something, but the force of Brandy's hands, arms, and being shoved him, knocking him to the stone floor before any words could escape.

CHAPTER TWENTY-FIVE

Draco took the lead through the shadowy halls of the castle as if he had lived in the cold gloomy fortress most of his days. Forrest kept a close pace behind, followed by Volan and Puppis, with Steve bringing up the rear, alert for any danger. As they neared the place of their capture upon entering the castle, three gobioids stood lazily, eating what looked to be a large rat, and talking loudly in their guttural language.

Draco roared with the ferocity of an untamed wasteland beast and launched himself forward in a headlong rush at the dumb witted creatures. Forrest and others followed the lead of their elder elf and mimicked his war cry with just as much enthusiasm. The gobioids turned in their direction and stared with mouths hanging open with surprise. They never even had the chance to draw their weapons before the band of filthy prisoners were on them like a pack of beserkers.

The elder elf grabbed two of the gobioids, slamming their heads together with a tremendous crash. The creatures skulls split like ripened melons on a hot day. Forrest leapt at the remaining gobioid catching him full in the chest with an outstretched foot. The creatures ribs cracked easily from the force of his blow, sending it to the ground in a crumpled heap.

"Gee whiz," Steve complained with a grin, looking at the elves handiwork. "You didn't leave any for us."

"I am just getting warmed up," Forrest replied with a wicked smile. He picked up the three swords that the gobioids no longer needed, handing one to Volan, one to Draco, and keeping the third for himself.

"Well, let us at least find two more, so that Steve and I can get a blade before we walk into Lacerta's den," Puppis added with her own grin.

They continued on, following Draco closely. They did not go far until they came across another small group of gobioids. Just as before they were easily and swiftly dealt with. Leaving no survivors to tell what had befallen them. By the time they had reached the opening of the huge chamber that held Lyra they were heavily armed with knives, swords, and a few maces.

"This is it," Draco whispered over his shoulder to his companions. "Lyra is held there." All followed his pointing finger and saw Lyra held in suspension in the glimmering crystal.

"Heavens help us," Puppis murmured, tears rushing to her eyes. "How can such a thing be happening?"

"I know not, child," Draco remarked. "We are here to change it."

"That we are," Volan said in a low grumble. "I owe these scum quite a debt."

"I think we all do," Steve agreed solemnly.

They watched in silence as Lacerta floated gracefully down the narrow staircase on the far side of the chamber. She was dressed in blazing silver, the firelight and torches reflecting brilliantly off of her clothing's surface. Behind her Carina followed meekly. Head bowed and seeing nothing around her. The pair crossed the chamber, and approached the black marble table that sat imperiously on top of a thick blood red carpet. As if in a trance, Carina approached the table and laid down upon, becoming still.

"Carina," Steve gasped a the lovely vision of the princess. She looked like a delicate flower in her simple gown of white. He started forward but was stopped by the strong grip of Draco. He shot a questioning glance at the elder elf.

"We must not give up our presence just yet. Let us survey that in which we will meet soon enough," Draco said with gentle kindness. He easily saw the feelings that raged on the human's face for the plight of their princess. How strange these human's were about their emotions, he thought.

They watched a group of gobioid's filed into the heavy chamber from some side entrance that they could not see from their vantage point. The gobioids were armed, but not very heavily. It seemed almost more symbolic than for protection, for Lacerta believed herself to be quite safe.

The Dark Queen stood before the crystal and smile triumphantly at her sister, trapped within. She turned and looked up at the ceiling of the chamber, as if she could see through the stones, and the many other floors that were above her, to the sky outside.

"In minutes, my dear sister, I will be the one that all in our land bow down to," she crowed, laughing in total victory.

Lacerta turned her attention from the crystal and walked over to Crimm. The mighty dragon bled from many wounds upon his scaled hide. He hung his head limply, keeping his large eyes closed.

"The time is at hand, my pet," Lacerta crooned to the green beast, stroking his drooping head. "Your blood will make it so that I can not fail."

Crimm lifted his head with great effort and stared at the lovely vision before him. "You will not win, my Queen," he hissed slowly, almost with sarcastic laughter. "There are things at work that you did not count on. You will see when it is too late." With that Crimm closed his eyes once more and lowered his head.

"You are near death," Lacerta said, after taking many long moments to ponder the dragon's ominous words. "You speak of foolish hope filled dreams."

The Dark Queen turned her back on the tethered creature when he did not respond and positioned herself between Lyra and the princess, who laid obediently on the table. Where was her mage, Chameleon? She needed him to add his power to hers in order to keep her sister locked away forever. She could do it alone, but then she would not have enough strength left to go out and face the elves, and proclaim herself their new leader, and then deal with those who refused her. Damn him and his black heart, where was he?

'Chameleon? Answer me mage. I demand to know of your presence,' Lacerta sent her thoughts out all about the keep waiting for his reply.

'I am close, my queen. Begin without me, for dawn is upon us. I will add my power to yours as soon as I arrive,' Chameleon answered, then closed off his thoughts, not wanting his queen to know what he was really planning. He would let her become weak, then he would take control of all, including her.

The band in the shadows of the tunnel watched transfixed as Lacerta began chanting in a slow steady rhythm. When she did so, Crimm twitched as if in pain. Carina made small movements on the marble table, and the gobioids watched as if they had been hypnotized. They could all feel the power that surged within the room.

"We can't wait any longer," Steve said, determined not to take no for an answer this time.

"He is right," Forrest agreed, anxiously gripping his sword.

Draco said nothing, only nodded and stepped into the chamber. "Something is not correct here," he whispered, hesitating for a moment with his hand upheld. "Something is out of place."

"What is it?" Puppis asked, losing more and more of her nerve with each passing second, for the odds were not in their favor at all.

"Chameleon is not here," Draco stated sweeping his gaze across the vast chamber again.

"So what," said Volan. "We will deal with him when he does get here. For now, lets take care those who are."

Draco grunted, but was cut off before he could say anything. A gobioid yelled in their direction. They had been spotted, and too soon for their own good.

Steve rushed at the group of five gobioids that stood closest to Carina's form on the marble altar. By taking them with complete surprise he was able to chop the sword arms from two of the creatures before they were even aware of his presence. The remaining three turned on him like vipers. They lashed out with their decorative blades. Steve slashed and parried for his life, but his enraged heart drove him on, making him quicker than he ever thought possible. Every time he caught a glimpse of Carina on the stone table he would strike faster and harder, wearing down the gobioids.

Draco, Volan, and Puppis engaged the main force of gobioids that ran at them when they were spotted. They formed a small three way circle with their backs to each other so that they would be protected from the rear, and hoped that none would fall to the ugly creatures. Draco gripped his sword with both hands and began a pile of fallen bodies before him. Volan fought easily against the light swords of the gobioids with a spiked mace, and Puppis dealt many casualties with the two long knives that she held; one in each hand. Nothing that came within reach of the three, stepped back unharmed.

Forrest hacked his way through the creatures, his sword dropping nearly one with every stroke. He cut a bloody path to the crystal that imprisoned Lyra. Lifting his gore covered weapon, he brought it down in a sweeping arc to the surface of the shimmering stone. It bounced ineffectively off of its gleaming face. With a roar of rage Forrest tried again and again to splinter the shining rock, but nothing seemed to damage it.

"Forrest. Look out!" a scream echoed to his sensitive ears.

The elf swung his gaze incredibly at the sound of the voice. It was Brandy, he would recognize it anywhere. How, he wondered, as he sought her out in the chamber. Suddenly there she was. Running without a care through the tangles of gobioids with weapons. Her hair billowed out behind her like a banner in the wind. She had on a silky green gown and was covered in soot. She rushed straight for him screaming something that he could not understand. He turned and looked behind him, only to see Chameleon a short distance away with an evil grin on his face. The mage held out his hand to the elf. Orange lightning crackled from his fingertips.

Forrest turned his gaze back to Brandy as she reached him, knocking him forward with a tremendous shove. The impact of her force careened him into the crystal. The edge of his sword tapped the glittering surface. At first a tiny crack appeared. Then it began to move with a life of its own. The line of breakage moved with amazing speed all around the crystal, cracking it like some giant egg.

The elf stood transfixed, watching the crystal fall to pieces before his eyes. A small moan behind him caused him to tear his gaze from the sight.

"Brandy," he barely whispered, his throat constricting at what he saw. He rushed to the crumpled form on the stone floor and dropped to his knees beside the human girl. A horrible hole had been burned through her chest. A thin line of blood trickled from the corner of her mouth. She was pale, and barely breathing. Her hair was tangled and had mingled with the blood of the gobioids who laid dead all about her fallen form. Forrest scooped her up in his arms and held her close to his chest.

"Brandy," he choked hoarsely, a huge lump settling in his throat, nearly suffocating him. "You promised not to save me," he began, but could not finish. Tears blurred his vision. Emotions he had never felt before, flooded over him in a thunderous wave. Why her? Why this beautiful human girl? She who bore a brave spirit greater than any he had met before.

"Don't," Brandy gasped weakly, quieting his words with a frail small hand placed lightly against his lips. She opened her eyes and struggled to smile. "You really are handsome, Forrest," she rambled incoherently.

"I have got to get you out of here."

"No," she murmured softly, stroking his cheek and placing her hand on his strong chest. She was surprised, the blast hadn't hurt that much. She felt it when the bolt of power had slammed into her chest, but the burning sensation had only lasted for seconds. She had felt herself lifted off her feet, and sliding, no tumbling, across the battle littered floor, but that had been all. What really hurt was seeing Forrest's face. The pain and guilt he felt was evident to her, and she did not want to be responsible for that.

"Don't mourn for me, please. Just finish Chameleon," she trailed off to silence, closing her eyes. Her hand fell limply from his chest to the stone floor next to her.

"Brandy?" Forrest called to her, gently rocking her in his arms, tears of anguish spilling freely from him.

"Love you," she whispered upward with a gentle smile. The words were barely spoken, more of a wisp on the breeze. Then she became very still.

"No!" Forrest bellowed in rage, his anger shaking the foundations of the castle. He brought his gaze up and met the eyes of Chameleon. Hate boiled within him. Softly placing Brandy on the floor, he leapt to his feet and stalked forward without heed to the mage.

"You die now!" Forrest yelled at the stunned face of Chameleon.

"I did not mean for her to die," he said tonelessly. "I wanted her for myself."

"Only because you knew you could not. You knew she would not give in to you," accused Forrest angrily. He lifted his sword and swung it at the mage, who stepped back just in time to miss the blow.

Chameleon quickly grabbed a sword from a fallen gobioid and stood to meet the elf's challenge. "I fear you not, elf."

"Then we are even, you devil," Forrest spat. "You said before that I feared you, but you were very wrong. You make me ill that we share some form of elfin blood. I condemn you to death."

The mage laughed in contempt. "You speak loudly for such a small insignificant being."

Forrest said nothing. The time for words was over. Revenge burned deeply in his soul. Even knowing what the results of her actions would be, Brandy did not hesitate to place her life in danger for him. She would be avenged, even if he died trying.

Chameleon wasted no time in sizing up his opponent. His plans were being destroyed by this ragged band. The crystal was breaking, soon Lyra would be free. Lacerta was struggling to keep control. He could sense that Carina had not feebly given in as she had first appeared to. She fought his queen's power with ever ounce of her being from the altar, making it harder for Lacerta to contain her sister, and the elves fought with the strength of ten their number. The gobioids were taking all of the losses.

Forrest kept advancing on Chameleon, bring his sword forward with almost every breath. The mage was too used to his magic, he thought to himself, for the dark elf could barely keep him at bay. Forrest shot his weapon out again and again, slicing and slashing through the robes of the mage, wounding him more and more. At first they were minor nicks, they soon gave way to bigger bites.

Finally Chameleon stumbled. He fell backward over the prone form of a gobioid. He let his sword fall from his grasp and pointed a finger at the elf.

"Enough of this barbaric foolishness," he croaked tiredly. "You die now." He sent his hands of unseen death to wrap themselves about Forrest's neck, squeezing the air from him.

Forrest halted, groping blindly at his throat with his left hand. He stared at the mage on the floor before him. Chameleon grinned triumphantly, assured victory would be his. Forrest sneered in distaste, lifted his sword, and with a mighty heave, threw it, point first into the chest of the grinning magician, then fell to the floor out of breath.

Chameleon's mouth fell open in disbelief. He dropped his hand, a gurgling sound escaped his lips. He had underestimated the elf before and realized that his plan had gone severely wrong before he saw no more.

Forrest slowly rose to his feet, rubbing his bruised neck. The gobioids around him rushed away in panicked fear at what they saw. Their Master Chameleon was defeated by one inferior to him, and their queen seemed to be faring no better. Forrest went to Crimm, who still barely lived and yanked the chain that bound him to Lacerta's magic. The golden links crumpled to dust at his touch.

Lacerta's eyes flew opened, her chanting trance halted. She turned in his direction. "What have you done?" she bellowed, looking from the free Crimm to the fallen form of her mage.

"It is over, sister," a gentle voice floated over the air.

"It cannot be," Lacerta wailed, childlike at what she saw. Lyra was free. She stood among the shards of broken crystal all about her feet. All of the gobioids fled in terror, tripping over one another in their haste. All that remained before her now were the bodies of the dead, and the small band that had invaded her castle and she whom she had imprisoned below in her dungeon. With the last ounce of power that she possessed, Lacerta made her form invisible from sight and vanished from the room.

"Where did she go?" Puppis asked, looking about in wide eyed awe. She gripped Draco tightly around the waist. The elder elf had been severely wounded in the leg, and bled profusely.

"I do not now," Volan said. "Lyra lives, and is well. We have succeeded."

The trio slowly picked their way through the bodies that littered the floor, the spilled gore making the stones slippery. Steve helped a groggy, but unhurt Carina from the stone altar. He smiled deeply into her sky colored eyes. She hugged him close, but her smile faded instantly at what she saw over his shoulder.

He felt Carina stiffen in his arms. "It's all right," he said softly into her hair. "You are safe now."

"I know," Carina said with a gentle sigh of relief. "Only your friend, Brandy, is harmed," she faltered badly. The words seemed to stick on in her throat.

Steve released his grip on Carina and spun around, his eyes meeting the massive wound that covered the chest of his dearest friend. Forrest stood silently over her still form as Steve rushed to her side.

"Brandy, wake up," he mumbled, poking her lightly on the arm as if that would rouse her. He stared despondently at her blank peaceful face. Tears blurred his vision until he could no longer see. "This is our adventure to finished together," he choked. "Don't leave. Not now."

Puppis knelt beside the human male, wanting to speak, but could find no words. Tears spilled unheeded down her dirty face. Pain and loss washed over her like a wave. "Good bye my friend," she sobbed, dropping her face into her hands, her shoulders shaking under the burden.

Volan supported Draco. Neither tried to hide their sorrow. Brandy had shown her worth better than any elfin warrior. Many tales would be told of her deeds in the future.

Carina wrapped a soothing arm around Steve. She struggled to control her words, her sadness threatening to overcome. "I do not know how to express my words of thanks or gratitude for your friend. It was she who freed Lyra and brought about the defeat of Lacerta. She who is not even of the elfin world. A human who gave her life for the lives of all of our kind."

Steve looked up from Brandy to stared deeply into the tear glittered eyes of Carina. He wanted to scream that it wasn't fair, that it shouldn't have happened to Brandy, but he couldn't. Brandy would have laughed at him and told him that it was worth the risk to have the adventure of a life time.

"I am so sorry, Steve," Carina wailed, unable to keep her tears in control any longer.

"Do not mourn, my children," Lyra spoke with the softness of the wind. Her warmth radiated all around them. "Life is but a large circle. My human child knew this very well. Perhaps better with the losses that she herself had already faced. With each passing brings a new beginning. A new beginning for all."

"Not for me," Forrest said hoarsely. "Not ever."

He bent down and gently gathered the human girl into his powerful arms. Standing, he turned and walked away. Taking her away from the carnage of her death.

CHAPTER TWENTY-SIX

"Quiet or you will wake her."

A giggling sound slowly filtered its way down into Brandy's troubled dreams. She didn't know what she was dreaming, but knew it was uncomfortable and unpleasant. Uncertainly she opened her eyes. She hurt. Her chest hurt the worst. Breathing hurt, blinking hurt, everything hurt. Squinting into the dim light she realized that she was in the same room she had been in the first time she woke up in this crazy land. They were at Carina's home, in the comfortable tree colored bedroom.

"Good day." Steve smiled brightly, looking intently at his groggy friend. "How did you sleep?"

"How long?" Brandy managed to grate out. Her throat burned with the attempt.

"Almost a week." Steve grinned, back to his old reckless self. He showed almost no signs from their passed experiences, only a few scars that would remind him for a lifetime. "I didn't think you were ever going to wake up. How do you feel?"

"Like crap. What do you think?" Brandy croaked out a sarcastic laugh.

Steve laughed again. "Glad to know you're better," he whispered sincerely, kissing her lightly on the brow.

"I thought I was dead," she whispered back, not really wanting to speak, but feeling the need to.

"You were," her friend answered somberly. "Chameleon tried to kill Forrest, but you took the blast instead."

"Then how?" Brandy began, shaking her head, not understanding.

"Your selfless sacrifice is what freed Lyra," said Carina, sitting down on the side of the bed by Brandy. She took a cool damp cloth and wiped the girl's forehead before continuing. "Many things happened after that. Many things changed. When we emerged from the castle a host of elves from many different clans were there to greet us. They were brought to the castle by the dragons, in case we failed in our task to defeat Lacerta."

"Did we defeat her?" asked Brandy, gratefully accepting the minty tea brew that Steve held to her lips.

"No, not really." Carina shook her head. "Her castle was destroyed, burned to the ground, but she disappeared, as did many of the gobioids. They must have went deeper south into the wastelands."

"What about Chameleon?"

"He is toast," Steve announced grimly. "Forrest finished him after what he did to you."

Brandy's heart pounded at the sound of the elf's name. She scanned every inch of the room, looking for signs of him. "Where is he?"

Steve looked at Carina, not sure what to say.

"He's not dead is he?" Brandy asked, her throat constricting fearfully.

"No," Steve assured his friend. "He stayed here with you until we were sure that you would pull through. And then," he shrugged uncertainly, "no one has seen him since."

Brandy said nothing. She turned her head to the wall not wanting her friends to see the tears that threatened to escape. Why would he leave her? Did he not care?

"Why am I even alive?" Brandy asked after a moment, looking at Steve blankly.

"Lyra brought you back. She used the living essence of Spring to pull you back before your spirit got too far away from us. That's what she told us anyway," he added in a whisper. "It was magic either way."

Brandy grinned. "You're bonkers, you know that?"

"Yes. I believe you are right." Steve nodded with a laugh.

"There are others who have been waiting to see you," Carina said with a smile at her friend. "Can they come in?"

"Sure." Brandy laughed hoarsely. "I don't think they've seen me any worse than this."

Puppis and Volan rushed into the room. Both hugged her gently and beamed with happiness.

"I am overjoyed that you are well," Puppis said, all smiles. "We were quite worried."

"I'm fine, really," said Brandy with a wave of her hand, stifling a yawn.

"She is tired, we should leave," Volan commented.

"Not before I get this squeaking creature in here to say hello, or he is going to drive me out of control," Draco's deep voice chuckled as he entered the room with a squirming mass of fur.

"Tar? Is that you?" Brandy asked incredulously.

"Pretty Brandy," Tar squeaked, jumping on the bed and rushing up to his mistress. "Tar miss pretty Brandy. Tar so happy to see pretty Brandy."

"I am happy to see you too, Tar," Brandy said, smiling affectionately at the rodent. "And you, Draco," she added to the limping elder elf, who gently squeezed her hand.

"I am joyful to see you still with us," Draco beamed, kissing Brandy on both cheeks.

"What of your leg?" she asked, aware of the pain it must be causing him.

"It is nothing but a reminder," he said with a chuckle. "Old men should have battle scars."

"We should leave. Brandy needs her rest," Carina said rising from her seat, indicating the others to follow. "We will be back soon," she promised her friend with a smile.

"Thanks," Brandy croaked, taking the princesses hand for a moment.

"C'mon, Tar. That means you too," Steve told the rodent, reaching from him.

"No. Tar no leave. Tar protect pretty Brandy," Tar demanded, stamping his small feet all about the bed linens.

"It's okay, let him stay," Brandy said, smiling. She absently stroked the rodents back as if he were a puppy until he fell into a contented sleep. She soon followed his lead.

It took another week for Brandy to regain enough strength to begin walking again, and another after that until she was fully recovered. The second day after she was given a clean bill of health, Volan and Puppis held the ceremony of partnership. It was a wondrous event. Elves from all clans were present for the celebration. All were joyous and happy, especially those who had spent a fateful few days together, depending upon each other for their very lives.

And for the first time, in the known history of the elfin clans, dragons attended the festivities. A tearfully happy Suun and her mate stood with the couple as they exchanged their vows. Sith and Soth bounced joyfully around a serious Garn, and a severely scarred, but fully recovered Crimm, were in attendance.

Two days after the joining ceremony, Brandy decided it was time to go home. She rode slowly to the edge of the woods, on horseback, with Steve, Carina, Volan, Puppis, and Draco. When they reached the place where she was to pass through the barrier, Lyra was waiting for them.

"Thank you, Lyra." Brandy smiled at the woman. "Thank you for my life, and thank you for letting me go home."

"You know this is your home also," she indicated gently to her human child.

"Thank you, but it would not be the same."

"I understand," replied Lyra, nodding her head. "The trees and all of its inhabitants will be part of you forever."

Brandy smiled, taking a deep breath. "Yes, I can feel them somehow."

"It is my gift to you." Lyra hugged her human child warmly.

"Thank you," she whispered again, turning face her other friends.

Draco hugged the slender human girl closely. "You are the child I never had. I will hold you in my heart as such."

"I will always remember you," Brandy promised with glistening lashes.

Puppis and Volan hugged their human friend tightly. "We will miss you," Puppis said quietly, tears misting in her bright eyes.

Volan pulled his mate close. "Our first female child will bear your name," he promised Brandy.

"Thank you." Brandy smiled, not sure what to say. Their gift was appreciated more than she could tell them.

"Good bye, Brandy," Carina said, kissing Brandy on each cheek and hugging her close. "I will never forget what you have done. If you reconsider, come back to us."

"I will."

Steve took his friend's arm and led her away from the group. "I don't know what to say Brand," he began awkwardly, glancing at the others. "I won't be coming back with you."

"I know." She smiled at her friend.

"You know?"

"I think I knew from the beginning."

"You did?"

"Of course stupid. You don't love someone the way I care for you and not know what they are thinking. It is very obvious to me that you are not going to let Carina slip through your fingers. If you did, then you would be a jerk." Brandy laughed aloud, hugging Steve tightly.

"Bye, Brandy. I love you, you know," Steve said, grinning recklessly.

"I know, but how am I going to get into my house? Never mind, don't answer that. Take care of Tar for me, okay? I didn't tell him I was leaving, because he would have insisted on coming, and what would I do with a talking rat?" Brandy shrugged. "Well, I better go."

Brandy looked back at her friends and smiled sadly. She was going to miss them. Maybe she was making a mistake. No, it was better like this. A clean break, back to what she knew best. Back to her own home. She waved at Lyra, and walked slowly forward into the thick swirling mist.

"Stop!" A shout rang out through the still air.

Brandy froze, not sure what to do. She knew the voice, it was Forrest. She didn't dare turn around. Her heart pounded loudly in her chest. Footsteps raced up behind her, and a light touch on her shoulder, caused her breathing to stop.

"You are leaving?" Forrest asked softly, barely making his words audible.

Brandy spun around and faced him, anger blazing in her large eyes. "Well, what the hell do you care? You didn't even bother to come visit me. You act like I have the plague or something. I mean really, the nerve you've got!"

Forrest reddened and looked to the ground. "I am sorry," he mumbled miserably. "I thought after all that had happened you would not want to see me."

"Why?" Brandy snapped irritably.

"Because I had caused your death," Forrest answered, looking deep into those blazing eyes.

Brandy's anger faded in a flash and she laughed loudly, throwing her hands upward.

"What is so amusing?" Forrest asked indignantly.

"You are," she replied, poking her finger into his chest. "Why do you think I even bothered to save you? Because I hate you? Duh, wake up here Forrest. I . . . love . . . you," Brandy said slowly, staring evenly at the elf male.

A slow boyish smile spread across Forrest's face. Quickly it vanished, and he cleared his throat. "You know, I am rather opinionated," he began.

"So, I talk too much."

"And I am still not too sure about humans."

"And I tend to be bossy." Brandy grinned slyly.

"Yes, you do," Forrest agreed, taking Brandy into his arms, pulling her close. "I think we will do fine."

"Yes, I think we will," Brandy agreed, wrapping her arms around her elf's neck and kissing him gently on the lips.

THE END